THE RAILWAY VIADUCT

When a landscape artist witnesses a body plummeting from a train speeding over the Sankey Viaduct into the canal below, Inspector Robert Colbeck and Sergeant Victor Leeming face their most complex case. They are unable to identify the disfigured corpse and press appeals bring forward no information, but observing his clothes have a Continental cut, they travel to France where a new railway is being built by a British contractor. Anti-British feeling is rife, and Colbeck and Leeming must put their own lives in danger to pick up the murderer's trail. Has Colbeck finally met his match?

THE RAILWAY VIADUCT

THE RAILWAY VIADUCT

by

Edward Marston

Magna Large Print Books
Long Preston, North Yorkshire,
BD23 4ND, England.

British Library Cataloguing in Publication Data.

Marston, Edward
    The railway viaduct.
    A catalogue record of this book is
    available from the British Library

    ISBN   978-0-7505-2637-1

First published in Great Britain in 2006 by Allison & Busby Ltd.

Copyright © 2006 by Edward Marston

Cover illustration © The Old Tin Dog by arrangement with
Allison & Busby Ltd.

The moral right of the author has been asserted

Published in Large Print 2007 by arrangement with
Allison & Busby Limited

Magna Large Print is an imprint of Library Magna Books Ltd.

Printed and bound in Great Britain by
T.J. (International) Ltd., Cornwall, PL28 8RW

CHAPTER ONE

1852

Something was missing. His preliminary sketch of the Sankey Viaduct was both dramatic and satisfyingly precise but it needed something to anchor it, a human dimension to give a sense of scale. He knew exactly where to place the figures, and he could easily have pencilled them in, but he preferred to rely on chance rather than imagination. Ambrose Hooper had been an artist for over forty years and his continued success could not simply be attributed to his sharp eye and gifted hand. In all that he did, luck played a decisive part. It was uncanny. Whenever he needed to add a crucial element to a painting, he did not have to wait long for inspiration to come. An idea somehow presented itself before him.

Hooper was a short, slim, angular man in his sixties with a full beard and long grey hair that fell like a waterfall from beneath his battered old straw hat. On a hot summer's day, he had taken off his crumpled white jacket so that he could work at his easel in his shirtsleeves. He wore tiny spectacles and narrowed his lids to peer through them. An experienced landscape artist, it was the first time that he had turned his attention to the massive railway system that had changed the face of the English countryside so radically over the previous twenty years. It was a challenge for him.

Viewed from below, the Sankey Viaduct was truly imposing. It had been opened in 1830 as part of the Liverpool and Manchester Railway and was roughly halfway between the two places. Straddling a valley that contained both a canal and a brook, the viaduct was supported by nine identical arches, each with a span of fifty feet. Massive piers rose up with perpendicular certitude from the piles that had been driven deep down into the waterbeds, and the parapet coping reached a height of almost seventy feet, leaving ample room to spare for the tallest vessels that sailed on the canal. It was a predominantly brick structure, finished off with dressings and facings that gave it an added lustre. In the bright sunshine, it was a dazzling piece of architectural masonry.

Hooper's sketch had caught its towering simplicity. His main objective, however, was to show the stark contrast between the valley itself with its verdant meadows and the man-made intrusions of canal and viaduct. A few cattle grazed obligingly on his side of the waterway and Hooper was able to incorporate them in his drawing, timeless symbols of rural life in the shadow of industry. What he required now were human figures and – as ever, his luck held out – they not only appeared magically before him, they stood more or less in the spot where he wanted them to be.

Two women and a small boy had come to look up at the viaduct. From the way that she held the boy's hand, Hooper decided that the younger woman must be his mother and his guess was that the other woman, older and more fastidious, was her spinster sister, less than happy at being there. She was wearing too much clothing for such a hot day and was troubled by insects that flew in under her poke bonnet. While the boy and his mother seemed quietly excited, the other woman lifted the hem of her dress well above the ground so that it would not trail in any of the cowpats. The visit was clearly for the boy's benefit and not for that of his maiden aunt.

As he put them into his sketch with deft flicks of his pencil, Ambrose Hooper gave each of them a name to lend some character. The mother was Hester Lewthwaite, the wife of a provincial banker perhaps, her son, eight or nine years of age at most, was Anthony Lewthwaite, and the disagreeable third person was Petronella Snark, disappointed in love, highly critical of her sister and not at all inclined to indulge a small boy if it entailed trudging across a meadow in the stifling heat. Both women wore steel-ringed crinolines but, while Hester's was fashionable, brightly coloured and had a pretty flounced skirt, Petronella's dress was dark and dowdy.

He knew why they were there. When he took his watch from the pocket of his waistcoat, Hooper saw that a train was due to cross the viaduct at any moment. It was something he had always planned to use in his painting. A railway viaduct would not suffice. Only a locomotive could bring it to life and display its true purpose. Gazing up, the artist had his pencil ready. Out of the corner of his eye, he then caught sight of another element that had perforce to be included. A sailing barge was gliding serenely along the canal towards the viaduct with three men aboard. Before attempting to sketch the vessel, however, Hooper elected to wait until the train had passed. It was usually on time.

Seconds later, he heard it coming. Mother and child looked up with anticipatory delight. The other woman did not. The men on the barge raised their eyes as well but nobody watched with the same intensity as Ambrose Hooper. Just when he wanted it, the locomotive came into sight, an iron monster, belching clouds of steam and filling the whole valley with its thunder. Behind it came an endless string of gleaming carriages, rattling noisily across the viaduct high above the spectators. And then, to their amazement, they all saw something that they could not possibly have expected.

The body of a man hurtled over the edge of the viaduct and fell swiftly through the air until it landed in the canal, hitting the water with such irresistible force that it splashed both banks. The mother put protective arms around her son, the other woman staggered back in horror, the three men in the barge exchanged looks of utter disbelief. It had been an astonishing sight but the cows accorded it no more than a cursory glance before returning to the more important business of chewing the cud. Hooper was exhilarated. Intending to portray the headlong dash of the train, he had been blessed with another stroke of good fortune. He had witnessed something that no artist could ever invent.

As a result, his painting would now celebrate a murder.

CHAPTER TWO

After a couple of tedious hours in court, Detective Inspector Robert Colbeck was glad to return to Scotland Yard so that he could write a full report on the case, and clear up some of the paperwork cluttering his desk. He got no further than his office door. Superintendent Tallis loomed into view at the end of the corridor and beckoned him with an imperious crook of a tobacco-stained finger. When they went into the superintendent's office, Colbeck could smell the pungent smoke still hanging in the air. It was a telltale sign that a serious crime had been committed. His superior's response to any crisis was to reach for his cigar box. Tallis waved a piece of paper at him.

'This message came by electric telegraph,' he said.

'From where?'

'Liverpool. That's where the body was taken.'

'Another murder?' asked Colbeck with interest.

'Another *railway* murder. It's the reason I'm sending you.'

The inspector was not surprised. After his

success in capturing the gang responsible for the daring robbery of a mail train, the press had dubbed him unanimously as the Railway Detective and he had lived up to the name subsequently. It gave him a kudos he enjoyed, a popularity that Tallis resented and a burden of expectation that could feel very heavy at times. Robert Colbeck was tall, lean, conventionally handsome and dressed as usual in an immaculate black frock coat, well-cut fawn trousers and an Ascot cravat. Still in his thirties, he had risen swiftly in the Detective Department, acquiring a reputation for intelligence, efficiency and single-mindedness that few could emulate. His promotion had been a source of great pride to his friends and a constant irritation to his detractors such as the superintendent.

Edward Tallis was a stout, red-faced man in his fifties with a shock of grey hair and a neat moustache that he trimmed on a daily basis. His years in the army had left him with the habit of command, a passion for order and an unshakable belief in the virtues of the British Empire. Though invariably smart, he felt almost shabby beside the acknowledged dandy of Scotland Yard. Tallis derided what he saw as Colbeck's vanity but he was honest enough to recognise the inspector's rare qualities as a detective. It encouraged him to suppress his instinctive dislike of the man. For his part, Colbeck, too, made allowances.

Seniority meant that Tallis had to be obeyed and the inspector's natural antipathy towards him had to be hidden.

Tallis thrust the paper at him. 'Read it for yourself,' he said.

'Thank you, sir.' Colbeck needed only seconds to do so. 'This does not tell us very much, Superintendent.'

'What did you expect – a three-volume novel?'

'It claims that the victim was thrown from a moving train.'

'So?'

'That suggests great strength on the part of the killer. He would have to pitch a grown man through a window and over the parapet of the Sankey Viaduct. Unless, of course,' he added, handing the telegraph back to Tallis, 'he opened the door of the carriage first.'

'This is no time for idle speculation.'

'I agree, Superintendent.'

'Are you in a position to take charge of the case?'

'I believe so.'

'What happened in court this morning?'

'The jury finally brought in a verdict of guilty, sir. Why it should have taken them so infernally long, I can only hazard a guess. The evidence against Major Harrison-Clark was overwhelming.'

'That may be,' said Tallis with gruff regret, 'but I hate to see a military man brought down like that. The major served his country honourably for many years.'

'That does not entitle him to strangle his wife.'

'There was great provocation, I daresay.'

A confirmed bachelor, Tallis had no insight into the mysteries of married life and no taste for the company of women. If a husband killed his spouse, the superintendent tended to assume that she was in some way obscurely responsible for her own demise. Colbeck did not argue with him or even point out that, in fact, Major Rupert Harrison-Clark had a history of violent behaviour. The inspector was too anxious to be on his way.

'What about my report on the case?' he asked.

'It can wait.'

'Am I to take Victor with me, sir?'

'Sergeant Leeming has already been apprised of the details.'

'Such as they are.'

'Such – as you so rightly point out – as they are.' Tallis looked down at the telegraph. 'Have you ever seen this viaduct?'

'Yes, Superintendent. A remarkable piece of engineering.'

'I don't share your admiration of the railway system.'

'I appreciate quality in all walks of life,' said Colbeck, easily, 'and my fondness for railways is by no means uncritical. Engineers and contractors alike have made hideous mistakes in the past, some of which have cost lives as well as money. The Sankey Viaduct, on the other hand, was an undoubted triumph. It is also our first clue.'

Tallis blinked. 'Is it?'

'Of course, sir. It was no accident that the victim was hurled from that particular place. My belief is that the killer chose it with care.' He opened the door then paused to give the other man a farewell smile. 'We shall have to find out why.'

Sidney Heyford was a tall, stringy, ginger-haired individual in his forties who seemed to have grown in height since his promotion to the rank of inspector. When he had first joined the local constabulary, he had been fearless and conscientious, liked by his colleagues and respected by the criminal fraternity. He still worked as hard as ever but his eminence had made him arrogant, unyielding and officious. It had also made him very proprietorial. When he first heard the news, he let out a snort of disgust and flung the telegraph aside.

'Detectives from Scotland Yard!'

'Yes, sir,' said Constable Praine. 'Two of them.'

'I don't care if it's two or twenty. We don't want them here.'

'No, Inspector.'

'We can solve this crime on our own.'

'If you say so.'

'I do say so, Constable. It was committed on our doorstep.'

'That's not strictly true,' said Praine, pedantically. 'The Sankey Viaduct is halfway between here and Manchester. Some would claim that *they* have a right to take over the case.'

'Manchester?'

'Yes, Inspector.'

'Poppycock! Arrant poppycock!'

'If you say so.'

'I do say so, Constable.'

'The train in question did depart from Manchester.'

'But it was coming here, man – to Liverpool!'

In the eyes of Inspector Sidney Heyford, it was an unanswerable argument and the constable would not, in any case, have dared to quarrel with him. It was not only because of the other man's position that Walter Praine held his tongue. Big, brawny and with a walrus moustache hiding much of his podgy young face, Praine nursed secret ambitions to become Heyford's son-in-law one day, a fact that he had yet to communicate to the inspector's comely daughter. The situation made Praine eager to impress his superior. To that end, he was ready to endure the brusque formality with which he was treated.

'I'm sure that you are right, Inspector,' he said, obsequiously.

'There is no substitute for local knowledge.'

'I agree, sir.'

'We have done all that any detectives from the Metropolitan Police would have done – much more, probably.' Heyford turned an accusatory glare on Praine. 'How did they get to know of the crime in the first place?' he demanded. 'I hope that nobody from here dared to inform them?'

'It was the railway company who sent the telegraph.'

'They should have shown more faith in us.'

The two men were in the central police station in Liverpool. Both wore spotless uniforms. Inspector Heyford had spent most of the day leading the investigation into the murder. When he finally returned to his office late that afternoon, the waiting telegraph was passed to him. It had immediately aroused his possessive streak.

'This is our murder. I mean to keep it that way.'

'We were the first to receive reports of it.'

'I'll brook no interference.'

'If you say so, sir.'

'And, for heaven's sake, stop repeating

that inane phrase,' said Heyford with vehemence. 'You're a police constable, not a parrot.' Praine gave a contrite nod. 'What time should we expect them?'

'Not for another hour or so at least.'

'How did you decide that?'

'I checked the timetables in *Bradshaw*,' said Praine, hoping that his initiative might be rewarded with at least a nod of approval. Instead, it was met with a blank stare. 'They could not have set out much before the time when that telegraph was sent. If they arrive at Lime Street by six-thirty, they will be here not long afterwards.'

'They shouldn't be here at all,' grumbled Heyford, consulting his pocket watch. 'I need to master all the details before they come. Get out of here, Constable, and give me plenty of warning before they actually cross our threshold.'

'Yes, Inspector.'

'Make yourself scarce, then.'

Walter Praine left the room, acutely aware of the fact that he had failed to ingratiate himself with his putative father-in-law. Until he managed to do that, he could not possibly muster the confidence that was needed to make a proposal of marriage. Glad to be rid of him, Heyford began to read carefully through the statements that had been taken from the witnesses. It was only minutes before there was a timid knock on the door.

'Yes?' he barked.

The door opened and Praine put a tentative head around it.

'The gentlemen from Scotland Yard are already here, sir,' he said, sheepishly. 'Shall I show them in?'

Heyford leapt to his feet. 'Here?' he cried. 'How can that be? You told me that we had at least an hour.'

'I was mistaken.'

'Not for the first time, Constable Praine.'

Quelling him with a glare, Sidney Heyford opened the door wide and went into the outer office, manufacturing a smile as he did so. Robert Colbeck and Victor Leeming were studying the Wanted posters on the walls. Both men had bags with them. After a flurry of introductions, the detectives were taken into the little office and invited to sit down. Heyford was not impressed by Colbeck's elegance. With his stocky frame and gnarled face, Leeming did at least look like a policeman. That was not the case with his companion. To the man in uniform, Colbeck's debonair appearance and cultured voice were completely out of place in the rough and tumble world of law enforcement.

'I'm sorry that it's so cramped in here,' Heyford began.

'We've seen worse,' said Leeming, looking around.

'Much worse,' agreed Colbeck.

'Ashford in Kent, for instance. Six thousand people and only two constables to look after them from a tiny police house.'

'Some towns still refuse to take policing seriously enough. They take the Utopian view that crime will somehow solve itself without the intercession of detective work.' He appraised Heyford shrewdly. 'I'm sure that Liverpool displays more commonsense.'

'It has to, inspector,' said Heyford, sententiously, 'though we are woefully short of men to police a population of well over three hundred thousand. This is a thriving port. When the ships dock here, we've foreigners of all kind roaming our streets. If my men did not keep close watch over them, we'd have riot and destruction.'

'I'm sure that you do an excellent job.'

'That's how I earned my promotion.' He looked from one to the other. 'May I ask how you got here so soon?'

'That was the inspector's doing,' said Leeming, indicating his companion. 'He knows everything about train timetables. I prefer to travel by coach but Inspector Colbeck insisted that we came by rail.'

'How else could we have seen the Sankey Viaduct?' asked Colbeck. 'A coach would hardly have taken us across it. And think of the time we saved, Victor. Travel between Manchester and Liverpool by coach and it will take you up to four and a half hours. The train got us here in far less than half that time.' He turned to Heyford. 'I've always been fascinated by the railway system. That's why I know how to get from London to Liverpool at the fastest possible speed.'

'Inspector Colbeck!' said Heyford as realisation dawned. 'I thought I'd heard that name before.'

'He's the Railway Detective,' explained Leeming.

The information did not endear them to Heyford. If anything, it only soured him even more. Newspaper accounts of Colbeck's exploits had reached Liverpool in the past and they were invariably full of praise. Sidney Heyford felt that he deserved the same kind of public veneration. He took a deep breath.

'We are quite able to handle this case ourselves,' he asserted.

'That may be so,' said Colbeck, briskly, 'but your authority has been overridden. The London and North-West Railway Company has asked specifically that the Detective Department of the Metropolitan Police Force intercede. Last year, Sergeant Leeming and I were fortunate enough to solve an earlier crime for the same company so we were requested by name.'

Leeming nodded. 'They were very grateful.'

'So, instead of haggling over who should be in charge, I suggest that you give us all the information that you have so far gathered. We shall, of course, be glad of your assistance, Inspector Heyford, but we have not come all this way to have our credentials questioned.'

Colbeck had spoken with such firm politeness that Heyford was slightly stunned. He retreated into a muted surliness. Snatching up the papers from his desk, he told them about the progress of the investigation, reciting the details as if he had learned them by heart.

'At 10.15 a.m.,' he said, flatly, 'a train passed over the Sankey Viaduct on its way to Liverpool. The body of a man was thrown over the parapet and landed in the canal. When some people on a barge hauled it out of the water – their names were Enoch and Samuel Triggs, a father and son – it was found that the victim had been killed before he was flung from the train. He had been stabbed in the back though there was no sign of any weapon.'

'What state was the body in?' asked Colbeck.

'A bad one, inspector. When he hit the water, the man's head collided with a piece of driftwood. It smashed his face in. His own mother wouldn't recognise him now.'

'Was there anything on his body to

identify him?'

'Nothing. His wallet and watch were missing. So was his jacket.'

'Where is the body now?'

'In the mortuary.'

'I'd like to examine it.'

'It will tell you nothing beyond the fact that he was a young man and a very healthy one, by the look of it.'

'Nevertheless, I want to see the body this evening.'

'Very well.'

'If you don't mind, sir,' said Leeming, squeamishly, 'it's a treat that I'll forego. I hate morgues. They unsettle my stomach.'

Colbeck smiled. 'Then I'll spare you the ordeal, Victor.' He looked at Heyford again. 'There were two men on the barge, you say?'

'Actually,' replied the other, 'there were three, the third being Micah Triggs. He owns the barge but is very old. His son and grandson do most of the work.'

'But he was another witness.'

'Yes, Inspector. He confirmed what the others told me. When they had pulled the man out of the canal, they moored the barge. Samuel Triggs clambered all the way up to the station and caught the next train here to report the crime.' He puffed out his chest. 'He knew that Liverpool had a better police force than Manchester.'

25

Leeming was puzzled. 'Why didn't the train from which the body was thrown stop at the Viaduct? We did. Inspector Colbeck wanted to take a look at the scene of the crime.'

'This morning's train was an express that does not stop at all the intermediate stations.'

'The killer would have chosen it for that reason,' said Colbeck.

'Once he had jettisoned his victim, he wanted to get away from there as swiftly as possible.' He pondered. 'So far, it would appear, we have three witnesses, all of whom were in a similar position. Was anyone else there at the time?'

'According to Enoch Triggs, there were two ladies and a boy on the bank but they fled in fear. We have no idea who they were. Oh, yes,' he went on, studying one of the statements, 'and there seems to have been a man there as well but he, too, vanished. The truth is that Enoch Triggs and his son were too busy trying to rescue the body from the water to notice much else.'

'That takes care of those at the scene of the crime. I presume that you have details of where this barge can be reached?'

'Yes, Inspector.'

'Good. What about the other witnesses?'

'There *were* none,' asserted Heyford.

'A train full of passengers and nobody sees a man being tossed over the side of a viaduct? That's not an everyday event. It's something that people would remember.'

'I'd remember it,' agreed Leeming.

'Well?' said Colbeck. 'Did you make any effort to contact the passengers on that train, Sergeant Heyford?'

'How could I?' asked the other, defensively. 'By the time we were made aware of the crime, the passengers had all dispersed throughout the city.'

'Many of them may have intended to return to Manchester. It may well be that some people live there and work here. Did it never occur to you to have someone at the railway station this afternoon to question anyone leaving Liverpool who might have travelled on that train this morning?'

'No, sir.'

'Then we'll need to meet the same train tomorrow. With luck, we should find at least a few people who make the journey daily.'

'Wait,' said Heyford, leafing through the papers. 'There was something else. Oddly enough, it was the old man who told me this.'

'Micah Triggs?'

'He thought the man was thrown from the last carriage.'

'So?'

'That might explain why nobody saw it happen.'

'What about the guard?' said Leeming.

'His van would be behind the last carriage. Why did he see nothing?'

'Because he could have been looking the other way,' said Colbeck, thinking it through, 'or been distracted by something else. It would only have taken seconds to dispose of that body and the last carriage would be the ideal place.' His eyes flicked back to Heyford. 'I take it that you've spoken to the guard, inspector.'

'No,' said the other. 'When I got to the station, that train had long since left for Manchester with the guard aboard.'

'He would have been back at Lime Street in due course. Guards work long hours. I know their shift patterns. All you had to do was to look at a copy of *Bradshaw's Guide* and you could have worked out when that particular train would return here. We need every pair of eyes we can call on, Inspector. The guard must be questioned.'

'If he'd had anything to report, he'd have come forward.'

'He *does* have something to report,' said Colbeck. 'He may not have witnessed the crime being committed but he would have seen the passengers boarding the train, perhaps even noticed who got into the carriage next to his van. His evidence could be vital. I find it strange that you did not realise that.'

'I had other things to do, Inspector Col-

28

beck,' bleated the other, caught on the raw. 'I had to take statements from the witnesses then arrange for the transfer of the body. Do not worry,' he said, huffily, 'I'll meet that very train tomorrow and interview the guard in person.'

'Sergeant Leeming will already have done so.'

'Will I?' gulped Leeming.

'Yes, Victor. You'll catch an early train to Manchester so that you can speak to the staff at the station in case any of them remember who got into that last carriage. Then you must talk to the guard who was on that train today.'

'What then?'

'Travel back here on the same train, of course,' said Colbeck, 'making sure that you sit in the last carriage. You'll get some idea of how fast you go over the Sankey Viaduct and how difficult it would have been to hurl a dead body into the canal.'

Leeming goggled. 'I hope you're not expecting me to throw someone out of the carriage, sir.'

'Simply use your imagination.'

'What about me?' asked Heyford. 'Is there anything I can do?'

'Several things.'

'Such as?'

'First of all, you can recommend a hotel nearby so that Sergeant Leeming can book some rooms there. Second, you can conduct me to the mortuary and, after that, you can point me in the direction of the local newspapers.'

'Newspapers?'

'Yes,' said Colbeck, tiring of his pedestrian slowness. 'Papers that contain news. People have a habit of reading them. We need to reach as many of them as we can with a description of the victim.'

Heyford was scornful. 'How can you describe a faceless man?'

'By concentrating on his other features – age, height, build, hair colour and so on. His clothing will give us some idea of his social class. In short, we can provide enough details for anyone who knows him to be able to identify the man. Don't you agree?'

'Yes, Inspector.' There was a grudging respect. 'I suppose I do.'

'Have you reached any conclusion yourself?' asked Leeming.

'Only the obvious one, Sergeant – it was murder for gain. The victim was killed so that he could be robbed.'

'Oh, I suspect that there was much more to it than that,' said Colbeck. 'A lot of calculation went into this murder. Nobody would take so much trouble simply to get his hands on the contents of another man's wallet. Always reject the obvious, Inspector Heyford. It has a nasty tendency to mislead.'

'Yes, sir,' grunted the other.

Colbeck stood up. 'Let's get started, shall we? Suggest a hotel then lead me to the mortuary. The sooner we get that description in the newspapers, the better. With luck, he may read it.'

'Who?'

'The other witness. I discount the two ladies and the boy. They'll have been too shocked to give a coherent account. But there was a man on that bank as well. He's the person who interests me.'

Ambrose Hooper put the finishing touches to his work then stood back to admire it. He was in his studio, a place of amiable chaos that contained several paintings that had been started then abandoned, and dozens of pencil drawings that had never progressed beyond the stage of a rough sketch. Artist's materials lay everywhere. Light was fading so it was impossible for him to work on but he did not, in any case, need to do so. What he had achieved already had a sense of completeness to it. The sketch he had made of the Sankey Viaduct was now a vivid watercolour that would serve as model for the much bigger work he intended to paint.

It was all there – viaduct, canal, train, sailing barge, lush green fields, cows and, in the foreground, two women and a small boy. What brought the whole scene together,

31

giving it life and definition, was the central figure of the man who was tumbling helplessly through the air towards the water, a bizarre link between viaduct and canal. Hooper was thrilled. Instead of producing yet another landscape, he had created a unique historical document. It would be his masterpiece.

CHAPTER THREE

Victor Leeming was a walking paradox. The more things he found to dislike about his job, the more attached he became to it. He hated working late hours, looking at mutilated corpses, appearing in court to give evidence, facing the wrath of Superintendent Tallis, having to arrest women, being forced to write endless reports and travelling, whenever he ventured outside London, by rail instead of road. Most of all, he hated being separated for a night from his wife, Estelle, and their children. Notwithstanding all that, he loved being a detective and having the privilege of working alongside the famous Robert Colbeck. Slightly older than the inspector, he had none of the latter's acuity or grasp of detail. What Leeming could offer were tenacity, commitment and an unflinching readiness to face danger.

He slept fitfully that night. The bed was soft and the sheets were clean but he was never happy when Estelle was not beside him. Her love could sustain him through anything. It blinded her to the patent ugliness of her husband. His broken nose and jagged features would have tempted few women. His squint would have repelled most wives. Estelle adored him for his character rather than his appearance, and, as he had discovered long ago, the most hideous man could look handsome in the dark. Night was the time for confidences, for catching up on domestic events, for making plans, for reaching decisions and for sharing those marital intimacies that never seemed to dull with the passage of time. Leeming missed her painfully. Instead of waking up in his wife's arms, he had to go on another train journey. It was unjust.

Over an early breakfast at the hotel the next morning, he had difficulty in staying fully awake. Leeming's yawns punctuated the conversation. Colbeck was sympathetic.

'How much sleep did you get last night, Victor?' he said.

'Not enough.'

'I gathered that.' Colbeck ate the last of his toast. 'Make sure that you don't doze off on the train. I need you to remain alert. When you get to Lime Street, buy yourself a newspaper.'

'Why?'

'Because it will contain a description of the man we need to identify. Memorise it so that you can pass it on to the various people you question in Manchester.'

'Wouldn't it be easier simply to show them the newspaper?'

'No. You must master all the facts. I'm not having you thrusting a newspaper article under their noses. It's important to look everyone in the eye when you talk to them.'

'If I can keep mine open,' said Leeming, wearily. He drained his teacup in a gulp. 'Is it true that the man's shoes were missing?'

'His shoes and his jacket.'

'I can imagine someone stealing the jacket. It would have his wallet and other things of value in it. Why take his shoes as well?'

'They were probably of high quality. The rest of his clothing certainly was, Victor. It is no working man we seek. The murder victim dressed well and had a comfortable income.'

'How much is comfortable, Inspector?'

'More than we get paid.'

Leeming gave a hollow laugh. He finished his breakfast then checked the time. He had to be on his way. Colbeck accompanied him out of the hotel dining room and into a lobby that was decorated with unsightly potted plants. When someone opened the front door, the noise of heavy traffic burst in. Liverpool was palpably alive and busy. Leeming had no enthusiasm for stepping out into the swirling maelstrom but he steeled himself to do so. After an exchange of farewells with Colbeck, he strode off in the direction of Lime Street.

The first thing he noticed when he reached

the railway station was the visible presence of uniformed policemen. Inspector Heyford had obviously taken Colbeck's strictures to heart. Leeming bought a return ticket to Manchester then picked up a copy of the *Liverpool Times* from a vendor with a stentorian voice. The murder attracted a banner headline on the front page. Colbeck's appeal for information was also given prominence. There was no mention of Inspector Sidney Heyford. The Liverpool constabulary had been eclipsed by the arrival of two detectives from Scotland Yard. Leeming was glad that nobody in the bustling station knew that he was one of the men dispatched from London. In his present somnambulistic state, he was hardly a good advertisement for the Metropolitan Police.

The platform was crowded, the noise of trains was deafening and the billowing steam was an impenetrable fog that seemed to thicken insidiously with every minute and invade his nostrils. In the previous year, Lime Street Station had been considerably enlarged, its majestic iron structure being the first of its kind. Leeming was unable to see this marvel of industrial architecture. His mind was on the harrowing journey ahead. When the train pulled in and shed its passengers, he braced himself and climbed aboard. The newspaper kept him awake long enough for him to read the front page.

Then the locomotive exploded into action and the train jerked forward like an angry mastiff pulling on a leash.

Within seconds, Victor Leeming was fast asleep.

Inspector Robert Colbeck also spent time at Lime Street that morning but he made sure that he saw every inch of it, struck by how much railway stations had improved in the past twenty years. It did not have the classical magnificence of Euston but it had a reassuring solidity and was supremely functional. Even though it was used by thousands of passengers every week, it still had an air of newness about it. Colbeck was there to meet the train from which the murder victim had been hurled on the previous day, hoping that Sergeant Leeming's visit to Manchester had borne fruit.

Blackboards had been set up along the platform with a question chalked on them in large capitals – DID YOU TRAVEL ON THIS TRAIN YESTERDAY? – and policemen were ready to talk to anyone who came forward. Colbeck watched with approval. Long before the train had even arrived at Lime Street, however, Constable Walter Praine bore down purposefully on the detective.

'Excuse me, Inspector,' he said. 'May I have a word, please?'

37

'Of course,' replied Colbeck.

'There's someone at the police station who refuses to speak to anyone but you. He saw your name in the newspaper this morning and says that he has important information for the person in charge of the investigation.' Praine rolled his eyes. 'Inspector Heyford was most upset that the fellow would not talk to him.'

'Did this man say nothing at all?'

'Only that you'd got it wrong, sir.'

'Wrong?'

'Your description of the murder victim.'

'Then I look forward to being corrected,' said Colbeck, eagerly. 'Any new facts that can be gleaned are most welcome.'

Praine led to the way to a waiting cab and the two of them were soon carried along bumpy streets that were positively swarming with horse-drawn traffic and handcarts. When they reached the police station, the first person they met was an aggrieved Sidney Heyford.

'This is *my* police station in *my* town,' he complained, 'and the wretched man spurns me.'

'Did he give you his name?' asked Colbeck.

'Ambrose Hooper. He's an *artist*.'

Heyforth pronounced the word with utter contempt as if it were a heinous crime that had not yet come within the purview of the statute book. In his codex, artists were shameless outcasts, parasites who lived off others and who should, at the very least, be transported to a penal colony to reflect on their sinful existence. Heyforth jerked his thumb towards his office.

'He's in there, Inspector.'

'Thank you,' said Colbeck.

Removing his hat, he opened the door and went into the office. A dishevelled Ambrose Hooper rose from his chair to greet him.

'Are you the detective from London?'

'Yes, Mr Hope. I am Inspector Colbeck.'

'I thought you didn't come from around here,' said Hooper, looking him up and down. 'Liverpool is a philistine place. It has no real appreciation of art and architecture. It idolises conformity. Those of us who cut a dash with our clothing or our way of life could never fit easily into Liverpool. I hate towns of any kind myself. I choose to live in the country and breathe in free air.'

Ambrose Hooper was wearing his crumpled white jacket over a flowery waistcoat and a pair of baggy blue trousers. A fading blue cravat was at his neck. His straw hat lay on the table beside a dog-eared portfolio. Some paint had lodged in his beard. Wisps of grey hair stood up mutinously all over his head. Colbeck could see that he was a man of independent mind.

'I'm told that you believe I am wrong,'

said Colbeck.

'I don't believe it, sir – I *know* it.'

'How?'

'I was there, Inspector.'

'At the Sankey Viaduct?'

'Yes, I saw exactly what happened.'

'Then why didn't you give a statement to the police?'

'Because that would have meant waiting an age until they arrived on the scene,' explained Hooper. 'Besides, there was nothing that I could do. The body was hauled aboard that barge. I felt that it was important to record the event while it was still fresh in my mind.'

Colbeck was delighted. 'You mean that you went home and wrote down an account of all that you'd seen?'

'I'm no wordsmith, sir. Language has such severe limitations. Art, on the other hand, does not. It has an immediacy that no author could match.' He picked up the portfolio. 'Do you want to know what I saw at the Sankey Viaduct yesterday?'

'Very much so, Mr Hooper.'

'Then behold, my friend.'

Untying the ribbon, the artist opened the cover of the portfolio with a flourish to reveal his work. Colbeck was flabbergasted. An unexpected bounty had just fallen into his lap. What he was looking at was nothing less than a detailed photograph of what had

40

actually happened. Having read the statements from the three witnesses on the barge, Colbeck had built up a clear picture of the situation in his mind's eye. Hooper's work enlarged and enlivened that mental image.

'A perfect marriage of artistic merit and factual accuracy,' said Hooper, proudly. 'This is merely a rough version, of course, hastily finished so that I could offer it as evidence. I'll use this as the basis for a much larger and more dramatic painting.'

'It could hardly be more dramatic,' opined Colbeck, scrutinising the work. 'You are a man of talent, sir. I congratulate you.'

'Thank you, Inspector.' He pointed to the three small figures in the foreground. 'I moved the ladies slightly but this is more or less the position they were in. Not that they stayed there for long, mark you. When that poor man suddenly dived over the parapet, Aunt Petronella jumped back as if she'd seen a ghost.'

Colbeck was surprised. 'She was your aunt?'

'Not mine – the boy's. At least, that's what I assumed. They were complete strangers to me but I always like to give people names if I include them in a painting. It lends a sense of familiarity.' He indicated each one in turn. 'This is Hester Lewthwaite – this is her son, Anthony – and here is his maiden aunt,

Petronella Snark.' He gave a sly chuckle. 'I suppose that if you've preserved your virginity as long as she had, the sight of a man descending on you from a great height would be quite terrifying.'

Colbeck could not believe his good fortune. Ambrose Hooper had provided the best and most comprehensive piece of evidence he had ever received from a member of the public. It answered so many important questions and saved him so much time. He was pleased to note that Micah Triggs had been so observant. The victim did appear to have been thrown from the last carriage. He remembered his own description of the victim.

'Ah,' said Colbeck, jabbing a finger at the man in the centre of the painting. 'This is where I got it wrong. He's wearing a jacket.'

'And a pair of shoes,' added Hooper.

'Are you absolutely sure that was the case?'

'That's the kind of detail an artist doesn't miss. The shoes were gleaming. They caught the sun as he plummeted down. They're only minute in the painting, of course, but, if you look closely, you'll see that the shoes are definitely there.'

'They are indeed.'

'I'm a stickler for precision.'

'This is remarkable, Mr Hooper,' said Colbeck, shaking him warmly by the hand.

'I can't thank you enough.'

'We also serve who only stand and paint.'

'You've made our job so much easier. What a blessing that you happened to be in the right place at the right time!'

'I have a habit of doing that, Inspector. At first, I used to put it down to coincidence but I've come round to the view that I'm an agent of divine purpose. God *wanted* me to bear witness. I daresay it was also true of Aunt Petronella but she was unequal to the challenge.' He looked at the tiny figure of the murder victim. 'What I'd like to know is how he brought off that wonderful conjuring trick.'

'Conjuring trick?'

'Yes,' said Hooper. 'When he left the train, he was wearing a jacket and a pair of shoes. How did he get rid of them by the time that the police arrived on the scene?'

'There's no mystery there,' said Colbeck with a wry smile.

'No?'

'He clearly had some assistance.'

Victor Leeming talked to every member of staff he could find at the station. By the time he finished, he felt that he had spoken to half the population of Manchester and all to no avail. Ticket clerks, porters, the station-master, his assistants, the engine driver, the fireman, even those who sold newspapers at

Victoria Station were asked if they had seen anyone suspicious around the same time on the previous day. In effect, they had all given him the same answer – that it was difficult to pick out any one person from the sea of faces that passed in front of them. Least helpful of all had been the guard in charge of the train on which the murder had occurred. His name was Cyril Dear, a short, skinny, animated individual in his fifties who was highly offended even to be approached by the detective. As he talked to him, his hands were gesticulating madly as if he were trying without success to juggle seven invisible balls in the air.

'I saw nobody getting into the last carriage, Sergeant,' he said. 'I've got better things to do than to take note of where every passenger sits. Do you know what being a guard means?'

'Yes,' said Leeming. 'It means that you have responsibilities.'

'Many responsibilities.'

'One of which is to ensure the safety of your passengers.'

'And that's what I do, Sergeant.'

'It must entail being especially vigilant.'

'I *am* especially vigilant,' retorted Dear, hands now juggling five additional balls. 'I defy any man to say that I'm not. I see things that most people would never notice in a hundred years.'

'Yet you are still quite unable to tell me who occupied the last carriage yesterday morning. Think back, sir,' encouraged Leeming, stifling a monstrous yawn. 'When the train was filling up, what did you observe?'

'What I observe every day – paying passengers.'

'Did none of them stand out?'

'Not that I recall.'

'This is very serious,' said Leeming, as people surged past him to walk down the platform. 'A man who travelled on this same train only twenty-four hours ago was murdered in cold blood then flung over the Sankey Viaduct.'

'I know that.'

'We simply must catch his killer.'

'Well, don't look at me, Sergeant,' said Dear, as if he had just been accused of the crime. 'I have an unblemished record of service on this line. I worked on it when it was the Liverpool and Manchester Railway, all of twenty-two years ago. Cyril Dear's name is a by-word for loyalty. Speak to anyone. They'll tell you.'

Leeming groaned inwardly. 'I have no wish to talk to another human being in Manchester,' he said, ruefully. 'My throat is sore enough already. Very well, Mr Dear. You are obviously unable to help me at the moment. But if you should happen to remember anything of interest about yesterday's journey –

45

anything at all – please let me know when we reach Liverpool.'

'Climb aboard, sir. We leave in two minutes.'

'Good.'

Leeming had turned to get into the last carriage, only to find, to his dismay, that it was already full. Men and women had taken every available seat. With a sinking feeling, he realised why. Manchester newspapers had carried full details of the murder as well. Ghoulish curiosity had dictated where some of the passengers sat. They wanted to be in the very carriage where it was believed the crime had been committed. As it passed over the Sankey Viaduct, they would no doubt all rush to the appropriate window in a body to look out over the parapet. He found it a depressing insight into human nature.

Colbeck had instructed him to travel in the last carriage. Since he could not obey the order, he decided to solve another problem that had vexed them. He swung round to face Cyril Dear again and asserted his authority.

'I'll travel in the guard's van with you,' he declared.

Dear was outraged. 'It's against the rules.'

'Is it?'

'I could never allow it, sir.'

'But you're not allowing it, Mr Dear. I'm

forcing myself upon you.' He summoned up his most disarming smile. 'When we reach Liverpool, you'll have the pleasure of reporting me, won't you?'

When he was angry, the freckles on Inspector Heyford's face stood out more than ever. As he stared at the painting, they seemed to glow with a rich intensity. He turned to confront Ambrose Hooper.

'Concealing evidence is a crime,' he warned.

'But I haven't concealed it,' argued the artist. 'I've brought it to you. There it lies, for all to see.'

'A day late.'

'I can see that you are no painter, Inspector Heyford.'

'I prefer to do an honest job sir.'

'Art cannot be rushed. I had to finish the watercolour before I presented it to the public. I have my reputation to consider.'

'It remains intact,' Colbeck assured him.

'There is still the question of delay,' insisted Heyford. 'You were a witness, Mr Hooper. Yet you sneaked away from the scene of the crime. Action should be taken against you.'

'Then it should also be taken against Mrs Lewthwaite, her son and her unmarried sister, Miss Petronella Snark. They had just as good a view of the whole thing as me.'

Heyford gaped. 'Who on earth *are* these people?'

'I'll explain later, Inspector,' said Colbeck. 'The fact of the matter is that Mr Hooper has shown us crucial evidence that may help us to identify the dead man.'

'How?'

'He had an expensive tailor. I could see that from his trousers. In all likelihood, the name of that tailor will be sewn inside his jacket.'

'But we do not have his jacket, Inspector Colbeck.'

'We will do in due course. As for Mr Hooper, the only action that should be taken is to commend his skill as an artist and to thank him for his assistance.' He closed the portfolio. 'It's been invaluable, sir.'

'It's the least I could do for the victim,' said Hooper, tying up the ribbon. 'His loss was, after all, my gain. Like any true artist, I paint out of a compulsion but there is, alas, a commercial aspect to my work as well. As a result of the publicity surrounding this crime, my painting will fetch a much higher price.'

Heyford was scandalised. 'It should not be allowed.'

'It should,' said Colbeck. 'You deserve every penny, sir.'

Since they were in Heyford's office, Colbeck felt an obligation to let him see the

48

painting even though the inspector did not appreciate either its quality or its significance. When the artist had left, Colbeck tried to mollify Heyford by praising the way that he had deployed his men at the railway station. The freckles slowly lost their glint though they did flare up again when Colbeck told him how Petronella Snark and her companions had come by their names.

'And what's all this about the jacket?' asked Heyford.

'I'll reclaim it from the person who stole it.'

'And who might that be?'

'A member of the Triggs family, of course,' said Colbeck. 'Before you got there, he also relieved the corpse of its shoes. Now that really is a case of withholding evidence.'

There was a tap on the door. In response to Heyford's invitation, it opened to admit Victor Leeming, drooping with fatigue. He removed his hat to wipe perspiration from his brow with the back of his hand.

'What did you find out, Victor?' asked Colbeck.

'That I never wish to travel by train ever again, sir,' replied Leeming, rubbing his back. 'The journey back to Liverpool rattled every bone in my body.'

'Did you discover any witnesses in Manchester?'

'Nobody saw a thing.'

'Not even the guard?'

'No, Inspector. When the train is in motion, he always sits on the other side of the van so he saw the wrong side of the viaduct as the train passed over it yesterday. I made the fatal mistake of sharing the guard's van with him,' he went on, massaging a sore elbow. 'It's no better than a cattle truck.'

'Did he remember *anything* about yesterday's journey?' said Heyford. 'What about the occupants of that last carriage?'

'They could have been a tribe of man-eating pygmies, for all that he cared. The guard's only concern was that the train was on time.' Undoing his coat, he flopped into a chair. 'Do you mind if I sit down for a while? I'm aching all over.'

'I'm sorry, Victor,' said Colbeck. 'I need you to come with me.'

'Where?'

'To retrieve some stolen property. While you were away, we had an interesting development in the case.' He eased the sergeant to his feet. 'Come on – I'll tell you about it on the way.'

Leeming blenched. 'Not another train journey?'

'Two of them, I'm afraid.'

The *Red Rose* was moored in the canal basin. Micah Triggs sat on the bulwark of his barge and puffed contentedly on his pipe. Well into his seventies, he had a weather-beaten face and a shrunken body but he remained unduly spry for his age. Curled in his lap, basking in the afternoon sunshine, was a mangy black cat. When he saw three figures walking towards him along the towpath, Micah stood up suddenly and catapulted the animal on to the deck. With a squeal of protest, the cat took refuge beneath the sail.

'Mr Triggs?' asked Colbeck as they got near. 'Mr Micah Triggs?'

'The same,' grunted the old man.

Colbeck introduced himself and his companions, Victor Leeming and Walter Praine. He explained that he was leading the investigation into the murder and thanked Micah for the witness statement that he had given.

'If you work on a barge,' said Micah, shifting his pipe to the other side of his mouth, 'you fish all sorts of odd things out of the canal but this is the first time we found the dead body of a man.'

'Your son and grandson were with you, I believe.'

'Yes, Inspector – Enoch and Sam.'

'How tall would your son be?'

'That's a strange question. Why do you ask it?'

'Curiosity, Mr Triggs. Would he be around your height?'

'No,' replied Micah. 'Enoch is a good foot taller than me and twice as broad. Sam is shorter and has more of my build.'

'Then it's your grandson we need to speak to, sir,' said Colbeck, glancing around. 'Where might we find him?'

'What business do you have with Sam?'

'We just want to clarify something in his statement.'

Micah was suspicious. 'It takes *three* of you to do that?'

'I think I know where he might be, Inspector,' said Constable Praine, sensing that they would get little help from the old man. 'Most of the bargees spend their spare time in the Traveller's Rest.' He pointed to the inn further along the towpath. 'My guess is that he and his father will be in there.'

'Shall I roust them out, sir?' volunteered Leeming.

'No, Victor,' replied Colbeck. 'This is a job for Constable Praine, I think. And no rousting out is required. The only person we need is Samuel Triggs. He sounds as if he'd be the right size. Constable.'

'Yes, Inspector?' said Praine.

'Invite him, very politely, to come and talk to me.'

'I will, sir.'

Pleased with his assignment, Praine went off willingly towards the inn. On the journey there, Colbeck had questioned him closely about the Liverpool Constabulary and, in the course of describing activities at the central police station, the constable had let slip the information that he had conceived a romantic interest in Heyford's daughter. Since Praine was too frightened of the inspector to pursue it any further, Colbeck hoped that he could put in a good word for the young lover by praising his conduct as a policeman. It was the reason he had dispatched Walter Praine to the Traveller's Rest.

'What's going on?' said Micah, warily.

'You tell us, sir,' suggested Colbeck.

'We've done nothing wrong. We helped you.'

'That's true, Mr Triggs, and we were grateful. But another witness has come forward and his statement contradicts all three that were made on the *Red Rose*.'

Micah became aggressive. 'Is someone calling me a liar?'

'Not at all.'

'I told those policemen exactly what I saw.'

'I'm sure, sir.'

Colbeck looked around the barge. Sailing along the canal, the *Red Rose* had a certain grace about it. Close to, however, its defects were glaringly obvious. It was old, dirty and neglected. The sail had been repaired in several places and some of the planks in its deck were badly splintered. Also, it stank. Micah could read his mind.

'It's not my fault,' he said, bitterly. 'I can't

53

afford a new barge. There's not the same money in the canal any more. That bleeding railway is to blame. It's took lots of our trade away from us. And what has it given us in return – a bleeding corpse!'

'I'd much prefer to travel by water,' said Leeming.

'It's in our blood.'

'By water, horse or on my own two feet. Anything but a train.'

Leeming was about to explain his dislike of the railway when he saw two people emerge from the Traveller's Rest. Constable Praine was strolling towards them with Samuel Triggs by his side. Triggs was wearing the same rough clothing as his grandfather and a similar hat, but the sun picked out something that set him apart from the other bargees. On his feet was a pair of expensive, shiny, black leather shoes. He was a slim young man in his twenties with a defiant smile and an arrogant strut. Triggs saw the detectives looking at his shoes.

'Finders, keepers,' he said.

'They belong to someone else,' Colbeck told him.

'Yes, but 'e's got no bleedin' use for 'em, poor devil.'

'That doesn't give you the right to steal from him, Mr Triggs.'

'It was my reward for pullin' 'im out of the canal.'

'Where's the jacket?'

'What jacket?' returned Triggs with a blank expression on his face. 'There *was* no jacket. Grandpa?'

'No,' said Micah, firmly. 'He had no jacket on, Inspector.'

'Father will tell you the same. Ask 'im.'

'Constable Praine,' said Colbeck, smoothly, 'we are confronted here with what amounts to a collective loss of memory. Three people have somehow forgotten that the corpse was wearing a suit when it fell into the canal. How do you deal with this sort of problem when you come across it?'

'Like this, sir.'

Seeing an opportunity to impress, the policeman grabbed Triggs by the collar and lifted him bodily before dangling him over the edge of the canal. Triggs squawked in protest but he could not get free.

'If I hold him under the water long enough, we might eventually get an honest answer out of him.'

'Leave him alone,' yelled Micah, snatching up a wooden pole to brandish at Praine, 'or I'll split your skull open.'

'That wouldn't be very wise, Mr Triggs,' said Leeming as he squared up to the old man. 'We're already in a position to arrest your grandson for the theft of a pair of shoes. Do you want to share the same cell on a charge of assaulting a police officer?'

Micah spat into the water with disgust then flung the pole aside. 'That's better, sir.'

'Now, then,' said Praine, dipping Triggs in the water before pulling him out again, 'have I jogged your memory?'

'Yes!' cried Triggs, capitulating. The constable set him down again. 'It's under the tarpaulin. I was goin' to wear it on special days.'

'But it must have a hole in the back,' observed Colbeck.

'It's only a slit – and you can 'ardly notice the bloodstains.'

Samuel Triggs climbed aboard the barge and lifted the tarpaulin so that he could haul out the smart jacket. Like the black shoes, it looked incongruous against the rest of his apparel. Before he surrendered it, he put a hand to his heart.

'I swear to God there was nothin' in the pockets, Inspector.'

'Sam's right,' confirmed Micah. 'If there'd been a wallet or some papers, we'd have given them to the police. We're not criminals. If we had been, we'd have stripped all his clothes off and slung him back in the canal for someone else to find.'

Colbeck could see that they were telling the truth. He put out a hand. With great reluctance, Triggs passed the jacket to him. Colbeck turned it over and held it up. There was a neat slit where the knife had gone

56

through the material and an ugly stain left by the blood. Its unexpected visit to the dark water of the canal made the jacket lose a little of its shape. Colbeck examined the front of it.

'This was not made by an English tailor,' he decided, studying the cut of the lapels. 'You'll not see this fashion in London.'

'Then where *does* it come from?' asked Leeming.

Colbeck checked the label inside the jacket then looked up.

'Paris,' he said. 'The murder victim was a Frenchman.'

CHAPTER FOUR

Superintendent Edward Tallis had dedicated himself to his work with a missionary zeal. Faced with what he saw as a rising tide of crime, he put in far more hours than anyone else in the Detective Department in the hope of stemming its menacing flow. With too few officers covering far too large an area, he knew that policing the capital city was a Herculean task but he was not daunted. He was determined that the forces of law and order would prevail. Tallis was not the only man to leave the army and join the Metropolitan Police but the others had all retained their rank to give their names a ring of authority. The only rank that he used was the one confirmed upon him in his new profession. It filled him with pride. Being a detective superintendent was, for Tallis, like sitting at the right hand of the Almighty.

Accustomed to arrive first at Scotland Yard, he was surprised to find that one of his men was already there. Bent over his desk, Robert Colbeck was writing something in his educated hand. Spotting him through the half-open door, Tallis barged into the room.

'What the devil are *you* doing here, Inspector?' he said.

'Finishing my report on the Harrison-Clark trial, sir,' replied the other. He turned to face Tallis. 'If you recall, I had to postpone it.'

'You are supposed to be in Liverpool.'

'We came back to London last night.'

Tallis was astounded. 'Are you telling me that the murder was solved in the space of two days?'

'Alas, no,' said Colbeck, rising to his feet, 'but the investigation has reached the stage where our presence is no longer required in Liverpool. To be honest, I'm heartily relieved. It's an unlovely place and Victor Leeming was missing his wife badly.'

'Wives do not exist in the Detective Department,' said Tallis, acidly. 'Duty always comes before any trifling marital arrangements. Leeming knows that. He should have been ready to stay in Liverpool for a month, if called upon to do so.'

'That necessity did not arise, Superintendent.'

'I expected the pair of you to spend more than one night there.'

'So did I, sir,' said Colbeck, 'but events took an interesting turn. You'll find a full explanation in the report I left on your desk earlier on. I also took the liberty of opening a window in your office. When I got here, the stench of cigar smoke had still not dispersed

60

from the room.'

'It's not a stench, man – it's a pleasing aroma.'

'Only to those who create it.'

Tallis glowered at him before stalking off to his office. Colbeck sat down again to finish the last paragraph then he put his pen aside. After blotting the wet ink, he picked up the pages and put them in the right order. When he took the report into the superintendent's office, Tallis was reading about the murder inquiry. Colbeck waited until his superior had finished. The older man nodded.

'Admirably thorough,' he conceded.

'Thank you, sir.'

'Though I'm not sure that it's altogether wise to accept the testimony of an artist at face value. In my experience, they're rather shifty fellows whose imagination tends to get the better of them.'

'I put my trust in Ambrose Hooper unreservedly. Those three witnesses on the barge confirmed everything that was in the painting.'

'Thieves and an artist.' Tallis sucked his teeth. 'Such men are hardly reliable.'

'It was only one member of the Triggs family who kept hold of property that did not belong to him, and he is not what anyone would describe as a thief. Samuel Triggs simply seized an opportunity.'

'That's what villains do,' said Tallis, crisply.

'This fellow stole a jacket and a pair of shoes, thereby impeding the investigation. I trust that you arrested him on the spot.'

'I left that to Constable Praine.'

'You mentioned him in your report.'

'A good policeman, sir – strong, quick-thinking and obedient. I told Inspector Heyford that I would be happy to see Praine in the ranks of the Metropolitan Police. It made the inspector look at the man through new eyes.'

What he did not tell the superintendent was that he had also been able to oil the wheels of Walter Praine's romance. Faced with the threat of losing him, Sidney Heyford had been at his most proprietary, offering all manner of blandishments for the constable to stay. At long last, Praine had been able to broach the sensitive subject of marriage to the inspector's daughter.

'I see that you resorted to the press again,' noted Tallis.

'Yes,' said Colbeck. 'I put the same advertisement in Liverpool and Manchester papers even though the victim is not a local man.'

'How do you know that?'

'Someone would have reported him missing by now, sir. There are not all that many young Frenchmen living in that part of the country, even fewer with this man's income and taste in clothes. We must remember that he was travelling in a first class carriage. Most people on that train settled for second or third.'

Tallis wrinkled his nose. 'I could never lower myself to either.'

'My hope is that our man was visiting someone in Liverpool without warning. Though he had no face, the description of him is very detailed. If he has friends there, he'll be recognised.'

'He could just have been on his way to the docks.'

'Why?'

'To sail home to France, of course.'

'From Liverpool?' said Colbeck. 'I doubt that, sir. He'd choose one of the Channel ports. No, he had another reason for visiting the place and we need to discover what it was.'

'Why didn't you stay there until someone came forward in answer to your request in the newspapers?'

'Because it might take days and I had no intention of sitting there and twiddling my thumbs. We did not exactly have the most cordial welcome from the local police. They felt – quite rightly – that we were treading on their toes.'

'Supposing that nobody responds to your plea?'

'Oh, I'm fairly certain that someone will, Superintendent.'

'What makes you so confident?'

'A reward was offered,' said Colbeck. 'The railway company is anxious for the crime to be solved as soon as possible. They want to assure their passengers that this is an isolated incident. That's only possible if we catch the killer.'

'Quite so.'

'As long as the man is at large, people will fear that he's likely to strike again even though that possibility is remote.'

'Is it?'

'I believe so. Look at the facts. This murder is unique. It was committed in a particular way and at a particular point on the line. It was at a particular time of day as well – when the express train was running. All of the others stop at the Sankey Viaduct though, rather confusingly, that station was renamed Warrington Junction in 1831. Victor and I changed trains there to get to the canal basin.'

'What this does not explain,' said Tallis, tapping the report in front of him, 'is how the killer came to be sharing the carriage alone with his intended victim.'

'There are two possible answers to that, sir.'

'I fail to see them.'

'They could have been known to each other and travelled as friends. That would have meant that the victim was caught off guard.'

'And the second possibility?'

'That's the more likely one,' said Colbeck. 'The carriage may have been first class but other passengers might have wished to choose it. Had they done so, of course, the murderer would have been foiled. Once his victim had entered the carriage, he had to ensure nobody else did.'

'How could he do that?'

'By posing as someone in authority and turning people away.'

'You mean that he pretended to be a railway employee?'

'No, sir. He was wearing a uniform that would deter other passengers while at the same time reassuring the victim when he joined him in the carriage at the time of departure.'

Tallis was furious. 'Only one uniform would do that.'

'Exactly,' said Colbeck. 'The killer was dressed as a policeman.'

Much as he loved his daughter, there were times when Caleb Andrews found her profoundly exasperating. For the third time in a row, Madeleine had beaten him at draughts, a game in which he had once considered himself invincible. The previous evening, she had trounced him at dominoes. Andrews was not a man who suffered defeat with good grace. He began to wish that he had never taught her how to play the games. It was humiliating for him to lose to a woman.

'Another game?' she suggested.

'No, no, Maddy. I've had enough.'

'Your luck may change.'

'It's not a question of luck,' he said, gathering up the counters and putting them back in their box. 'Draughts is a game of skill. You have to be able to out-think your opponent.'

'I just play it for the pleasure.'

Andrews grimaced. It was even more annoying to be beaten by someone who did not take the game seriously. For him, it was a real contest; for Madeleine, it was simply fun. Seeing that he was so discomfited, she got up, kissed him on the forehead and went into the kitchen to make a pot of tea. They were in the little house that they shared in Camden. Andrews was a short, wiry man in his fifties with a fringe beard dappled with grey. There was a suppressed energy about him that belied his age. Since the death of his wife six years earlier, his daughter had looked after him with a mixture of kindness, cajolery and uncompromising firmness.

When the tea had been brewed, Madeleine brought the pot into the living room and set it down on the table with a cosy on it. Now in her twenties, she had inherited her mother's good looks and had the same auburn hair, but Madeleine Andrews possessed an assurance that was all her own. As

66

her father had learned to his cost, she also had a quick brain. To stave off the pangs of defeat, he tried to lose himself in his newspaper. One item of news immediately caught his jaundiced eye.

'He should have consulted me,' he said.

'Who?'

'Inspector Colbeck. I work for that railway company. I know every inch of our track.'

'Yes, Father,' she agreed, 'but you're only an engine driver.'

'So?'

'You're not a detective like Robert.'

'I could have helped. I could have made suggestions.'

'I'm sure that he appreciates that,' said Madeleine, tactfully, 'but he had to act quickly. As soon as word of the crime reached him, Robert went straight off to Liverpool. He had no time to contact you.'

'Is that what he told you?'

'More or less.'

It was a white lie to appease her father. Caleb Andrews had been the driver of the mail train that was robbed in the previous year and he had been badly injured in the process. Since he was leading the investigation, Colbeck had got to know both Andrews and his daughter well. A warm friendship had soon developed between the detective and Madeleine and it had matured into something far more. Andrews liked to pretend that Colbeck called at the house to increase his knowledge of the railway system by discussing it with a man who had spent his working life on it. But he knew that it was his daughter who brought the detective to Camden.

'When are you likely to see him again, Maddy?' he asked.

'Soon, I hope.'

'Make a point of telling him about my offer.'

'Robert will be very grateful to hear of it,' she said, fetching two cups and saucers from the dresser. 'At the moment, I'm afraid, he's extremely busy.'

'Not according to this.' Andrews peered at the newspaper. 'It's been five days since the murder took place and they've got nowhere. Inspector Colbeck is making another appeal for someone to help the police by identifying the victim. He was a Frenchman,' he added with a loud sniff. 'Fifty years ago, we'd have cheered anyone who killed a Froggy. Now, we arrest them – if we can find them, that is.'

'Robert will find him in due course,' she said, loyally.

'Meanwhile, he's just sitting on his hands.'

'He'd never do that, Father. While he's waiting for information to come in, he'll be helping to solve crimes here in London. Robert never rests. He works terribly hard.'

'So do I,' boasted Andrews. 'Hard and long. I've been at it for over forty years, man and boy. I could have told Inspector Colbeck exactly what it's like to take a train over the Sankey Viaduct because I've done it. He should have come to me, Maddy.'

'I'll tell him that,' she soothed, removing the tea cosy and lifting up the pot. 'When Robert has a moment to spare.'

Nobody was allowed to rest at Scotland Yard. Superintendent Tallis made sure of that. He kept a watchful eye on what his detectives were doing and cracked the whip over any he felt were slacking. There was never any cause to upbraid Robert Colbeck. He was intensely busy. While awaiting further developments in the murder case, he was reviewing the evidence on a daily basis, giving instructions by letter to Inspector Heyford, deploying his men on other cases, attending meetings within the Detective Department and acting as a legal consultant to his colleagues.

Unlike the majority of those at Scotland Yard, he had not worked his way up through the Metropolitan Police. Colbeck had trained as a barrister and been a familiar figure in the London courts. The murder of someone very dear to him had affected him deeply and made him question the efficacy of what he was doing. He felt that he could make a far better contribution to law enforcement by catching criminals than simply by securing their convictions in court. Fellow detectives made great use of his legal knowledge but Tallis merely envied it. Colbeck's career as a barrister was one more reason why there was so much latent hostility between the two men.

That afternoon began badly. The superintendent's patience was wearing out. After a bruising interview with him – 'You are supposed to be the Railway Detective – prove it!' – Colbeck returned to his office and began to go painstakingly through all the evidence yet again, hoping that there was some hitherto unnoticed detail that might help to illumine the whole investigation. He was so absorbed in his work that he did not hear Victor Leeming enter the room.

'Excuse me, sir,' said the sergeant. 'You have a visitor.'

'Oh.' Colbeck glanced up. 'Thank you, Victor. Show him in.'

'It's a lady and a very handsome one at that.'

'Did she say what her business was?'

'No, sir. The only person she wishes to see is you.'

Colbeck got to his feet. 'Then you'd better bring her in.'

Moments later, a tall, stately woman in her thirties came into the office and waited until the door had been closed behind her before she yielded up her name.

'Inspector Colbeck?'

'That's correct.'

'My name is Hannah Critchlow,' she said, 'and I've come in response to the request you inserted in the *Liverpool Times*.'

He was curious. 'You've come all the way from Liverpool?'

'This is not something I wished to discuss with the local police. I had other reasons for being in London so I decided to speak directly to you. I hope that I can rely on your discretion.'

'Completely,' he said. 'Do sit down, Mrs Critchlow.'

'*Miss* Critchlow,' she corrected.

'I beg your pardon.'

Hannah Critchlow lowered herself into a chair and he resumed his seat behind the desk. Colbeck was surprised to hear that she was unmarried. She had a sculptured beauty that was enhanced by her costly attire. She also had a distinct poise about her and would never go through life unnoticed by members of the opposite sex. Without being told, he knew that she had travelled by train to London in a first class carriage. Colbeck felt a quiet excitement. Given the trouble she had taken to see him, he believed that she would have something of value to impart.

'Before we go any further,' she said, 'there

is one thing that I must make clear. I am not here in search of any reward.'

'But if you can provide information that will lead to the arrest of the murderer, the railway company will be very grateful to you.'

'I don't want their gratitude.'

'What do you want, Miss Critchlow?'

'The satisfaction of knowing that this villain is caught. From the reports in the newspaper, it seems to have been an appalling crime. The culprit should not be allowed to get away with it.'

'He won't,' said Colbeck, levelly. 'I can assure you of that.'

'Good.'

While he had been appraising her, she had been sizing him up and she seemed pleased with what she saw. It encouraged her to confide in him. After clearing her throat, she leaned slightly forward.

'I believe that they call you the Railway Detective,' she said.

'My nickname is immaterial. The only name that interests me at this point in time is that of the murder victim.'

'When I tell you what it is, Inspector, you will see that your nickname is not at all irrelevant. The gentleman who was thrown from the Sankey Bridge was – if I am right – a railway engineer.'

'Does he have a name, Miss Critchlow?'

'Yes.' There was a long pause. 'Gaston Chabal.'

'What makes you think that?'

'I happen to know that he was coming to England around this time to take a closer look at our railway system. He had an especial interest in the London and North-West Railway so that would account for his presence on the train in question.'

'Gaston Chabal.'

'Yes, Inspector – if I am right.'

'I have a feeling that you are,' he said, writing the name down on a piece of paper in front of him. 'Would it be impertinent of me to ask how you come to know this gentlemen?'

'Not at all,' she replied, adjusting her skirt. 'My sister and I visited Paris earlier this year. In a small way, we are art collectors. We attended the opening of an exhibition one afternoon. M. Chabal was one of the guests.'

'Could you describe his appearance?'

'He was very much like you, Inspector.'

'Me?'

'Yes. M. Chabal was not what I had expected a railway engineer to be any more than you are what I envisaged as a detective. I mean that with the greatest of respect,' she went on. 'Most policemen I've encountered have had a more rugged look to them. As for Gaston – for M. Chabal – he seemed to be far too modish and fastidious to be involved

73

in work on the railways.'

'He was French. They pay attention to their appearance.'

'Yes,' she murmured. 'He was very French.'

'Did he live in Paris?'

'I believe so.'

'You have no address for the gentleman?'

'It was only a casual encounter, Inspector,' she said, 'but I do know that he was an admirer of our railway system. It's much more advanced than the one in France. He felt that he could learn useful lessons by studying it.'

'To some extent, that's true,' said Colbeck, 'but our system has many vices as well as virtues. We do not have a standard gauge on our railways, for a start. That causes immense problems.'

'I would blame the Great Western Railway for that. Mr Brunel insists on using the broad gauge instead of coming into line with the others. And we have too many companies competing with each other to serve the same towns and cities.'

'You seem to know a lot about railways, Miss Critchlow.'

'I've spent a lot of time travelling on them.'

'So have I,' said Colbeck. 'To come back to M. Chabal, do you happen to know if he was married or not?'

Her reply was prompt. 'He was a bachelor.'

'Nevertheless, he'll have had a family and friends who need to be informed of his death, not to mention his employers. Have you any idea how we might contact them?'

'No, Inspector.'

'Do you know if he was engaged on any particular project?'

'Yes,' she replied, a finger to her chin. 'He did mention that he would be working with a British contractor in northern France, but I can't remember exactly where.'

'It must be the railway between Mantes and Caen. It's the only large project in that part of the country. Thomas Brassey is in charge of its construction. Yes, that must be it,' decided Colbeck. 'Thank you, Miss Critchlow. At least I know where to start looking now.'

'I hope that I've been able to help your investigation.'

'Without question. You've cleared up one mystery for us. Is there anything else you can tell me about Gaston Chabal?'

'I'm afraid not. I only met him that once.'

'Was he a handsome man? Did he speak good English?'

'Most people would have thought him handsome,' she said, choosing her words with care, 'and his English was faultless. He once gave a lecture here in London on railway engineering.'

'Bold man. That's rather like carrying coals to Newcastle. Do you know when and where he delivered this lecture?'

'No, Inspector.'

'A pity. It might have been another way to track him.'

'If it really is the man I think.' She rose to her feet. 'Well, I won't take up more of your time, Inspector Colbeck. I've told you all I can so there's no point in my staying. Goodbye.'

'I'll see you out,' he insisted, getting up to cross to the door. 'Are you staying in London?'

'Only until tomorrow.'

'Then permit me to call a cab for you, Miss Critchlow. And if you are an art collector, allow me to recommend the name of a British painter – Ambrose Hooper. I think very highly of his work.'

He opened the door to let her go out first then followed her down the corridor. When they left the building, he hovered on the pavement until an empty cab came into sight. Flagging it down, Colbeck assisted her into the vehicle and made sure that he heard the name of the hotel that she gave to the driver. The man flicked his reins and the horse set off at a steady trot in the direction of Trafalgar Square. Colbeck did not return to his office. Hannah Critchlow had given him a crucial piece of information but he was much more interested in what she was concealing than in what she had actually divulged. When the next empty cab came along Whitehall, therefore, he put out an arm to stop it.

'Where to, guv'nor?' asked the driver.

'Camden.'

Madeleine Andrews had always been fond of drawing but she did not know that she possessed a real talent until Robert Colbeck had come into her life. Not for her a rural landscape, or a jolly scene at a fair or even a flattering portrait of her sitter. Like her father, her passion was for locomotives and she had sketched dozens of them over the years, honing her skills without even realising that she was doing it. With Colbeck's encouragement, she had shown some of her sketches to a dealer and actually managed to sell two of them.

Bolstered by her modest success, Madeleine always tried to find at least some time in a day to work on her latest drawing. When she had cleaned the house, finished the washing-up and been out to do the shopping, she was back at her easel. Sitting near a window in the living room to get the best of the light, she was in the perfect position to see the cab as it drew up outside. When she saw Colbeck alight, she put her work aside and rushed to open the door.

'Robert! How lovely to see you!'

'I need your help,' he said, kissing her on the cheek. 'Is there any chance that you could spare me an hour or two?'

'Of course,' she replied. 'Where are we going?'

'I'll tell you in the cab.'

'Give me a moment.'

Madeleine went back into the house to leave a short note for her father then she collected her hat and coat. Colbeck was waiting to help her into the cab before climbing up to sit beside her. Their conversation was conducted to the rhythmical clip-clop of the hooves. He told her about his visitor from Liverpool. Madeleine was interested.

'What made you think she was hiding something?'

'When a married woman tells me that she is single, then I know that she is lying to me. Nobody as fetching as Hannah Critchlow could reach that age without having had dozens of proposals.'

'She might have turned them all down,' said Madeleine.

'That was not the impression I got. She not only has a husband,' Colbeck went on, 'but my guess is that he's connected with a railway company in some way – though not the GWR.'

'Why do you say that?'

'Because of a criticism she made to me

about the broad gauge. It was not the kind of remark I'd expect a woman to make – unless her name was Madeleine Andrews, that is. But then, you have a genuine fascination with railways.'

'It's only natural. Father is an engine driver.'

'Hannah Critchlow is different,' he said. 'When she talks about railways, she sounds as if she's quoting somebody else – her husband, most probably. It was another instance of her concealing something from me. And I didn't believe for a second that she had chanced upon this railway engineer at an art exhibition.'

'Why not?'

'Wait until you meet her, Madeleine.'

'What do you mean?'

'She's a very self-possessed woman with typical English reserve. Such people do not make casual conversation with foreigners. I fancy that she and Gaston Chabal became friends elsewhere. You'd be doing me a huge favour if you could find out the truth.'

'What makes you think that she'd confide in me, Robert?'

'You're a woman. You might be able to break through her defences. It took an enormous effort for her to come forward like this. She must have found Scotland Yard – and me, for that matter – rather intimidating.'

'You're not in the least intimidating,' she

said, squeezing his arm affectionately. 'You're always extremely charming.'

'Well, my charm did not work on her, Madeleine – yours might.'

He spent the rest of the journey schooling her in what to say and how to say it. Madeleine was an attentive pupil. It was not the first time he had employed her on an unofficial basis and she had proved extremely helpful in the past. Colbeck knew that he could rely on her to be gently persuasive.

'Does the superintendent know about this?' she said.

'Mr Tallis?' He gave a dry laugh. 'Hardly. You know his opinion of women – they should be neither seen nor heard. If he realised what I was doing, he'd probably roast me over a spit.'

'Even if your methods bring results?'

'Even then, Madeleine.'

They eventually reached their destination in the Strand and pulled up outside a fashionable hotel. He gave her another kiss.

'Good luck!' he said.

It had taken Hannah Critchlow almost a week to gather up enough courage to get in touch with Inspector Colbeck. Now that she had done so, she felt both relieved and anxious. But her overriding emotion was sadness and, no sooner did she return to her hotel, than she burst into tears. It took her a long time to compose herself. When there was a tap on her door, she assumed that it would be a member of the hotel staff. Opening the door, she saw instead that she had a visitor.

'Miss Critchlow?'

'Yes,' said the other, guardedly.

'My name is Madeleine Andrews. I wonder if I might have a private word with you? I'm a friend of Inspector Colbeck.'

'Then why are you bothering me? We've nothing to say to each other. I told the Inspector all that I know.'

'That's untrue,' said Madeleine, holding her ground.

'Good day to you.'

'As Hannah Critchlow, you gave him a certain amount of information but, as Mrs Marklew, you may be able to provide more. Why give him one name when you are staying here under another?'

Hannah was suspicious. 'Who *are* you?'

'I told you. I'm a friend of the inspector. If I explained how he and I came to meet, you'll understand why I'm here.'

Hannah Marklew hesitated. She was unsettled by the fact that her disguise had been so easily pierced and she knew that she could be severely reproached for misleading a detective. At the same time, she found Madeleine personable and unthreatening. There was another telling factor. Her visitor had a sympathetic manner. She was on Hannah's side.

'You'd better come in, Miss Andrews. It is "Miss", I presume?'

'Yes, Mrs Marklew.'

Madeleine went into the room and the other woman shut the door behind them. Hannah indicated a chair but she remained standing when Madeleine sat down.

'What did Inspector Colbeck tell you about me?' said Hannah.

'That you had provided the name of the murder victim and thereby moved the investigation on to another stage. He also told me how eager you were to see the killer brought to justice.'

'I am, Miss Andrews.'

'Then he needs all the help he can get in order to do that.'

Hannah was still wary. 'How do you know the inspector?'

'The same way that you do,' replied Madeleine. 'As a result of a crime. Somebody I know was attacked on the railway in the course of a robbery and Inspector Colbeck was put in charge of the case. Luckily, the injured man survived but it took him months to recover and he still carries the scars from that assault. Because of Inspector Colbeck's efforts, the villain responsible was eventually apprehended with his accomplices.'

'And who exactly was the victim?'

'My father. He almost died.'

Madeleine spoke with quiet intensity. She explained that her father had been in a deep coma and was not expected to live. More suffering had followed. In a desperate attempt to impede the police investigation, she had been abducted and held in captivity until rescued by Robert Colbeck.

'You can see why I have such faith in the inspector,' she said.

'Yes, Miss Andrews.'

'It's the reason I'm so willing to help him now.'

'But I have nothing else to add.'

'I believe that you do, Mrs Marklew. You came all the way from Liverpool to see Inspector Colbeck in person. That suggests it was a matter of importance to you. Otherwise,' Madeleine pointed out, 'you could simply have informed the local police or even made contact with Scotland Yard by anonymous letter. The inspector believes that you have a personal reason to see this crime solved.'

Hannah studied her carefully as if weighing her in the balance. It was certainly easier talking to a woman in the confines of a hotel room than discussing the case with a detective inspector in an office. Madeleine, she sensed, was discreet. Also, there was a bond between them. Both had endured great pain as a result of a crime committed on the London and North-West Railway. Hannah wondered if she could ease her pain by talking about it.

'Inspector Colbeck is very perceptive,' she said. 'I did know Gaston Chabal rather better than I indicated but I did not wish to admit that. It might have caused complications.'

'With your husband?'

'Yes, Miss Andrews.' Hannah sat down. 'I love him very much and I do not want to hurt him in any way. The simple fact is that Alexander – my husband – is somewhat older than me and is always preoccupied with business affairs.'

'The inspector thought that he had a connection with railways.'

'It's more than a connection. He's one of the directors of the London and North-West Railway. That's what seems so cruel. Gaston was murdered on a railway in which my husband is so closely involved.' She hunched her shoulders. 'I suppose that some might see that as an example of poetic justice.'

'How did you first meet M. Chabal?' asked Madeleine.

'It was at a reception in Paris. A major rail link was planned between Mantes and Caen. Since he already has some investments in French railways, my husband was interested in buying shares.'

'And you were invited to go with him?'

'All that I saw was an opportunity to visit Paris,' said Hannah. 'To be candid, I expected the reception itself to be very boring – they usually are. When you get a group of men talking business, you can feel very isolated. Fortunately,' she went on, a wan smile touching her lips, 'Gaston was there. We began talking. A few months later, there was a meeting in London for investors in the project. My husband had to be there so I made sure that I was as well.'

'Did you meet M. Chabal again?'

'Yes. I suppose that it all sounds a trifle sordid to you. I'm a married woman. I had no right to let a friendship of that nature develop. But the simple fact was that he made me feel unbelievably happy. Gaston reminded me that I was a woman.'

'How did you keep in touch?'

'By letter.'

'So you have an address for him?'

'Yes, Miss Andrews – it's in Mantes. His home was in Paris but he took a lodging in Mantes when they began to build the railway. My letters went there.'

'Inspector Colbeck would like that address, Mrs Marklew.'

'Of course.'

'And any details you have of his life in Paris.' Hannah nodded sadly. 'It must have

85

come as a terrible blow to you when you realised that he was the murder victim on that train.'

'It did. I cried for days.'

'And are you absolutely sure that it was Gaston Chabal?'

'There's no possible room for error, Miss Andrews.'

'How can you be so certain?'

'My husband was away from Liverpool on business,' said Hannah, frankly. 'I was waiting at Lime Street station that day to meet the train. Gaston was coming to see me.'

CHAPTER FIVE

'France!' exclaimed Superintendent Tallis, reaching for a cigar to absorb the shock of what he had just been told. 'Heavens above! For centuries, they were our mortal enemies until we put paid to them at Waterloo. Why must you go to France?'

'Because that's the only place we'll find out the full truth,' said Robert Colbeck. 'The crime may have taken place on British soil but I believe that its roots lie across the Channel.'

'We have no jurisdiction there, Inspector.'

'I'm sure that the French police would cooperate with us. The murder victim was a Parisian, after all. They have a stake in this.'

'But they would insist on being in charge,' said Tallis, irritably. 'Before we know it, we'd have their officers crawling about over here.'

'I dispute that, sir.'

'I've had dealings with them before.'

'So have I,' said Colbeck, 'and I found members of the Police de Surêté very help- ful. We are kindred spirits.'

'If only that were the case! You seem to have forgotten that the man responsible for founding the Surêté was a known villain who had served time in prison.'

'Vidocq saw the folly of his ways, Super-intendent. It was to his credit that he chose to work on the right side of the law. And he achieved some remarkable results.'

'Yes,' said Tallis, lighting his cigar and puffing on it until the end glowed. 'But how did Vidocq get those remarkable results? There was a suspicion that many of the crimes he solved were actually committed by his henchmen. I'd not have allowed any-body under me to resort to that kind of skulduggery. Vidocq was a born criminal. Look what happened to him.'

'He became a private detective twenty years ago, sir.'

'And then?'

'The police eventually closed down his agency because he was using dubious methods.'

'I rest my case – as you barristers say.'

'But that does not invalidate all the good work that he did earlier,' affirmed Colbeck. 'Besides, the Surêté is a much improved police force now. It's not full of men like Eugene Vidocq. How could it be? He was inimitable.'

'He was French,' said Tallis, darkly. 'That's enough for me.'

He pulled on his cigar then exhaled a cloud of thick smoke. It was one more problem with which Colbeck had to contend as he stood before the superintendent's desk. He was not merely hampered by the other man's prejudices against the French, he was forced to conceal both the source and extent of the information that he had received. In using Madeleine Andrews as his unauthorised assistant, Colbeck had risked dismissal but he felt that it had been worth it. What she had discovered from Hannah Marklew had been extraordinary. Once the older woman had started talking about her relationship with Gaston Chabal, she had not stopped. When she reported back to him, Madeleine was able to tell Colbeck a great deal about the character and career of the Frenchman.

'In the first instance, sir,' said Colbeck, 'we do not have to deal with the French police at all. It would be a preliminary inquiry.'

'To what end?'

'Establishing if there were any clear motives why someone would seek the life of the victim.'

'How could you hope to do that in a country full of foreigners?'

'I have a fair command of the language, Superintendent, so I would not be at a disadvantage. In any case, most of the people to whom I intend to speak are English.'

'Really?' said Tallis in surprise.

'You are obviously not familiar with French railways.'

'I regard that as a virtue, Inspector.'

89

'Their system is far less developed than ours,' said Colbeck, 'so it was natural that they looked to us for expertise. Many of the locomotives they use over there were designed by Thomas Crampton and three-quarters of the mileage of all French railways so far constructed was the work of Thomas Brassey and his partners.'

'What relevance does this have to the case in hand?'

'Gaston Chabal worked for Mr Brassey.'

'Then you do not have to go haring off to France,' said Tallis, flicking cigar ash into a metal tray. 'If this contractor is English, you can call on him at his office.'

'He is not in this country at the moment.'

'How do you know?'

'Because he always supervises major projects in person. This line will run for well over a hundred miles, sir, so it will take a long time to build. Until it's finished, Mr Brassey has moved to France.'

'What about his family?'

'They've gone with him, sir. His wife, Maria, I believe, speaks tolerable French and acts as his interpreter. It's a language that her husband cannot bring himself to learn.'

'Then he's a man after my own heart. Dreadful lingo!'

'Perhaps you can understand now why I need to go there,' said Colbeck. 'Mr Brassey will be wondering what's happened to one of his senior engineers and Chabal's family need to be informed of his death so that they can reclaim the body.'

Edward Tallis thrust the cigar between his teeth. He was loath to send Colbeck abroad on what he believed might be an expensive and unproductive visit. At the same time, he could appreciate the logic of the inspector's argument. Unless the crime was solved, the railway company would keep hounding him. Worse, in his view, was the intensive scrutiny of the press. Newspapers were very willing to trumpet any success the Detective Department achieved but they were equally ready to condemn any failures. Having christened Colbeck as the Railway Detective, they would have no qualms about finding a more derisive nickname for him.

'How long would you be away?' growled Tallis.

'Impossible to say, sir, but we'd be as quick as possible.'

'Would you take Sergeant Leeming with you?'

'With your permission.'

'It's his wife's permission you need to seek, by the sound of it.'

'Victor will do what he's told,' said Colbeck. 'While I'm talking to Mr Brassey, he can question some of the men who work for him.'

Tallis was astounded. 'Are you telling me

that the sergeant speaks French?'

'No, sir, and nor will he need to. For a number of reasons, Mr Brassey prefers to employ men from this country. When he built the Paris to Rouen railway, he took five thousand navvies, miners, carpenters, smiths, brick-makers, bricklayers and other trades-men with him. He had his own private army.'

'That's what you need over there – for protection.'

'Hostilities with France ceased many years ago, sir.'

'Some of us have long memories.' Tallis chewed on his cigar and regarded Colbeck from under bushy eyebrows. 'How do you come to know so much about Thomas Brassey?'

'I read a number of railway periodicals, sir.'

'What manner of man is he?'

'A very successful one,' said Colbeck. 'He's a good businessman and a caring em-ployer. That's why his men are so loyal to him. He also has the courage to admit his mistakes.'

'Mistakes?'

'Even the best contractors go astray at times, Superintendent. Six years ago, Mr Brassey built the Barentin Viaduct about twelve miles from Rouen.'

'Don't mention viaducts to me, Inspector.'

'This was a massive construction, much

higher and longer than the one over the Sankey Valley. There was only one problem with it.'

'And what was that?'

'After a period of heavy rain, it collapsed in ruins. Some people would have invented all manner of spurious excuses, but not Thomas Brassey. His reputation as a contractor was in serious danger. So he admitted liability and at his own cost – some £30,000 – he had the viaduct rebuilt.'

'Did it stay up this time?'

'Oh, yes,' replied Colbeck. 'I've been over it. I think it's one of the most inspiring sights on the French railways. And because it was rebuilt in a mere six months, it meant that he completed the whole project well ahead of schedule, earning himself a bonus of £10,000.'

'The only viaduct that concerns me at the moment is the one from which that fellow was thrown. Why couldn't he have the decency to get himself killed in his native country?'

'I doubt if he was given any choice, Superintendent.'

'I agree,' said Tallis, becoming serious. 'A murder victim is a murder victim, whatever nationality he holds. We must bring his killer to book and do so with all speed.'

'Does that mean you sanction our visit to France?'

'I'll give it my consideration.'

'You just said that speed was essential, sir.'

'I'm treating it as a matter of urgency.'

'Shall I warn Victor that he may be going abroad?'

'Do not run ahead of yourself, Inspector. There are many things to take into account. Leave me alone while I mull them over.'

'Of course, Superintendent.'

The decision had been made. When Tallis stopped making protests about a course of action, it invariably meant that he would in time approve of it. Colbeck left the room with a feeling of triumph. After a period of inertia, the murder investigation had been given a new lease of life. He and Victor Leeming were going to France.

Thomas Brassey came out of the wooden hut that he used as an office and went off to see the damage for himself. He wore his habitual frock coat, waistcoat and check trousers and, although in his late forties, moved briskly across the ground. When he passed a group of navvies, he was given warm smiles or cheerful greetings, and coarser language was immediately suppressed within his earshot. Brassey was a true gentleman with an innate dignity. He lacked the rough and ready appearance of some self-made men and had none of their arrogance or assertive manner.

'When did you discover it?' he asked.

'This afternoon,' replied Aubrey Filton. 'We'd suspended work on the tunnel until fresh materials arrived, but, in view of what's happened, I thought that I'd carry out an inspection.'

'Very sensible of you.'

'This is what I found, sir.'

Filton led the way down the embankment to the mouth of the tunnel. As it was dark inside, he picked up a lantern that was already burning. Brassey followed him into the long cavern. Halfway along it, the contractor expected to see two sets of parallel rails, laid across timber sleepers and bolted tight, the whole track resting on ballast. Instead, he was looking at a confused mass of wood, iron and rock chippings. Rails and sleepers had been levered out of position. The fishplates and bolts that held one length of rail against the end of another had been either broken or twisted out of shape.

'This was done on purpose, Mr Brassey,' said Filton.

'I can see that. Was nobody guarding the tunnel last night?'

'They claim that they were but my guess is that they either fell asleep or were paid to look the other way. This is the fourth incident in a row. Someone is trying to stop us building this railway.'

'Then they'll have to do a lot better than this,' said Brassey, assessing the cost of the damage. 'It's annoying but it won't hold us up for long. As soon as a fresh supply of rail arrives on site, we'll start work in the tunnel again. Meanwhile, we'll post more guards.'

'Yes, Mr Brassey.'

'*Armed* guards.'

'What are their orders?'

'I'll issue those directly.'

They walked back towards the mouth of the tunnel, stepping over the accumulated debris as they did so. Filton, one of the engineers working on the Mantes-Caen railway, was a tall, thin, nervous man in his thirties with a tendency to fear the worst. Brassey had a much more robust attitude to life. What his companion saw as a disaster, he dismissed as a minor setback. Sensing the other man's anxiety, he put a consoling arm around Filton's shoulders.

'Do not worry about it, Aubrey,' he said. 'If someone is trying to hinder us, we'll catch them sooner or later. The important thing is that these delays do not interfere with our overall schedule.'

'I hate the thought that we have enemies in our midst.'

'For every bad apple, we have a thousand good ones.'

'I wonder that you can shrug it off like this, sir,' said Filton.

'Oh, I'm not shrugging it off, I assure you. I take this very seriously – but I'll not let my

96

anger show. I prefer to carry on as if nothing had occurred to halt our progress. I've signed a contract that has time limits on it. I intend to meet them.'

They walked on until they emerged into broad daylight. All around them, men of various trades were working hard. Brassey stopped to watch them. It was very hot and the navvies were dripping with sweat as they toiled away. Many of them were bare-chested in the baking sun. The ceaseless pandemonium of industry rang out across the French countryside as picks, shovels, axes, sledgehammers and other implements pounded away. Birds flew overhead but their songs went unheard beneath the cacophony.

'Is there any finer sight on earth than men building a railway?' said Brassey, removing his top hat. 'It lifts my spirit, Aubrey.'

'It would lift mine as well if we were not plagued by problems.'

'Four incidents can hardly be called a plague.'

'I think the number might be five, sir.'

'What do you mean?'

'Well,' said Filton, brow corrugated with disquiet, 'I can't help remembering what happened to Mr Ruddles the other week.'

'That was an accident, man.'

'Was it?'

'Of course,' said Brassey, airily. 'It's a law of averages that a scaffold will collapse from time to time. Bernard Ruddles and I had the misfortune to be standing on it when it gave way.'

'You could have been badly injured, sir.'

'I was lucky. I had a nasty fall and was shaken up but I lived to tell the tale. Bernard, alas, was not so fortunate.'

'He broke his leg in two places.'

'I know,' said Brassey. 'I was right beside him at the time. Had we listened to the advice of the French doctors, he would have lost the leg altogether. They were queuing up to amputate. Bernard had the good sense to wait for an English doctor to give an opinion. As a consequence, the leg can be saved.'

'That's not the point, Mr Brassey.'

'Then what is?'

'The scaffold could have been tampered with.'

'It was badly erected, that's all,' Brassey told him. 'I sacked the men responsible. They were not trying to inflict injury on me or on Bernard Ruddles. How could they know when either of us would stand on that particular scaffold?'

'But suppose it had been you who'd broken a leg, sir?'

'I did suppose it, Aubrey, and it made me offer up a prayer of thanks. I landed on level ground but Bernard, alas, hit some rocks. It could so easily have been the other way around.'

'How could we have managed without you, sir?'

'You wouldn't have had to do so.'

'No?'

'Once the leg had been put into a splint, I'd have used a pair of crutches to get round. Nothing would stop me from keeping an eye on a project like this,' he went on, stoutly. 'If I'd broken both legs and both arms, I'd have men to carry me around on a stretcher.'

'Heaven forbid!'

'Never give in, Aubrey – that's my motto.'

'Yes, sir.'

'And always complete a railway ahead of time.'

Brassey put on his hat. They clambered up the embankment and strolled back towards the office. Filton was not reassured by his employer's brave words. Clearly, they had enemies. That was what alarmed him. He felt certain that it was only a matter of time before those enemies struck again.

'By the way,' said Brassey, 'have you seen Gaston Chabal?'

'No, sir.'

'He was due back here days ago.'

'Well, I've seen no sign of him. Wherever can he be?'

'Find out.'

'I'll try, sir.'

'When I engage a man, I expect him to

fulfil his duties or give me an excellent reason why he's unable to do so. Gaston has left us in the dark,' said Brassey. 'We need him back here. Unless he turns up soon, he may well find that he is no longer working for me.'

Victor Leeming had been horrified to learn that he had to go to France with Robert Colbeck. Apart from the fact that he would miss his wife, Leeming knew that he would be condemned to spend long and uncomfortable hours on trains, a form of transport he had come to loathe. There was an even deeper cause for concern. Leeming was uneasy about the temper of the French nation.

'What if they have another revolution while we're here?' he said.

'Then we'll be privileged spectators,' replied Colbeck.

'It wasn't long ago that the barricades went up in Paris.'

'France was not alone, Victor. In 1848, there were revolutions in other parts of Europe as well. Superintendent Tallis feared that we might have riots in London if the Chartists got out of hand.'

'We've had nothing to match the bloodshed over here,' said Leeming, looking through the window of the carriage at some peasants working in the fields. 'There's something about the French. It's in their nature to revolt. They make me feel uneasy.'

The two men were on their way to Mantes. Having crossed the English Channel by packet boat, they had boarded a train at Le Havre and were steaming south. Colbeck had been pleased to note that the locomotive was of English design and construction but the news brought no comfort to the sergeant. The name of Thomas Crampton was meaningless to him. If the train had been pulled by a herd of giant reindeer, Leeming would have shown no interest. The only thing about France that would bring a smile to his craggy face was the date of their departure from the country.

'Look upon this as an adventure,' urged Colbeck. 'You are seeing a foreign country for the first time and you'll get some insight into the way that it's policed.'

'It seems such a long way to come, sir.'

'Be grateful that the murder victim was not Italian or Swiss. Had that been the case, we'd have had to go much farther afield.'

'I'd prefer to be in London.'

'Amid all that crime and squalor? There's far less danger out here in the countryside, Victor, and it's so much healthier for us to get away from the city.' A beautiful chateau appeared on the horizon. He pointed it out to his companion. 'Isn't it superb?' he said. 'Now there's something you wouldn't see in Whitechapel.'

Leeming was unimpressed. 'I'd still much rather be there.'

'You're too insular,' said Colbeck with a laugh.

'I like my country, that's all. I'm patriotic.'

'I have no quarrel with that.'

The railway had been built in defiance of geography. There were so many hills, valleys and rivers to cross that there was a long sequence of tunnels, cuttings, bridges and viaducts. As they sped across the Barentin Viaduct with its striking symmetry and its panoramic views, Colbeck thought it better not to mention that it had once collapsed into the valley below. Teeth clenched and hands gripping the seat for safety, Leeming was already troubled enough by having to cross it. The magnificent construction had all the qualities of a death trap to him. Only when they were well clear of the viaduct did he find his voice again.

'Why didn't he choose that instead, Inspector?' he asked. 'Why didn't the killer throw his victim over that viaduct instead of coming all the way to England to do it?'

'You're assuming that the murderer was French.'

'Isn't that why we're here?'

'No, Victor,' said Colbeck. 'We are hunting a motive. I'm fairly certain that the man who killed Gaston Chabal was English and that only the Sankey Viaduct would suffice.'

'In that case, the lady's husband must be involved.'

'I think not.'

'His wife was unfaithful to him – there's the motive.'

'On the face of it, perhaps,' said Colbeck, 'but there are two very good reasons why we can eliminate Alexander Marklew from our enquiries. To begin with, he was quite unaware of the friendship that existed between his wife and M. Chabal.'

'It was more than a friendship, sir. Let's not beat about the bush. It was adultery, pure and simple – except that it was far from pure. I don't hold with it,' declared Leeming, thinking of his wife. 'Marriage vows should be kept.'

'We are not here to sit in judgement on Mrs Marklew. The fact is that, but for the information that she volunteered, we would still be scratching our heads back in Scotland Yard. But there's an even stronger reason why the husband must be discounted,' he went on. 'Mr Marklew is a director of the London and North-West Railway. He would never do anything to create bad publicity for it. Murder is the worst possible advertisement, Victor.'

Colbeck had given him an abbreviated version of what he had learned from Hannah Marklew, making no reference to the fact that it was Madeleine Andrews who had obtained most of the salient facts. While he did not share the superintendent's dismissive attitude towards women, Leeming would certainly have questioned the use of one in a murder investigation. That was why Colbeck told him only what the sergeant needed to know. Victor Leeming was an able detective but he was shackled to correct police procedure. When it served his purpose, the inspector was ready to ignore it.

'Are you hungry, Victor?' he asked.

'No, sir,' replied Leeming, feeling his stomach. 'Crossing the Channel took away my appetite completely. Besides, I don't think that I'd take to French food.'

'Why not?'

'They eat horses and frogs and snails.'

'Not on the same plate,' said Colbeck with amusement. 'Wait until you taste their wine. If we stay here long enough, you'll acquire a real taste for it. You may even learn some of the language.'

'There's only one thing I want to hear, sir.'

'What's that?'

'The French for "We're going home". Very soon, please.'

Having removed his coat and hat, Thomas Brassey was at his desk, poring over surveyors' maps as he planned the next stage of the Mantes-Caen railway. Each project threw up its own individual challenges and this one was no exception. There were a number of potential hazards to be negotiated. He was grappling with one of them when there was a firm tap on the door. In response to Brassey's call, it opened to admit Inspector Robert Colbeck and Sergeant Victor Leeming. When introductions had been made, Brassey was amazed to hear that they had come all the way from England in order to see him.

'Have I committed a crime of some kind?' he asked.

'Not at all, sir,' said Colbeck. 'We're here on other business. I believe that you employ an engineer called Gaston Chabal?'

'I did employ him, Inspector, but the fellow seems to have vanished into thin air. He's an extremely competent man. If he keeps me waiting any longer, however, he'll find that he no longer has a job here. Nobody is indispensable.'

'M. Chabal will not be returning here, I fear. He's dead.'

Brassey was shocked. 'Dead – poor Gaston!'

When he was told about the murder, he was aghast and felt guilty for harbouring so many unkind thoughts about the engineer's absence. It was no wonder that Chabal had been unable to return.

'Did you know that he went to England?' said Colbeck.

'No, Inspector. He told me that he was going to be in Paris for a few days to see his parents. I'd no idea that he crossed the Channel. Whatever could have taken him there?'

'We believe he went to see a friend, Mr Brassey, but that's not our major concern. What we are looking for is the reason why he was singled out in this way. That reason can only be found in France.'

'Nothing else would have brought us here,' said Leeming, sourly. 'We hope that the effort will have been worthwhile.'

'You must forgive Victor. Rail travel is a torment to him.'

'That boat was even worse, sir. Fair upset me, it did.'

'He misses London,' explained Colbeck. 'He hates to be away from his wife and children.'

'I always bring my family with me,' said Brassey.

Leeming scowled. 'I could hardly do that in my job, sir.'

'No,' agreed Colbeck. 'It might hamper you somewhat. But let's turn our attention to Chabal. He's the important person here. What sort of man was he, Mr Brassey?'

'An extremely able one,' said the contractor. 'Gaston had the sense to learn from good masters. Most of the engineers I employ are English but Gaston Chabal could match any of them.'

'Did he have any enemies?'

'None that I know of, Inspector. He was very popular. Some of the men used to tease him because he was French, but it was all in good fun. I can't think of any reason why anyone should conceive such a hatred of him that he wanted him dead.'

'And yet someone clearly did.'

'Yes.'

'Have you had any trouble in your camp, sir?' said Leeming.

'We've had the usual fights and drunkenness, but you expect that from navvies. They're a law unto themselves. If you employ them, you have to allow for a certain amount of boisterous behaviour.' Brassey grew pensive. 'On the other hand...'

'Well?' prompted Colbeck.

'No, no. It's probably just a coincidence.'

'Let us be the judge of that, sir.'

'The truth is,' confessed Brassey, running a hand across his broad forehead, 'that we've been having a spot of bother here. I've tried to ignore it but Aubrey takes it very seriously.'

'Aubrey?'

'Aubrey Filton, one of the senior engineers. He worked alongside Gaston and he'll be very distressed to hear what's happened to him. Anyway,' he continued, 'there have been three or four incidents here that look as if they're part of a worrying pattern.'

'What sort of incidents, Mr Brassey?'

'Aubrey would be the best person to tell you that.'

'Is he here at the moment?'

'Yes, Inspector. He has an office in the hut at the end.'

'Then I think you should pay him a visit,' said Colbeck, raising an eyebrow at Leeming. 'Break the sad news to him, Victor, and see what memories he may have of Chabal. And make a list of these incidents. They could be significant.'

Leeming nodded and went straight out. Colbeck was glad to be alone with the contractor. He had long been an admirer of Thomas Brassey and had always felt it rather unjust that those who designed locomotives or ran railway companies enjoyed public acclaim while those who actually built the endless miles of track remained in the shadows. The two men appraised each other.

'Do sit down, Inspector,' said Brassey, resuming his own seat.

'Thank you, sir.' Colbeck lowered himself on to a chair. 'This is a treat for me. I've always wanted to see a new stretch of line being laid. We hired a trap in Mantes to bring us out here so I was able to see what you've done so far.'

'Then you've also seen the problems created by the Seine.'

'We followed it for most of the journey.'

'Rivers are the bane of my life, Inspector Colbeck. Bridges and viaducts slow us down so much. If only we had a flat plain across which to construct a railway – flat and arid.'

'Then there would be no triumphs of civil engineering.'

'No triumphs, maybe, but far less sweat and toil.' He shook his head. 'I still can't accept that Gaston is dead. I always found him such an honest fellow. Why tell me that he was going to Paris when he intended to sail to Engand?'

'He was being discreet, I expect.'

'In what way?'

'There was a lady involved.'

'Ah, of course. Do you know who she was?'

'No,' said Colbeck, determined to honour his promise to keep Hannah Marklew's name out of it. 'But I'm convinced that Chabal was on his way to visit her when he was killed.'

Aubrey Filton was very upset to hear of his colleague's murder. It made him twitch slightly and glance over his shoulder. His office was in a much smaller hut but it was perfectly serviceable. Victor Leeming glanced at the array of drawings that had been pinned to the wall.

'What are these, Mr Filton?' he said.

'Part of the original survey.'

'Is this your work, sir?'

'I wish it was, Sergeant,' replied Filton, looking enviously across at the wall, 'but my drawings are not quite as neat and accurate as these. Gaston was very gifted.'

'Do you mean that Chabal did these?'

'Most of them. It's all we have to remember him by.'

Leeming was pleased to have the responsibility of questioning Aubrey Filton. It gave him something to do and took his mind off the queasiness that he still felt. Having heard so many French voices since their arrival, he was relieved to be talking to an Englishman.

'Mr Brassey mentioned some incidents,' he said, taking out a notebook and pencil. 'Could you tell me what they were, sir?'

'The most recent happened only yesterday. When I inspected a tunnel, I discovered that someone had levered the rails off their sleepers and scattered the ballast everywhere. A week earlier, we had a more serious setback.'

'Go on, Mr Filton.'

'A fire had been started in one of our storage huts. We were able to stop it spreading but it destroyed everything inside. It slowed us down, Sergeant Leeming. Time costs money in this business.'

110

'And were there any other incidents?'

'The first was a case of simple theft – at least that's what we thought at the time. But who would want to steal gunpowder?'

'Someone who needed to blast through rock.'

'The second incident was a week later,' said Filton. 'A stack of our timber was pushed into the river. By the time we became aware of it, the sleepers had floated over a mile away.'

'Stolen gunpowder, missing timber, arson in a storeroom and wreckage in a tunnel. These are all serious crimes, Mr Filton. Have you reported them to the police?'

'Mr Brassey chose not to, Sergeant.'

'Oh.'

'He believes that we should take care of our own security and he does not want too much interference from the French. We have enough of that, as it is. In any case,' he continued, 'there's no police force out here in the wilds. The nearest constable is ten miles away. What can one man on a horse do?'

'Travel in comfort,' said the other with feeling. 'From what you tell me, it's evident that somebody is taking pains to delay the building of this railway. This is not wanton damage. It's deliberate.'

'That's what I feel about the scaffolding.'

Filton told him about the way that Brassey

and his companion had fallen when the scaffolding had collapsed under them. Leeming duly noted the information down. It was Filton who discerned a clear connection with the murder.

'It's all part of the same plot,' he decided.

'Is it, sir?'

'In killing Gaston Chabal, they've inflicted yet another blow.'

'A critical one at that, Mr Filton.'

'They'll stop at nothing to wreck this railway.'

'Have you any idea who these people might be?' asked Leeming. 'Do you have any suspects in mind?'

'Several of them.'

'Such as?'

'Business rivals, for a start,' said Filton. 'This contract is worth a large amount of money. Mr Brassey was not the only person to put in a tender. He was up against others.'

'French or English?'

'Oh, French. They resent the fact that a contractor has been brought over from England, in spite of the fact that Mr Brassey has such an outstanding record of work in this country.'

'Anybody other than jealous rivals, sir?'

'Resentful navvies. We brought most of our labour with us because it's more reliable, but we've had to take on some Frenchmen as well. They bear grudges.'

'Why would that be?'

'They get paid less than our own men,' said Filton, 'and it's caused a lot of bad blood. Yes,' he went on, warming to his theme, 'I fancy that's where the trouble is coming from – French labour. It's their way of making a protest.'

'Then it has no connection with M. Chabal's death, sir.'

'I believe that it does.'

'Why would someone track him all the way across the Channel,' asked Leeming, 'when they could have killed him here? More to the point, how could a mere labourer possibly know that Chabal was going to England in the first place? I'm sorry, Mr Filton. I think you are forging links where they may not exist.' He consulted his notebook. 'Let's go back to the first incident, shall we? You say that gunpowder was stolen – for what purpose?'

'I dread to think, Sergeant Leeming.'

They moved swiftly. While one man kept watch, the other scuttled along the track in the darkness until he reached one of the largest of the wagons. He packed the gunpowder firmly beneath it and ran a fuse alongside the iron rail. Both men made sure that they were well clear of the danger area before the fuse was lit. When they saw it burning away purposefully in the direction of the wagon, they ran off quickly to their hiding place. The explosion was deafening. Shattering the silence, it lifted the wagon high off the track and blew it into small pieces that were dispersed everywhere at great velocity. Rolling stock in the immediate vicinity was also destroyed in the blast. A section of rail was plucked from the sleepers and snapped apart. Fires started. Injured men screamed in pain. Falling debris killed a dog.

Another incident could be added to the list.

CHAPTER SIX

Robert Colbeck and Victor Leeming were staying at a cottage almost a mile away but the noise of the blast woke them up. Though railway companies often used gunpowder to shift awkward obstructions, they would never do so at night. To someone like Thomas Brassey, it would be anathema. He was renowned for the care he took to keep any disruption to an absolute minimum in the locality where his men were working. Instead of putting all his navvies in one camp, and risking the uncontrollable mayhem that usually followed the creation of a private town, he placed as many of them as he could in houses, inns and farms in the area to spread them out. It was also a means of developing ties of friendship with local people and that was important.

A nocturnal explosion meant trouble. The two detectives got up at once, dressed in the dark then walked swiftly in the direction from which the sound had come. There was no danger of their getting lost. They simply followed the track that had already been laid. As each new extension was added, it was used to bring fresh supplies of iron, timber, ballast, bricks and other materials required on site. Movement by rail was so much quicker and more efficient than having to rely on horses and carts or using barges on the river. It also helped to raise morale. When they saw that their track was already in operation, those working on it could measure the progress they had already made. They could take pride.

As they got closer, Colbeck and Leeming could see a mass of torches and lanterns. Raised voices were then carried on the breeze towards them. They quickened their step until figures were slowly conjured out of the gloom. Dozens of people were moving about as they tried to establish the full extent of the damage. Thomas Brassey was supervising the operation. Colbeck and Leeming walked through the scattered wreckage to get to him.

'What happened, Mr Brassey?' asked Colbeck.

'We're still not entirely sure,' replied the contractor, 'but it looks as if someone planted gunpowder beneath one of the wagons and blew it to pieces. We'll have to wait until dawn before we can make a complete inventory of the damage.'

'It must have been the stuff that was stolen earlier,' said Leeming, confidently. 'Mr Filton told me about it.'

'Whoever used it knew what he was doing,

Sergeant. One wagon was blown apart and four others were damaged beyond repair. As you can see, the track was ripped up as well.'

'Was anyone hurt?'

'Some of the nightwatchmen were injured by the debris but nobody was killed, as far as we know.' He looked around and sighed. 'This is the worst incident yet. Someone is trying to cripple us.'

'No, sir,' said Colbeck. 'This was simply another warning.'

'Warning?'

The detective recoiled from the clamour all round him.

'Is there somewhere a little quieter where we might talk?'

'Of course, Inspector. Come to my office.'

Carrying a lantern, Brassey picked his way carefully through the gathering crowd and led them to the wooden hut. Once inside, he put the lantern on a ledge and lit some oil lamps, one of which was set on the large safe that stood in a corner. Brassey waved them to chairs before sitting down behind his desk.

'What's this about a warning?' he said.

'Somebody wishes you to think again about building this railway. I know that you have a contract to do so,' said Colbeck before Brassey could protest, 'but contracts can be revoked. The object of the exercise, I believe, is to frighten you off.'

'I'm not a man who's easily frightened, Inspector,' said the other with defiance. 'Whatever happens, I'll press on.'

'I admire your courage, sir, but you must expect worse attacks than the one you suffered last night.'

'What could be worse than this?'

'Lots of things,' said Colbeck. 'Blowing up the locomotive, for instance. That would have been far more costly and inconvenient than destroying some wagons. Breaking in here would be another option,' he went on, pointing to the safe. 'If they stole whatever you keep in there, I should imagine that it could create some serious problems for you.'

'It could,' admitted Brassey. 'That safe holds money. My men like to get their wages on time. If the navvies were not paid when they expect it, there'd be ructions. That's why a nightwatchman always patrols this area in the hours of darkness – to guard the safe.'

'You had plenty of men on duty tonight, sir,' Leeming pointed out, 'but the explosion still took place.'

'It means the people responsible must work for you,' reasoned Colbeck. 'They know exactly where any guards are deployed and they can find their way around in the dark. In short, they're familiar with everything that happens on site. It enables them to stay one step ahead of you all the time.'

'What do you suggest?' said Brassey. 'Do I call in the police?'

'That's a decision only you can make, sir.'

'Well, I wouldn't make it lightly, Inspector. I've tried until now to contain the various setbacks we've suffered. Once I involve the police, our difficulties become common knowledge and newspapers start to take an interest. I'd hate that to happen,' he confided. 'Not everyone in this country is entirely happy to see an English contractor building a French railway. Adverse comment by the press could make things very awkward for us.'

'Then we tackle the situation another way,' decided Colbeck. 'We have to catch the men who are behind all these incidents.'

'And how do we do that?'

'By having someone working alongside them. At the moment, we're trying to solve the problem from the outside. That's a handicap. What we need is someone inside the labour force who can sniff out these villains by rubbing shoulders with them.'

'Such a man would be courting grave danger,' said Brassey.

'Only if he were found out.'

'Navvies are very close-knit. They resent outsiders.'

'Not if the outsider can win their confidence.'

'Inspector Colbeck is right,' said Leeming, glibly. 'We've used this device before and it's always worked. If the right man is chosen, he could unmask the villains in no time.'

'I'm glad that you agree,' said Colbeck, putting a hand on his shoulder, 'because you are the person I had in mind.'

Leeming gasped. '*Me*, sir?'

'Yes, Victor – you can start work this very morning.'

When light finally came, there was no shortage of volunteers to help in the work of clearing up the mess. The fires caused by the explosion had been swiftly put out but, ironically, another one now had to be lit to burn the remnants of the wagons. Two men had been badly hurt in the blast and half-a-dozen had sustained minor injuries. The dog was duly buried. When the work was finally done, the men stood in a circle around the railway lines that had been hideously distorted by the blast. Threats of violence were made against the culprits.

'They should be hung by their balls from the tallest tree,' snarled Pierce Shannon, 'then we could all throw rocks at the cruel bastards until they bleed to death.'

'I agree with the principle that they should suffer,' said Father Slattery, gently, 'though I'd express myself with more restraint.'

'That's because you're a priest. I can speak

120

the truth.'

'You'll certainly speak *something*, Pierce, for I've never known a man with such a runaway mouth on him as you, but I'm not always sure that it's the honest truth that passes those lips of yours.'

'Whoever did this deserves to be crucified!'

Slattery bristled. 'And I'll not have you filching from the Holy Bible like that. Our Lord died upon a cross – he was martyred on our behalf. Never forget that. It would be sheer sacrilege to punish these evildoers in the same way.'

'What would you do to them, Father?'

'First of all, I'd ask them why they've been harrying us.'

'I can tell you that,' said Shannon, vengefully. 'They're swinish Frenchmen who can't bear the thought that we build better railways than they do. They want to drive us all away.'

'Well, I'm not going anywhere, Pierce.'

'Neither am I – whatever the dirty buggers do to us.'

Many of the navvies had been found accommodation in the surrounding farms and villages but hundreds of them lived in the makeshift camp they had erected. Pierce Shannon was one of them, a short, compact, powerful Irishman in his thirties with a fondness for strong drink and a hard fight.

121

Since there were so many people like Shannon on his books, Thomas Brassey had allowed a Roman Catholic priest to join them as a kind of missionary among the large Irish contingent, acting as a soothing presence and trying to turn their minds to higher things than merely satisfying their immediate needs.

Eamonn Slattery was a white-haired man in his sixties with a haggard face and an emaciated body. Respected and reviled alike, he loved the community in which he worked and did his best to master the names of as many men as he could. Instead of preaching at them from an imaginary pulpit, he came down to their level and talked in terms that they could understand. He disapproved of the fact that some of the navvies lived with common-law wives – sharing them openly with other men in some cases – but he did not respond with outright condemnation. Instead, he turned his persuasive tongue on the women, telling them how much deeper and more fulfilling their relationships would be if they were blessed by the Church. Since he had been in the camp, he had already performed two marriages.

'Why do you blame the French?' asked Slattery.

'Because they're behind all this trouble we've been having.'

'I see no evidence of it.'

'That's because you weren't here when we were working on the Rouen to Le Havre Railway,' said Shannon, pronouncing the names in a way that any Frenchman would find incomprehensible. 'Because the ballasting was done before the mortar was properly dry, the viaduct at Barentin fell down with a bang. Jesus! The way they turned against us, you'd have thought we'd raped every fucking nun in the country and set fire to that Notre Damn Cathedral.'

'Moderate your language, please,' rebuked the priest.

'They treated us like criminals, Father. It's as well I can't read French because the newspapers went for us with a cat-o'bleeding-nine tails. Even when we rebuilt the viaduct,' continued Shannon, 'we got no credit for it. We were British scum, taking jobs off the French.'

'That's not the case here, though, is it? The majority of the work force is British but Mr Brassey has also engaged French navvies.'

'Yes, but he pays them only half what we get – quite right, too.'

'They do have cause for resentment, then.'

Shannon was aggressive. 'Whose bleeding side are *you* on?'

'If you could ask me more politely, I might tell you. As it is, I remain sceptical about your claim that Frenchmen were behind that explosion. I'll reserve my judgement, Pierce,' said the priest, meeting his glare, 'and I advise you to do the same.'

'My mind is already made up and the same goes for a lot of us. We're not going to sit back and let these bastards cause even more damage. When we come off shift this evening,' said Shannon, bunching both fists, 'we intend to settle a few scores with the French.'

'What are you going to do?'

'Well, we're not going to pray with them, I can tell you that.'

The visit to Mantes was a revelation. When he called at the house where Gaston Chabal had lodged, Robert Colbeck had to explain to the landlady why the engineer would not be returning. She was very upset to hear of the murder and had clearly been exceptionally fond of her lodger. Colbeck was allowed to inspect the man's room. The first things he found were some letters from Hannah Marklew, one of which set a date for their rendezvous in Liverpool. On his way to the assignation, her lover had been killed. It was clear from the missives that Hannah had never been involved in such a situation before. She was naïve and indiscreet. She not only signed her Christian name, she gave her full address as well. Colbeck tore up the letters so that they would not fall into anyone else's hands.

Hers were not the only *billets-doux* he found in the room. A Frenchwoman, signing herself with the letter 'D', wrote with even greater passion from somewhere in Paris. She was more circumspect. No address was given in her letters, only the city from where the mail was dispatched. Colbeck checked the rest of the correspondence. Business letters showed that Chabal had built himself a reputation that brought in several offers of work. One person, from England, invited him to return there in order to give some more lectures on his work as a civil engineer. The fee was tempting.

Even when working on a railway, Chabal kept an extensive wardrobe and Colbeck found a jacket identical to the one that had taken an unfortunate dip in the Sankey Canal. There were many other clues to the character of the deceased and they helped to give the inspector a full portrait of him. When he went downstairs, he found the landlady in tears, stunned by the loss of her charming lodger and horrified at the manner of his death. Colbeck told her that, once Chabal's family and friends were informed of his demise, someone would soon come to claim his effects.

Paris was his next destination. Boarding a train at the station, Colbeck went on the short journey from Mantes, intrigued to see what had been for so many years the capital of Europe. It was a city that celebrated the arts and composers, musicians, dancers, artists, poets and authors from many countries had flocked there in search of inspiration. Chopin, Liszt, Mendelssohn, Donizetti, Rossini, Verdi, Wagner and Heine had all resided there at one time or another. Two English authors whose novels were on Colbeck's bookshelves back home in London – Dickens and Thackeray – had also lived in the city. It was a place of cosmopolitan talent with superb art galleries, concert halls and opera houses to display it.

Colbeck was not disappointed. Driven in a cab along its broad boulevards, he marvelled at its sumptuous architecture and tried to take in its full wonder. The buildings of Paris reflected an empire that no longer existed but that could still stir the imagination. What he noticed was the abundance of outdoor cafes, where customers were enjoying a leisurely drink in the sunshine while reading a newspaper, playing dominoes or talking with friends. Like any major city, Paris had its share of slums and Colbeck saw something of them when he was taken through a maze of back streets. The grinding poverty in the mean tenements was exacerbated by the prevailing stink of the drains.

Before he reported the death of Gaston Chabal to the police, and left them to track down his family, Colbeck wanted to visit the address that Thomas Brassey had given him for the late engineer. The detective hoped to find out a little more about the man on his own account. Once the French police were involved, he would have to surrender the initiative to them. The address was in the Marais, one of the oldest and most interesting parts of the city, and it took its name from the marshes on which it was built. When the cab pulled up in a busy street, he saw that the dead man had owned a tall, narrow house with a hint of Gothic extravagance in its façade. It was large enough to require servants so Colbeck could expect someone to be at home.

He alighted from the cab and was immediately reminded how much taller he was than the average Frenchman. Most of those who bustled past him were distinctly shorter and had darker complexions. From the hostile glances he was given, Colbeck could see that the passers-by had guessed his nationality. He pulled the bell rope and heard it ring deep inside the house. The door was soon opened by a pretty young woman with a look of hope and expectation in her eyes. When she saw that a stranger had called, she let out a sigh.

Colbeck thought that she could be no more than sixteen or seventeen. It was clear from her manner and her elegance that she was no servant. Since he had been informed that Chabal was unmarried, he assumed that she might be a relative of his. Breaking the sad news to her would be painful but it had to be done. Lifting his hat in a gesture of courtesy, Colbeck gave a smile.

'*Bonjour, Mademoiselle,*' he said.

'*Madame,*' she corrected.

'*Ah.*' He looked down and saw her wedding ring.

'*Vous êtes un ami de Gaston?*' she asked.

It was an awkward question and Colbeck did not wish to answer it on a doorstep when people were walking past all the time. Since he had bad tidings to impart, he needed to do so in privacy. He reached for a polite euphemism.

'*J'ai fait sa connaissance.*'

'*C'est mon marie.*'

Colbeck was shaken. He was talking to Gaston Chabal's wife.

Victor Leeming had been startled when first given the assignment but he had adapted to the notion very quickly. He was very pleased to be directly involved in the business of detection again. Strong enough to do the work, he also had the facial characteristics to pass as a navvy. For once, his ugliness was a positive advantage. Wearing moleskin trousers, double-canvas shirt, velveteen square-tailed coat, hobnail boots and a mud-spattered felt hat with the brim turned up, he looked almost indistinguishable from the rest of the men. Like them, he even wore a gaudy handkerchief at his neck to add some colour.

Railway work covered a wide variety of skills, each trade commanding a different wage. Leeming met carpenters, blacksmiths, miners, quarrymen, masons, bricklayers, horse keepers and sawyers. Taken on as a navvy, he was responsible to a ganger, a huge man with the rasping tongue and bulging muscularity needed to keep such an unruly group of workers in order. Digging, loading, cutting and tipping were the navvies' traditional tasks. Unskilled work was left to the labourers. Leeming was a cut above them.

When they were building a railway in England, navvies had an allowance of two pounds of beef and a gallon of beer a day. Since they had been in France, however, they had discovered that brandy was cheaper than beer and more potent. It had become the drink of choice for many of them. The fact that they spent their money so freely in the local inns made them more acceptable to the indigenous population. Given a shovel, Leeming was ordered to load spoil into wagons. It was hard, tiring, repetitive work but he did it without complaint. Those alongside him were largely Irish and they tended to work in silence. A group of Welsh navvies further down the line, however, insisted on singing hymns as they used pick and shovel on the rocky ground.

'Will you listen to those bastards?' said Liam Kilfoyle, during a brief rest. 'They never stop.'

'I'm surprised they've got the breath to sing,' observed Leeming.

'They'll work all day, fuck all night and sing their heads off while they're doing both. It's unnatural, that's what it is.'

'They sound happy enough.'

'Little things please little bloody minds.'

Kilfoyle was a tall, stringy individual in his twenties with a pair of small, darting eyes in a face that reminded Leeming of a weasel. The sergeant had gone out of his way to befriend the young Irishman, feeding him the story that Brassey had prepared for his new recruit. The problem was that Leeming could only understand half of what Kilfoyle said because the latter kept using colloquialisms that were peculiar to the Irish. He knew the rhyming slang of the London underworld by heart but this was quite different. When in doubt as to his companion's meaning, he simply nodded. Kilfoyle seemed amiable enough. Putting his shovel aside, he undid his trousers and urinated against the wheel of a wagon, breaking wind loudly in the process. He did up his moleskin trousers again.

'Have you worked for Mr Brassey before?'

said Kilfoyle.

'No – what's he like?'

'He's a fair man and you'll not find too many of them in this line of business. Some contractors are bloody tyrants, so they are. Real bloodsuckers. Not our Mr Brassey. His only fault is that he won't allow beer to be sold on site. Shovelling earth is thirsty work.'

'You don't need to tell me that,' said Leeming, face and armpits streaming with sweat. 'My throat's as dry as a bone.'

'Mine, too.' Kilfoyle eyed him up and down. 'So where have you worked, Victor?'

'On the London to Brighton.'

'From what I heard, there were some really good fights there.'

'There were, Liam. We were at it hammer and tongs many a time. I've got friends who are still locked up in Lewes Prison because of a riot we caused. They had to call in the troops.'

'It was the same for us when we were building the Chester and Holyhead. A gang of mad Welsh bricklayers from Bangor attacked us and said that all Irish were thieves and rogues. We'd have murdered the buggers, if the soldiers hadn't stopped our fun. You look as if you could handle yourself in a fight,' he went on, noting the size of Leeming's forearms. 'Am I right?'

'I won't let anyone push me around.'

'Then you're one of us.' After slapping the other on the back, he picked up his shovel. 'What do you think of the French?'

'I don't like them, Liam.'

'Turd-faced sons of diseased whores!'

'It's that gibberish they speak.'

'They hate us, Victor.'

'I know. They see us as invaders.'

'That's why they're trying to stop us,' said Kilfoyle, angrily. 'That explosion last night was set off by those French fucking navvies, sure it was. Well, some of us are not going to let these greasy, bloody foreigners drive us away. We're going to strike back.'

'Strike back?' repeated Leeming, trying to keep the note of alarm out of his voice. 'And who is we, Liam?'

'The sons of Erin.'

'Oh, I see.'

'We'll attack their camp tonight and kick their pox-ridden arses all the way from here back to Paris. Are you with us, Victor?'

'I'm not Irish.'

'A strong arm and a stout heart is all we ask.'

'Tonight, you say? When and where?'

'That doesn't matter. Are you with us or are you not?'

Leeming had no choice in the matter. If he refused, he would earn Kilfoyle's derision and be ostracised by the rest of the Irish navvies. If that happened, he would find out nothing. He simply had to appear willing.

'Oh, yes,' he said with conviction. 'I'm with you, Liam.'

'Good man!'

They started working in earnest beside each other again.

'Married?' said Thomas Brassey, rising from his seat in surprise. 'I always thought that Gaston was a roving bachelor.'

'That was the impression that he liked to give,' confirmed Colbeck, 'and it obviously convinced some ladies. I now know of two seduced by him and there may be well be more. He seems to have been liberal with his affections.'

'That raises the possibility that Gaston was the victim of an enraged husband, Inspector.'

'But it is only a possibility, sir.'

Robert Colbeck had returned from Paris late that afternoon and called in at Brassey's office to report his findings. The contractor was fascinated to hear what he had learned.

'What did you think of Paris?' he asked.

'It's a beautiful city, so cultured, so exciting, so urbane.' He held up a small book. 'Do you know Galignani's work? This is a *Stranger's Guide through the French Metropolis*. I bought it on my first visit there several years ago. It's a veritable goldmine of information. I only wish I'd had time to visit some of the sights he recommends.'

'How did Gaston's wife take the news?'

'She almost fainted. Naturally, I suppressed most of the details. There's no need for her to know any of those. Nor did I tell what her husband was doing in England. That would have been cruel.'

'What had he said to her?'

'That he was going to London to deliver a lecture.'

'And she had no suspicion that another woman was involved?'

'None at all, Mr Brassey,' said Colbeck. 'She's young, innocent and very trusting. His death was a devastating blow to her. Luckily, her mother was staying at the house. She was able to comfort her.'

'That's something, anyway.'

'I didn't wish to trespass on private grief any longer so I left.'

'Did you go to the police?'

'Yes,' said Colbeck, 'I gave them a full report of the murder and told them that we were devoting all our resources to the arrest of the killer. They agreed to help in any way, a fact that Mr Tallis will no doubt treat as a phenomenon.'

'Mr Tallis?'

'My superintendent. He has a very low opinion of the French.'

'Oh, they're a civilised nation at bottom,' said Brassey with a guarded affection. 'They make me feel very parochial at times. The trouble is that they are so easily aroused. I was here four years ago when the revolution broke out.'

'That must have been quite frightening.'

'It was, Inspector Colbeck. I was in no personal danger but my business interests were. Success as a contractor depends on stability and France became very unstable. When Louis Philippe was swept from the throne, there was a deep financial crisis.'

'Yes – many people were ruined.'

'I could have been one of them,' admitted Brassey, flicking back his coat tails as he perched on the edge of his desk. 'Stocks and shares fell heavily, none more so than those of the railways.' He pulled a face. 'It was a testing time for us. How much do you know about the French railway system?'

'I know that it's far less developed than ours,' said Colbeck, 'and that it's never attracted anything like the private investment that we enjoy. For that reason, the French government has had to play more of a role – and that's all very well until you have a violent change of government.'

'It's made this project so much more difficult.'

'Do the government interfere?'

'I'm answerable to the Minister of Public Works and he expects to be kept up to date with our progress. That was why Gaston

Chabal was so useful to us – I got him to send regular reports in French. No,' Brassey continued, 'our real difficulty lay on the other side of the Channel.'

'In England?'

'It's where so many of our private investors live, Inspector.'

'I see.'

'Ten years ago, they were happy to put money into a venture of this kind, knowing that they'd get an excellent return on their capital. After the revolution, they were much more reluctant. One of them told me that the trouble with the French was that they were *too* French.'

'Emotional, unreliable and prone to overthrow governments.'

'The gentleman in question put it more bluntly than that. Mark you,' said Brassey, 'not all the British investors turned tail. Some had the foresight to see that this railway could pay handsome dividends in time. One of them had the sense to come here to see for himself.'

'Oh?' said Colbeck. 'Who was that?'

'Alexander Marklew. He understands railways.'

'And he's actually been here?'

'In the very early stages,' replied the other. 'I let Gaston Chabal talk to him about the potential of this railway. He had such a persuasive tongue. He managed to persuade

Mr Marklew to invest. He also showed him and his wife around Paris – I think that helped.'

'I'm sure that it did.'

Colbeck said nothing about the liaison with Hannah Marklew but it took on a slightly different aspect now. He suspected that part of the reason Chabal had cultivated the lady was to persuade her to urge her husband to buy shares in the railway. The intimacies of the bedroom were not without a commercial significance.

'Clearly,' said Colbeck, 'you were able to raise the finance.'

'Yes, Inspector, but the government remains our paymaster. They've built a whole series of time penalties into the contract. That's why these setbacks are so annoying,' said Brassey, pursing his lips. 'They slow us down and cost us a lot of money.' He saw someone through the window. 'Ah, here's Aubrey.' He crossed to the door to open it. 'Come on in,' he said. 'This is Inspector Colbeck.'

'How do you do, sir?' said Filton.

'Pleased to meet you,' said Colbeck, shaking his hand. 'I believe that you talked earlier to Sergeant Leeming.'

'Yes. I've just come from him.'

'Oh?'

'Now that he's working in disguise, of course, I did not disclose the fact that I knew him. But, as I walked past, he slipped this into my hand.' He gave a note to Brassey. 'It's for you, sir.'

'Thank you, Aubrey.' Brassey unfolded the note and read it. He then offered it to Colbeck. 'I think you should see this, Inspector.'

'Why?'

'More trouble ahead.'

'Really?' Colbeck took the note from him.

'We're going to have a fight on our hands.'

'Between whom?' asked Filton, worried at the prospect.

'The French and the Irish.'

'When?'

'Tonight, according to this,' said Colbeck, reading the message.

'Some Irish hotheads have decided that the French are to blame for all the attacks on us,' said Brassey. 'They're acting as judge and jury. They want summary justice.'

'Some of them just want a fight, I expect.'

'Yes, Inspector. They enjoy a brawl for its own sake.'

'Think what havoc they can wreak,' said Filton, wringing his hands. 'There'll be dozens on both sides who are unfit for work tomorrow. And it won't end there. If there's bad blood between the Irish and the French, there'll be another clash before long.' He spread his arms in despair. 'What on earth are we going to do?'

'He's a friend, I tell you,' said Liam Kilfoyle. 'I can vouch for him.'

'I don't care,' snapped Pierce Shannon. 'He's not coming.'

'But he looks like a real fighter.'

'He's not Irish.'

'Victor supports our cause.'

'After only one day? No, Liam. I don't trust him.'

'Well, I do. I worked alongside him. The French are not going to take this lying down, Pierce. They'll fight back. We need every man we can get. Victor Leeming is on our side.'

'We'll manage without the English bastard.'

It was late evening and, like everyone else who was gathering there, Shannon and Kilfoyle had been drinking. They had also armed themselves. Shannon was carrying a shillelagh that had drawn blood from many a skull in the past while Kilfoyle preferred a pick handle. The rest of the men had chosen an assortment of weapons, including sledgehammers, shovels and lengths of thick, tarred rope. Brandy had roused passions to a fever pitch. When he joined the others, Victor Leeming found them in a turbulent mood.

'Good evening, Liam,' he said, picking out Kilfoyle by the light of the lanterns. 'When are we going?'

'You're not going any-bloody-where,' retorted Shannon.

'Why not?'

'Because you can fuck off out of here.'

Leeming turned to Kilfoyle. 'What's happened?'

'Pierce is not happy about you,' said the other, shuffling his feet in embarrassment. 'I'm sorry, Victor. You can't come.'

'Why not – what's wrong with me?'

'You're a cock-eyed cunt of an Englishman, that's why,' said Shannon, waving his shillelagh. 'This is our fight, not yours.'

'I work on this railway as well as you.'

'Yes – for one fucking day!'

'If it was one pissing hour, I'd still want to take a crack at the French,' said Leeming, boldly. 'There's jobs at stake here – mine as well as yours. If the French have been trying to stop us working on this railway, then they deserve a good hiding.'

'See?' said Kilfoyle. 'He's got balls, Pierce.'

Shannon was contemptuous. 'We don't need this ugly bugger,' he said, raising his weapon again. 'Go on – get out of here!'

It was a decisive moment. A menacing ring of Irishmen surrounded him. If he backed down, Leeming knew that he would be finished as a spy because he would be marked down as an outsider. The others would shun him completely. To win them over, he had to convince them that he shared their beliefs and commitment.

'Stop waving that cudgel at me,' he warned, 'or I'll take it off you and stick it up your arse!'

'You and whose bloody army?' demanded Shannon.

'Calm down,' said Kilfoyle, standing between them. 'We don't want you falling out with each other. Our enemy is the French.'

'And the fucking English, Liam.'

'Does that include Mr Brassey?' challenged Leeming. 'Or do you only curse him behind his back? Is he a fucking Englishman as well? Do you sneer at all of us?'

'Mr Brassey is different,' conceded Shannon.

'So am I. That means I come with you.'

'Over my dead body.'

'What's this idiot's name, Liam?'

'Pierce Shannon,' replied Kilfoyle. 'He's one of our leaders. Whatever Pierce says, goes. That's the way it is, Victor.'

'Yes,' reinforced Shannon. 'That's the way it is, shit-face.'

Leeming pretended to accept the decision. He glanced at the leering Irishmen around him. They began to jostle him. Without warning, he suddenly threw a punch that caught Shannon on the ear and knocked him to the ground. Leeming stamped on the hand that was holding the shillelagh, forcing him to release it. Two men grabbed the detective from behind but Shannon wanted personal revenge.

'Leave go of the bastard!' he yelled, struggling to his feet. 'He's all mine. I'll tear out his heart and liver.'

The crowd moved back to give them room. The two men circled each other warily. Leeming could feel the hostility all around him. His one mode of escape was to earn their respect. Shannon lunged at him with both fists flying but the blows were all taken on the protective forearms that Leeming put up. He responded by hitting Shannon hard in the stomach to take the wind out of him, then followed with a relay of punches to the face and body. Blood spurted from the Irishman's nose. It made him launch another attack but Leeming was much lighter on his feet. As Shannon lurched at him, he dodged out of his way and felled him with a vicious punch to the side of his head.

As their leader went down in a heap, three men clung on to Leeming so tight that he was unable to move. Shannon got up very slowly, wiped the blood from his nose with a sleeve then picked up his shillelagh. Eyes blazing, he confronted Leeming. Then he gave a broad grin of approval and jabbed him in the chest.

'I like him,' he announced. 'He's one of us, lads.'

There was a rousing cheer and Leeming

was released. Everyone close patted him on the back. Kilfoyle came forward to pump his hand. Leeming was relieved. He had survived one test but a far worse one might lie ahead. In beating one Irishman in a fight, all that he had done was to earn the right to attack the French as part of a mob. It was frightening. Once battle had been joined, there would be many casualties. No quarter would be given. In the uninhibited violence, Leeming could well be injured. He thought about his wife and children back in England. At that moment, he missed them more than ever. The railway was to blame. He realised that. It had not only brought him to a foreign country he disliked, it was now putting his life at risk. Leeming wished that he were hundreds of miles away.

'Come on, Victor,' said Shannon, putting a companionable arm around his shoulders. 'Let's go and kill a few Frenchies.'

CHAPTER SEVEN

'Navvies are a race apart,' said Thomas Brassey. 'I've never met anyone like them for sheer hard work. I respect them for their virtues but I also condemn them for their vices.'

'They've caused so much trouble in England,' observed Robert Colbeck. 'When they've set up camps there, they've terrorised whole communities.'

'You can see why, Inspector. Ordinary, decent, law-abiding people are horrified when they have huge gangs of hooligans on their doorstep. In their place, I'd be scared stiff.'

'Yet you seem to have less problems with your navvies, sir.'

'That's because I won't employ known trouble-makers. If I find someone trying to stir up mischief, I get rid of him at once. I also try to reduce friction by keeping different nationalities apart,' he went on. 'The Irish and the Welsh don't always see eye to eye so I make sure they are never together. It's the same with the French. I never put them shoulder to shoulder with British navvies.'

'Yet you've now got a potential riot on your hands.'

'Only because we're in an unusual position.'

'Have you never faced this situation before, Mr Brassey?'

'No – thank heaven!'

They were travelling through the French countryside in a trap. The horse was moving at a steady trot across the uneven ground and they were shaken up as the wheels mounted the frequent bumps and explored the deep potholes. It was a clear night with a half-moon looking down dolefully from the sky. Behind them were two other traps and a couple of men on horseback. Most of them carried a firearm of some sort.

'What's the worst that could happen?' asked Colbeck.

'That we get there too late.'

'We'd have heard the noise of battle before now.'

'True,' said the other. 'I suppose that the very worst thing that could happen is that news of any violence would get out, and that would surely happen if the French are involved. Activities on this railway would then be reported in the newspapers.'

'You've had bad publicity before.'

'And plenty of it, Inspector, especially in this country.'

'But I understood that you were on good

terms with the French government. Mr Filton told me that you'd had dealings with Louis Napoleon himself.'

'A businessman should always cultivate his employers. That's sound commonsense. Not that I ever expected to be accountable to a man called Napoleon,' he added with a rueful smile. 'It's a name that conjures up too many ghosts for any Englishman. But I've had to put all that aside. As it happens, on the few occasions when I've met him, I've found him an amenable gentleman.'

'How amenable would he be if French navvies were badly wounded in a fight with the Irish?'

'I hope that I never find out, Inspector Colbeck. That's why I was grateful for your advice. The plan might just work.'

'I've dealt with angry crowds before.'

'I'm sure.'

'Facing a Chartist march was a sobering experience,' admitted Colbeck. 'There were thousands of them and, if truth be told, I had a lot of sympathy with their cause. But I was there to police them so my personal views were irrelevant. Fortunately, no real violence erupted.'

'I pray that we have the same outcome tonight.'

'So do I, Mr Brassey.'

'It's not just the future of *this* railway that's at stake,' said the contractor, 'the next one

147

would also be imperilled.'

'The next one?'

'Linking Mantes to Caen is only the first half of the project. The next stage is to build a railway from Caen to Cherbourg. We would be bidding for the contract to extend the track for that extra ninety miles or so. If we blot our copybook on this venture,' he said with a frown, 'then our chances of securing that contract will be slim.'

'Caen to Cherbourg?' asked Colbeck.

'Yes, Inspector.'

'That would provide a direct link between Paris and the dockyard at Cherbourg.'

'More than the dockyard – they have an arsenal there.'

'That's exactly what I was thinking.'

'Of course, it will take time to build,' said Brassey. 'At a rough guess, we'd not even be starting for another three years. The engineer I'd most liked to have had on the project was Gaston Chabal.'

'Why?'

'His surveys were brilliant and, being French, he got on well with local people while he was there. Gaston's preparatory work on the current railway helped us to land the contract and – because of its accuracy – saved us a lot of money in the process.' Colbeck seemed to have gone off into a reverie. 'Did you hear what I said, Inspector?'

'Every word, Mr Brassey, every single

word. I was also reminded of a remark you made a little earlier.'

'Oh – and what was that?'

'You told me that you never expected to be accountable to a man called Napoleon.'

'Well, we fought for so many years against his namesake.'

'Precisely,' said Colbeck. 'Imagine how much more danger we would have been in if Napoleon Bonaparte had had a rail link between Paris and a huge arsenal on the tip of the Normandy peninsular. In that event,' he went on, stroking his chin reflectively, 'you and I might well have been having this conversation in French.'

Victor Leeming was afraid. He was so accustomed to physical violence that, as a rule, it held no fear for him. Most criminals resisted arrest and it was necessary to overpower them. It was an aspect of his work that he enjoyed. But he was now locked into a very different kind of struggle, one in which he had no place to be. Along with over two hundred wild Irishmen, he was trudging across the fields toward the farm where the French navvies had set up their camp. Leeming had sent warning of the attack to Thomas Brassey but he could not see how the contractor could possibly stop it. Carried along by its own momentum, the drunken mob was bent on what it saw as justified revenge.

Leeming felt as if he were trapped on a runaway train that was heading at top speed towards a fatal collision.

'Isn't this wonderful?' said Kilfoyle alongside him.

'Yes, Liam.'

'We'll teach them a lesson they'll not bloody well forget.'

'Whose idea was it?' asked Leeming.

'Eh?'

'Launching this attack on the French. Who first thought of it?'

'What does it matter?'

'I was interested, that's all. Was it Shannon?'

'Pierce is one of the leaders,' said Kilfoyle, 'but I fancy it was someone else who made the decision. Pierce just went along with it like the rest of us.' He let out a cackle. 'Oh, we need this so much, sure we do. We've not had a proper fight for months.'

'What will Mr Brassey do?'

'He can't do anything, Victor.'

'I don't want to lose my job over this,' said Leeming, worriedly. 'I've got a family to feed back in England.'

'Your job is safe – and so is mine. That's the reason we stick together. Mr Brassey knows which bloody side his bread is buttered. He can't sack all of us or the rest of the Irish would walk out.'

'Safety in numbers, eh?'

'Only for us, Victor – not for the French.'

'How many of them are there?'

'Who cares? One Irishman is worth four of the buggers.'

'What about me?'

'You're the fella who knocked Pierce to the ground,' said Kilfoyle, admiringly, 'and I've never seen anyone do that before. You'll have to be in the front line. Pierce wants his best men at his side. Get yourself a weapon, man.'

'Why?'

'Because the French won't be fighting with bare hands, that's why.' He thrust the pick handle into Leeming's palm. 'Here – have this. I'll use my knife instead and poke out a few eyes with it.'

There was no turning back now. Victor Leeming was part of a ravening pack of Irish wolves that was closing in on their prey. They could smell blood. Shannon pushed through the crowd.

'Come on, Victor,' he urged. 'We need you for the first charge.'

'I'm here,' said Leeming, holding up his pick handle.

'Let's see who can open the most French skulls.'

'Where's the camp?'

'Just over the brow of the hill. In a few more minutes, we'll be haring down on them to massacre the bastards.' He punched

Leeming on the shoulder. 'Are you ready for a fight?'

'Ready and willing, Pierce.'

Leeming spoke with more confidence than he felt. He was not merely facing the prospect of injury, he was taking part in a criminal act. If the superintendent ever discovered that he had been party to an affray, he would chew Leeming's ears off. The sergeant was glad that he was well out of Edward Tallis's jurisdiction.

Shannon took him by the arm and dragged him to the front of the marchers. As they went up the hill, Leeming began to have more and more misgivings. He rarely criticised Colbeck's methods but this time, he believed, the inspector had been mistaken. In making his sergeant work as a navvy, he had exposed him to dire hazards. Yet Leeming could not break ranks now. The brow of the hill was only thirty yards away. Once they were over it, there would be carnage.

Then, out of the dark, three figures appeared on the top of the hill. Silhouetted against the sky, they were an imposing trio. Even in the half-dark, Leeming recognised Colbeck, standing in the middle, with Thomas Brassey beside him. He could not identify the third man. Colbeck took out a pistol and fired it into the air. The Irishmen stopped in their tracks.

'That's as far as you go tonight, gentlemen,' said Brassey.

'Why?' demanded Shannon.

'Because I say so – and so does Father Slattery.'

'Yes,' said the priest, stepping forward and raising his voice so that all could hear. 'It's a pity that some of you don't come to a church service with the same kind of enthusiasm. When you want a fight, there's no holding you. When I tell you to join me in fighting the Devil, then it's only the bravest who show their faces.'

'Out of our way, Father!' shouted Kilfoyle.

'I stand here as a representative of Roman Catholicism.'

'I don't care if you're the bleeding Pope!' cried someone.

'The French are Catholics as well,' returned Slattery. 'Would you attack your own kind?'

'Go back to your camp,' ordered Brassey. 'There'll be no brawl tonight. The French are not even here,' he lied. 'They were forewarned to pull out of their tents and shacks.'

'Who by?' called Shannon.

'Me. And I didn't do it to save your skins. Some of you deserve to take a beating – it's the only way you'll see sense. I did it so that you could keep your jobs. This gentleman here,' he went on, pointing at Colbeck, 'is M. Robert, assistant to the Minister of

Public Works.' Colbeck raised his hat to the mob and produced a barrage of jeers. 'Before you taunt M. Robert, let me tell that he's empowered to revoke our contract if he decides that we are not able to fulfil it peaceably. I don't think anyone could construe an invasion of the French camp as a peaceful act.'

'Had you firebrands insisted on a fight,' said Slattery, taking over, 'you'd not only have been sacrificing your jobs and those of all the other navvies from across the Channel. In your wisdom, you'd also have been handing over the work to a French contractor who would refuse to employ a single one of you.'

'Think on that,' said Brassey. 'You'd have been letting me, yourselves and your families down. You'd have had to sneak home in disgrace without any money in your pockets and no work awaiting you in England. Is that what you really want?'

'No, sir,' bleated Kilfoyle.

'What about the rest of you?'

In response came a lot of shamefaced muttering. The fight had suddenly been taken out of the navvies. Several began to slink away at once. Alone in the crowd, Leeming was delighted. A calamity had just been averted by the intervention of Thomas Brassey and Father Eamonn Slattery. But it was the presence of M. Robert that had tipped the balance. Fear of losing their jobs, combined with the certainty that Brassey would never hire any of them again, brought them to heel. More of them turned round and left. The danger was over.

The contractor and the priest had prevented a bloodbath but Leeming knew that they did not deserve all the credit. The ruse had worked well because Robert Colbeck had devised it. Not for the first time, Leeming had been rescued by the inspector's guile.

As soon as they got back to his office, Thomas Brassey lit a few oil lamps then he unlocked a cupboard and took out a bottle of whisky and three glasses. He poured a generous amount into the glasses then gave one each to Robert Colbeck and Aubrey Filton. The contractor raised his own glass with a smile.

'I think we're entitled to toast a job well done,' he said.

'I never thought that you'd pull it off, sir,' confessed Filton after taking his first sip. 'I thought someone might call your bluff.'

'That's why I suggested that we involve Father Slattery,' said Colbeck, impressed by the quality of the whisky. 'I felt that he would give credence to the whole exercise. I'm still troubled by guilt at having had to deceive an ordained priest like that.'

'He really thought that you were M. Robert.'

'In a sense, of course, that's what I am.' He adopted a French accent. 'M. Robert Colbeck.'

'You spoke the language so well, Father Slattery was taken in.'

'The main thing is that the mob was as well,' said Brassey. 'I shudder to think what chaos would have followed if they'd reached the French camp. They hadn't withdrawn at all.'

'I had a very good reason to make sure that the two parties didn't meet,' Colbeck explained. 'Victor Leeming was in that crowd somewhere. I need him to remain in one piece.'

'He deserves my congratulations for what he did, Inspector.'

'Save them until he delivers the real culprits up to us.'

'Are you sure they're part of the Irish contingent?'

'Yes, Mr Brassey. Their camp is almost adjacent to the railway so it would be easy for someone to slip out at night to cause damage. The French are nearly a mile away and none of them would be aware of how you deployed your nightwatchmen. The same goes for the Welsh and the rest of your navvies,' said Colbeck. 'They're too far away. No, I believe that the men we're after might well have been in that mob tonight.'

'Would they?' said Filton.

'What better way to take suspicion off themselves than by accusing someone else of the crimes? It's an old trick, Mr Filton.'

'Cunning devils!'

'We played a trick on them tonight,' recalled Brassey. 'It was all your doing, Inspector. You'll have to meet my wife. Her French is almost as fluent as yours. Have dinner with us some time.'

Colbeck smiled. 'That's very kind of you, Mr Brassey.'

'Sergeant Leeming can join us as well.'

'Only when he's finished the task he was set.'

'He was very brave to take it on.'

'Victor has already proved his worth. I just hope that he's not the victim of his own success.'

'In what way?' said Filton.

'Those men we turned back earlier on will know that they were betrayed by someone,' said Colbeck. 'They'll want his name.'

'Then I hope they never discover it.'

'No,' said Brassey with a shiver. 'I wouldn't like to be caught out in the middle of all those Irishmen. They have hot tempers and they don't take prisoners.'

'Sergeant Leeming will have to be careful.'

'Extremely careful, Aubrey.'

'He's done this kind of work before,' said

157

Colbeck, 'though he's never dealt with navvies. As you told me earlier, Mr Brassey, they're a race apart. My hope is that Victor doesn't stick out too much. After tonight, some of those men will be desperate for revenge.'

'It must have been you, Father Slattery,' he said, glowing with rage.

'It was not, Pierce – on my word of honour.'

'You betrayed your own fucking country-men.'

'That's something I'd never do,' vowed the priest, 'and I'm insulted that you should even suggest it.'

'They knew we were coming.'

'And I'm eternally grateful that they did. Otherwise, you and your drunken ruffians would have committed the most unholy crime.'

'We were fighting on Mr Brassey's behalf.'

'Try telling him that.'

'We were,' said Shannon, vehemently. 'The Frenchies are trying to wreck this railway so that we lose the contract. That way, they can take over. The bastards want us all out of their country.'

'If you conduct yourselves as you did tonight, I'm not surprised. When drink is taken,' said Slattery, 'you turn into wild beasts. You don't belong in civilised company.

Truly, I was ashamed of you all.'

They were in the Irish camp, talking by the light of a lantern outside one of the shacks. Most of those who had marched with Pierce Shannon had either gone off to bed or starting drinking again. Shannon himself had waited until Father Slattery had reappeared. It was all he could do to keep his hands off the priest.

'I still say that it was you, Father,' he accused.

'Then you'd best bring a Holy Bible so that I can swear on it. That won't mean much to you, God-forsaken heathen that you are, but it means all the world to me.' He put his face close to that of the other. 'I did not tell a soul about your plan.'

'But you did know about it.'

'Of course – thanks to you. To get support, you told everybody you could. That's how it must have leaked out. The person to blame is you and that jabbering mouth of yours. It never stops. Someone overheard you and reported it straight away.'

'Is that what Mr Brassey told you?'

'Yes,' replied Slattery. 'He called me to his office and said that he'd received information that there was to be an attack on the French camp. He asked me if I knew who was behind it.'

Shannon was disturbed. 'Did you tell him?'

'Of course not.'

'How do I know that?'

'Because I give you my word. If I'd named you and the other ringleaders, you'd all have been on the first boat back home. If nothing else does, that should prove my loyalty to my nation.'

There was an extended pause while Shannon pondered.

'Thank you, Father,' he mumbled at length.

'I named no names,' said Slattery. 'Tell that to the others.'

'I will.'

'And don't invent any more hare-brained schemes like this.'

'It wasn't me that thought of it.' Shannon lowered his voice. 'What else did Mr Brassey say?'

'Only that you were mad to turn on the French. It could've meant him losing the contract altogether. As it is, the delays have cost him a lot of money. Did you know that there are time penalties of five thousand pounds a month if work is behind schedule?'

'No, I didn't.'

'Well, there are. Mr Brassey showed me the contract.'

'Did he give you the name of the traitor?'

'No, but I still think he was called Pierce Shannon. You opened your mouth once too often.'

'Everybody knew that something was afoot tonight,' said Shannon, 'but only those who were coming knew the fucking time and place. Somehow, Mr Brassey got hold of those details.'

'God works in mysterious ways.'

'This was nothing to do with God. We've got a spy in our ranks.'

'Then you should thank him – he saved your jobs.'

'And what if these bloody raids go on, Father? What if we get another explosion or some more damage in the tunnel? What if someone starts a real fire next time? What would happen to our fucking jobs then? Answer me that.' Shannon was breathing heavily. 'And while you're at it,' he continued, angrily, 'you can answer another bloody question as well.'

'If you could phrase it more sweetly, maybe I will.'

'Since *you* didn't betray us, who, in the bowels of Christ, did?'

Victor Leeming had never spent such an uncomfortable night before. He was, by turns, appalled by what he saw, nauseated by what he smelled and disgusted that human beings could live in such a way. The Irish camp consisted of ragged tents, rickety wooden huts and ramshackle cottages built out of stone, timber, thatch and clods of earth. In such dwellings, there was no trace of mortar to hold things together. Gaps in the roof and walls would, in due course, let in wind, rain and snow. Vermin could enter freely. It was grim and cheerless. Leeming had seen farmyard animals with better accommodation.

When he had been invited to go to the flimsy shack where Liam Kilfoyle slept, he did not realise that he would be sleeping on flagstones and sharing a room with five other people. Two of them were women and Leeming was shocked when the men beside them each mounted their so-called wives and took their pleasure to the accompaniment of raucous female laughter. It was worlds away from the kind of tender union that Leeming and Estelle enjoyed. Simply being in the same room as the noisy, public, unrestrained rutting made him feel tainted. Kilfoyle, by contrast, was amused by it all. As he lay beside Leeming, he whispered a secret.

'The fat one is called Bridget,' he said, grinning inanely. 'I have her sometimes when Fergal goes to sleep. You can fuck her as well, if you want to.'

Leeming was sickened by the thought. 'No, thank you.'

'It's quite safe. Fergal never wakes up.'

'I'm too tired, Liam.'

'Please yourself. I'll have Bridget later on.'

162

Leeming wondered how many more nights he would have to endure such horror. During his days in uniform, he had raided brothels in some of the most insalubrious areas of London but he had seen nothing to equal this. He could not understand how anyone could bear to live in such conditions. What he did admire about the navvies was their brute strength. After one day, his hands were badly blistered and he was aching all over, yet the others made light of the exhausting work. Navvies had incredible stamina. Leeming could not match it for long. To take his mind off his immediate discomfort, he tried to probe for information.

'Liam.'

'Yes?'

'What if we were wrong?'

'Wrong about what?'

'The French,' said Leeming, quietly. 'Suppose that it wasn't them who set off that explosion?'

'It had to be them, Victor.'

'Yes, but suppose – only suppose, mind you – that it wasn't? If it was someone from this camp, for instance, who'd be the most likely person to have done it?'

'What a stupid question!'

'Think it through,' advised Leeming.

'What do you mean?'

'Well, it has to be someone who knows how to handle gunpowder, for a start. It's very easy to blow yourself up with that stuff. Is there anyone here who's had any experience of blasting rock before? I heard that the gunpowder was stolen from near here.'

'It was.'

'Who could have taken it?'

'Some bleeding Frenchie.'

'It's a long way to come from their camp.'

'Yes,' said Kilfoyle slowly, as if the idea had never occurred to him. 'You're fucking right, Victor.'

'So who, in this camp, knows how to handle gunpowder?'

'Not me, I can tell you that.'

'Somebody must have had experience.'

'So?'

'I just wondered who it might be, that's all.'

'He needs catching, whoever the bastard is.'

'Have you any idea at all who it could be?'

'No.'

'Think hard, Liam.'

'Don't ask me.' He fell silent and cupped a hand to his ear so that he could hear more clearly. A loud snore came from the other side of the room. 'That's Fergal,' he said with a snigger. 'Fast asleep. I'm off to shag his wife.' He sat up. 'Shall I tell Bridget you'll be over to take your turn after me?'

Leeming's blushes went unseen in the dark.

Caleb Andrews was late getting home that night. When he came off duty at Euston, he went for a drink in a public house frequented by railwaymen and tried to bolster his confidence by beating his fireman at several games of draughts. His winnings were all spent on beer. As he rolled home to Camden, therefore, he was in a cheerful mood. His supremacy on the draughts board had been restored and several pints of beer had given him a sense of well-being. He let himself into his house and found his daughter working by the light of an oil lamp.

'Still up, Maddy?' he asked.

'Yes, Father,' she replied. 'I just wanted to finish this.'

He looked over her shoulder. 'What is it – a portrait of me?'

'No, it's the Sankey Viaduct.'

'Is it? Bless my soul!'

Since his vision was impaired after so much alcohol, he needed to put his face very close to the paper in order to see the drawing. Even then he had difficulty picking out some of the pencil lines.

'It's good, Maddy.'

'You've been drinking,' she said. 'I can smell it on your breath.'

'I was celebrating.'

'Celebrating what?'

'I won ten games of draughts in a row.'

'Are you ready for another game with me?'

'No, no,' he said, backing away. 'I'll not let you take advantage of your poor father when he can't even see straight. But why are you drawing the Sankey Viaduct? You've never even seen it.'

'Robert described it to me.'

'I could have done that. I've been over it.'

'Yes, Father, but you were driving an engine at the time. You've never seen the viaduct from below as Robert has. According to him, it was a painting rather like this that will help to solve the murder.'

'I don't see how.'

Madeleine put her pencil aside and got up from her chair. She explained how Ambrose Hooper had witnessed the body being hurled over the viaduct, and how he had duly recorded the moment in his watercolour of the scene. She felt privileged that Colbeck had confided the information to her. What both she and the inspector knew was that the murder victim had been on his way to an assignation, but it was something she would not confide to her father. Caleb Andrews would have been alarmed to hear that she had been involved in a police investigation. More worrying from Madeleine's point of view was that fact that he was likely to pass on the information over a drink with his railway colleagues. Discretion was unknown to him.

'Why do *you* want to draw the Sankey Viaduct?' he wondered.

'I was just passing an idle hour.'

'You're never idle, Maddy. You take after me.'

'Robert told me so much about it that I wanted to put it down on paper. It's not something I'd ever expect to sell. I was just trying to do what Mr Hooper did and reconstruct the crime.'

'The real crime was committed by the guard on that train,' said Andrews with passion. 'He should have kept his eyes open. If he'd seen that body being thrown from the train, he could have jumped on to the platform at the next stop and caught the killer before he could sneak away.'

'But the guard didn't see a thing, Father.'

'That's my point.' Swaying uneasily, he put a hand on the back of a chair to steady himself. 'I'm for bed, Maddy. What about you?'

'I'll be up soon.'

'Next time you speak to Inspector Colbeck, tell him to consult me. I've got a theory about this crime – lots of them, in fact.'

'I know,' she said, fondly. 'I've heard them all.'

Madeleine kissed her father on the cheek then helped him to the staircase. Holding the banister, he went slowly up the steps. She returned immediately to a drawing that she had embarked on in the first instance because it kept Robert Colbeck in her mind. It was not meant to be an accurate picture of the viaduct. Madeleine had departed quite radically from the description that she had been given. She now added some features that were purely imaginary.

Using her pencil with a light touch, she removed the brook and canal that ran beneath the viaduct by drowning them completely in the foaming waves of the English Channel. On one side of the viaduct, she drew a sketch of a railway station and wrote the name Dover above it. On the other, she pencilled in a tall, elegant man in a frock coat and top hat. England and France had been connected in art. The drawing was no longer her version of what had happened to Gaston Chabal. It was a viaduct between her and Robert Colbeck, built with affection and arching its way across the sea to carry her love to him. As she put more definition and character into the tiny portrait of the detective, she wondered how he was faring in France and hoped that they would soon be together again.

Thomas Brassey did not only expect his employees to work long hours, he imposed the same strict regimen on himself. Accordingly, he arrived on site early that morning to discover that Robert Colbeck was there before him. The inspector was carrying a newspaper.

'You've read the report, I daresay,' noted Brassey.

'Yes, sir.'

'I got my wife to translate it for me. I'm glad that they described Gaston as an outstanding civil engineer because that's exactly what he was. My only concern is that the report of his murder will bring droves of people out here to bother me.'

'I doubt it,' said Colbeck. 'Since the crime was committed in England, reporters would have no reason to visit you. The police, on the other hand, may want to learn more about the deceased so I am sure that they will pay you a call at some time.'

'I hope that you're on hand when they come, Inspector.'

'Why?'

'I need an interpreter.'

'What about your wife?'

'Maria doesn't like to come to the site. And who can blame her?' he said, looking around at the clamorous activity. 'It is always so noisy, smelly and dirty here.'

'Building a railway means making a mess, Mr Brassey.'

The contractor laughed. 'I've made more mess than anybody.'

'All in a good cause.'

'I like to think so.'

169

Brassey unlocked the door of his office and the two of them went in. Various people began to call to get their orders for the day from the contractor. It was some time before Colbeck was alone again with him. Meanwhile, he had been studying the map of northern France that was on the wall.

'Compared to us,' he remarked, 'they have so few railways.'

'That will change in time, Inspector. Mind you, they've been spared the mad rush that we had. Everyone wanted to build a railway in England because they thought they would make a fortune.'

'Some of them did, Mr Brassey.'

'Only the lucky ones,' said the other. 'The crash was bound to come. When it did, thousands of investors were ruined, credit dried up and everything ground to a standstill. The Railway Mania was over.'

'You survived somehow.'

'We still had plenty of work on our books, in France as well as England. Many of our rivals went to the wall. It was the one good thing to come out of the disaster – we got rid of a lot of crooked promoters, incompetent engineers and contractors who gave us all a bad name. It stopped the rot, Inspector.'

'Is that why you prefer to work in France?'

'My partners and I will go wherever railways need to be built,' said Brassey. 'We've contracts in Canada, Italy and Denmark at this point in time.'

'But this one is your major concern.'

'At the moment.'

'I can understand why,' said Colbeck, glancing at the map. 'If you can secure the contract for the extension of this line from Caen to Cherbourg, you'll have work in France for years to come.'

'That's why nothing must jeopardise the project.'

'We headed off one big threat last night.'

'When will the next one come?'

'I hope that it won't Mr Brassey.'

'But you can offer no guarantee.'

'No, sir. I fear not. What I can tell you is this. Gaston Chabal was murdered in England for reasons that are connected to this railway. As you pointed out to me,' Colbeck went on, 'he was much more than an engineer. He obviously had a pivotal role to play here.'

'He did, Inspector. He was a sort of talisman.'

'In more ways than one, it seems.'

'I knew nothing of Gaston's private life when I took him on,' said Brassey. 'Even if I had been aware of his adulteries, I'd still have employed him. I'm a contractor, not a moral guardian.'

'That's clear from the vast number of navvies you employ.'

'Quite so, Inspector Colbeck. All sorts of

irregularities go on in their camps but it's none of my business. As long as a man can do the job he's paid for, he can have three wives and a dozen mistresses.'

'I don't think that Chabal went to that extreme.' Colbeck moved away from the map to look through the window. 'I fear that it will all have come as a great shock to Victor.'

'What?'

'The moral laxity in the camp. He's a married man who tries to lead a Christian life. Some of the antics here will shake him to the core. He won't have seen anything like this before.'

'It's one of the reasons I encouraged Father Slattery to join us.'

'He's a courageous man, taking on such a task.'

'And so is Sergeant Leeming,' said Brassey, a chevron of concern between his eyebrows. 'As a priest, Father Slattery is not in any physical danger. Your sergeant certainly is.'

'Police work entails continuous danger, sir.'

'I just wonder if you have him in the right place.'

'The right place?'

'Well, I agree that the people we are after may be somewhere among the Irish but we've hundreds and hundreds of those. The villains could be bricklayers or quarrymen or blacksmiths. Why do you think they are navvies?'

'Instinct,' replied Colbeck. 'Instinct built up over the years. I feel that it was endorsed last night when that mob went in search of a fight. That was another attempt to disrupt this railway and to put you out of business. The villains used the same device as on the previous night, Mr Brassey.'

'In what way?'

'On the first occasion they used gunpowder. On the second, they used an equally deadly device – human gunpowder. Those Irish navvies were set to explode by the time they reached the French camp. No,' he decided, 'Victor is definitely where he needs to be. He won't thank me for putting him there, but he's in exactly the right place.'

Working so hard left him little time for detection. Victor Leeming had to take on a convincing camouflage and that forced him to toil away for long hours with a shovel in his hands. There were breaks for food and times when he had to satisfy the call of nature. Otherwise, he was kept busy loading spoil into the wagons for hour after fatiguing hour. He talked to Liam Kilfoyle and to some of the others labouring alongside him but they told him nothing of any real use. It was only when the shift finally ended, and the men trooped off to the nearest tavern, that Leeming was able to continue his search. Since he had joined in the march on the French camp, he was accepted. It made it easier for him to talk to the navvies. With a drink in their hands, they were off guard.

Yet it was all to no avail. Most of them refused to believe that an Irishmen could be responsible for the outrages, and none of them could give the name of someone with expertise in using gunpowder. At the end of a long evening, he abandoned his questioning and started to walk back towards the camp with a group of navvies. He braced himself to spend another night in the shack with Kilfoyle and the others, hoping that he would soon be released from that particular torture. The notion of coupling with Bridget, a big, buxom, shameless woman in her thirties, made his stomach heave.

So preoccupied was he in fearful thoughts of what lay ahead that he did not notice he was being followed. When they reached the railway, the men struck. Grabbing him by the shoulders, they pushed Leeming behind a wagon then one of them hit him on the back of the head with something hard and unforgiving. He had no chance to put up any resistance. He fell to the ground like a stone. Sinking into oblivion, he did not even feel the repeated kicks that thudded into his body. In a matter of seconds, it was all over.

CHAPTER EIGHT

Superintendent Edward Tallis was almost hidden by a swirling fug of cigar smoke. He did not like what he saw and he was unhappy about what he heard. While the cigar helped him to relieve his tension, it had another important function. It largely obscured Victor Leeming from his gaze. Seated in front of the desk, Leeming was a sorry sight. His head was heavily bandaged, his face covered in ugly bruises and lacerations, his lower lip twice it normal size. One eye was almost closed, the other looked to the superintendent for a sympathy that was not forthcoming. When he shifted slightly in his chair, Leeming let out an involuntary groan and put a hand to his cracked ribs.

Robert Colbeck was sitting beside the sergeant.

'I think that Victor should be commended for his daring, sir,' he suggested. 'By working alongside the navvies, he was able to foil an attack on the French camp.'

'Yes,' said Tallis, rancorously. 'He was also in a position to get himself all but kicked to death. That's not daring, Inspector, that's tantamount to suicide.'

175

'I'd do the same again, Superintendent,' said Leeming, bravely, wincing at the pain of speaking.

'You'll do nothing at all until you've recovered, man. I'm giving you extended leave until you start to resemble a human being again.' He leaned forward to peer through the smoke. 'Has your wife seen the state you're in?'

'No, sir,' said Colbeck, trying to spare the sergeant the effort of talking. 'We felt that we should report to you first so that you understood the situation. For obvious reasons, we travelled back to England slowly. Victor could not be hurried in his condition. I thought it best if I speak to Estelle – to Mrs Leeming – before she actually sees her husband.'

'That's up to you, Inspector.'

'I'll tell her how courageous he was.'

'Tell her the truth – he could have been killed.'

'No, Superintendent,' rejoined Colbeck. 'The men who set on him drew back from murder. That would have brought the French police swarming to the site and they did not want that. The beating was by way of a warning.'

'It was my own fault,' admitted Leeming, his swollen lip distorting the words. 'I asked too many questions.'

'I accept my share of the blame, Victor.'

'No, sir. It was the correct decision.'

'I beg to differ,' said Tallis, mordantly. 'Correct decisions do not result in a vicious attack on one of my men that will put him out of action for weeks.'

'You approved of our visit to France,' Colbeck reminded him.

'I've regretted it ever since.'

After giving him a day and night to make a partial recovery from the assault, Colbeck had brought Leeming back to England by means of rail and boat, two forms of transport that only served to intensify the sergeant's discomfort. Scotland Yard had been their first destination. Colbeck wanted the superintendent to see the injuries that Leeming had picked up in the course of doing of his duty. Neither compassion nor congratulation had come from across the desk.

'And what was all that about a Catholic priest?' said Tallis.

'It was Father Slattery who found Victor,' Colbeck told him. 'In fact, he seems to have disturbed the attackers before they could inflict even more damage.'

'Even *more?* What else could they do to him?'

'I didn't have the opportunity to ask them, sir,' said Leeming, rashly attempting a smile that made his whole face twitch in pain.

'Father Slattery is a good man,' said

Colbeck. 'He acts as a calming influence on the Irish.'

Tallis indicated Leeming. 'If this is what they do when they're calm,' he said with scorn, 'then I'd hate to see them when they're fully aroused. Navvies are navvies. All over the country, police and local magistrates have trouble with them.'

'Mr Brassey's men are relatively well-behaved, sir.'

'Comment would be superfluous, Inspector.'

Tallis glowered at him before expelling another cloud of cigar smoke. He was trying to rein in his anger. In allowing the two men to go to France, he had had to raid his dwindling budget and account to the commissioner for the expenditure. All that he had got in return, it seemed, was the loss of a fine officer and a succession of tales about the problems encountered by a railway contractor in France.

'None of this has any bearing on the murder,' he announced.

'But it does, sir,' insisted Colbeck. 'If you look at the events carefully, you'll see how the death of Gaston Chabal fits into the overall picture. There's a logical development.'

'Then why I am not able to perceive it?'

'Perhaps you have the smoke of prejudice in your eyes.'

Tallis stubbed out his cigar then waved an arm to dispel some of the smoke that enveloped him. Before he could take Colbeck to task for his comment, the inspector went on.

'Everything we learned in France confirmed my initial feeling.'

'And what was that?'

'The answer to this riddle lies across the Channel.'

'It's true,' said Leeming. 'We could feel it.'

'Feeling it is not enough, Sergeant,' said Tallis, coldly. 'I want firm evidence and you have signally failed to provide it. Mr Brassey may be experiencing difficulties on his railway – in spite of the calming influence of this Catholic priest – but it's no concern whatsoever of ours. The Froggies must solve any crimes that take place on French soil. Mr Brassey should call in the local police.'

'I've explained why he's reluctant to do that,' said Colbeck.

'Not to my satisfaction.'

'There's an international dimension to this murder.'

'It took place in this country. That's all that matters to me.'

'We'll only apprehend the killer if we help to solve the crimes that are bedevilling the new railway in France. I must go back.'

Tallis was peremptory. 'Out of the question.'

'Then the murderer of Gaston Chabal will go unpunished.'

'No, Inspector, he must be caught.'

'In that case, sir,' said Colbeck with gentle sarcasm, 'I'll be interested to hear your advice on how we are supposed to catch him. You are clearly in possession of important details that have so far eluded Victor and me.'

'What I am in possession of are these,' said Tallis, lifting a pile of correspondence from his desk. 'They are letters from the railway company, demanding action, and they come on a daily basis. This morning, one of their directors was here in person to ambush me. Mr Marklew did not mince his words.'

'Would that be Mr Alexander Marklew?'

'Yes. Do you know him?'

'Not personally,' said Colbeck, 'but I gather that he's also invested in the Mantes to Caen line. When he hears about the setbacks in France, he may realise that this is a much wider investigation than he imagined.'

'Marklew is only one of my problems,' moaned Tallis. 'I've had the commissioner on my tail as well and an Inspector Sidney Heyford keeps writing from Liverpool, asking me why the great Robert Colbeck has failed to make any discernible progress. That's a theme taken up elsewhere,' he went on, bending down to retrieve a newspaper from his wastepaper basket. 'There's biting criticism of the way that we've handled this investigation and you are now referred to as the Railway Defective.' He thrust the newspaper at Colbeck. 'Take it.'

'I'm not interested in what newspaper reporters think,' said the other. 'They don't understand the complexity of the case. If you'll excuse me, sir, I'll take Victor back home then make arrangements to return to France.'

'No,' said Tallis, pounding the desk. 'You stay in London.'

'I must insist, Superintendent.'

'You are overruled. Nothing on earth would induce me to send you gallivanting off on another pointless French adventure. You belong to the Metropolitan Police not to the Surèté.'

'It looks as if I belong to neither, sir,' said Colbeck, rising to his feet with dignity. 'Since you refuse me permission to go as a member of the Detective Department, then I'll do so as a private individual.'

'Don't talk nonsense, man!'

'I'm quite serious, Superintendent. I feel very strongly that this case can only be solved in France and I mean to go back there on my own account, if necessary. Give me a few minutes,' he said, as he walked to the door, 'and you shall have my resignation in writing.'

'You can have mine, too,' added Leeming,

getting out of his chair with difficulty. 'Inspector Colbeck is right. If you do not have faith in our judgement, then I'll leave the Department at once.'

'Wait!' yelled Tallis.

He could see the futility of blustering. The two of them were in earnest. The loss of Victor Leeming would be a blow but he could be replaced by promoting someone from below. Robert Colbeck, however, was quite irreplaceable. He not only had an unrivalled record of success as a detective, he had a comprehensive knowledge of railways that was founded on a deep love of steam transport. Whenever serious crimes occurred on a railway, the company involved always asked for Colbeck to investigate. If he were to leave Scotland Yard, a huge vacuum would be created. Superintendent Tallis would have to explain to the commissioner why he had forced his best officer to resign and he could imagine the withering reprimand that he would get in return. It was time to give ground.

'How long would you need in France?' he growled.

'As long as it takes,' replied Colbeck, going back to the desk to pick up the cigar box. 'Perhaps I can offer you one of these, sir?' he said, holding it out. 'It might stimulate your thought processes while I compose my letter of resignation.'

Madeleine Andrews was preparing a meal in the kitchen and musing on the changes that had come into her life since she had met Robert Colbeck. He had not merely urged her to develop her artistic talent to the point where she had actually managed to earn money from it, he had enlarged her world in every way. Until she had met him, Madeleine was happy enough looking after her father and educating herself by means of books, magazines and lectures. It had never crossed her mind that she would one day assist a detective inspector in a murder investigation and become – albeit unofficially – the first woman to have a role at Scotland Yard. Colbeck had brought love, interest and excitement into the house in Camden. Entertaining fond thoughts of him made the most menial chores seem pleasant. When she worked on, there was a smile on her face.

Madeleine had just finished peeling the potatoes when she heard the rasp of wheels pulling up outside the house. Only one person would call on her in a Hansom cab. Tearing off her apron, she wiped her hands dry in it then cast it aside. As she rushed to the front door, she adjusted her hair. She flung the door open. When she let Colbeck in, she was enfolded in a warm embrace.

'I was just thinking about you, Robert,'

she confessed.

'Good.'

'I had no idea that you were back in England.'

'Only briefly,' he told her. 'I'll be sailing across the Channel again this evening.'

'Why? What's happened? Do you know who the killer is?'

'Stop firing questions at me and I'll tell you what we've managed to find out so far.' He kissed her then led her to the sofa. 'Sit down.'

Holding her hand, he gave her a concise account of the visit to France and made her gasp when he revealed that Gaston Chabal was married. Madeleine recalled her interview at the hotel.

'Mrs Marklew was certain that he was single,' she said.

'I suspect that that's what she wanted to believe.'

'He deceived her cruelly.'

'In two ways,' said Colbeck, sadly. 'He not only enjoyed her favours by posing as a bachelor. Chabal seems to have entered into the liaison for the prime purpose of getting her to persuade her husband to invest in the railway. The French government provided much of the capital required but private investors were desperately needed. Given the volatile political situation in France, very few people from this country were prepared to risk their money.'

'How callous of him!'

'He'd probably have seen it as a piece of clever engineering.'

Colbeck finished by telling her about the savage beating sustained by Victor Leeming when posing as a navvy. The information made her sit up in alarm.

'Do be careful, Robert!' she exclaimed.

'I always am.'

'I feel so sorry for Sergeant Leeming.'

'His time as a navvy was not wasted, Madeleine. He unearthed a lot of useful intelligence. It's a pity that it had to end this way.'

'I hope that you are not thinking of taking his place.'

'If only I could,' said Colbeck, wryly, 'but it's impossible. With a face like mine, I could never pass as a navvy. Victor could. He looked the part – though he could never have lived that sort of life.'

'Was the work too hard?'

'I think it was the sleeping arrangements that upset him.'

'His wife must have been shocked by what happened.'

'That's why I went into the house first,' said Colbeck. 'I felt that it would be considerate to prepare Estelle beforehand. In fact, she took it very well. She went straight to the cab and helped Victor out. She's been a policeman's wife for years now. It's toughened her.'

'Will the sergeant be replaced?' asked Madeleine.

'Not from the Detective Department.'

'Who else would you take to France?'

'Someone who will fit more easily into the scene than Victor,' he told her. 'The last I heard of him, he was working as a dock labourer so I fancy that a trip to France might appeal to him.'

'Who is he, Robert?'

'The genuine article.'

Nature seemed to have destined Aubrey Filton to be the bearer of bad news. He had a face that could transform itself instantly into a mask of horror and a voice that rose by two octaves when he was really disturbed. His arms semaphored wildly.

'It's happened again, Mr Brassey!' he cried.

'Calm down, Aubrey.'

'We must have lost thousands of bricks.'

'How?'

'Somebody carried them to one of the ventilation shafts and dropped them down into the tunnel,' said Filton. 'The bricks were smashed beyond repair and the line has been blocked.'

'When did this happen?' asked Thomas Brassey.

'In the night, sir. They chose a shaft that was furthest away from the camp so that nobody heard the noise. When they'd unloaded the wagon that carried the bricks, they smashed it to pieces. There's no sign of the horse that pulled it.'

Brassey did his best to remain calm but exasperation showed in his eyes. He was in his office with Filton. On its walls were the maps and charts drawn as a result of various surveys. Had work proceeded at the stipulated pace, they would have been ahead of schedule and Brassey could have marked their progress on one of the charts. Instead, they were hamstrung by the sequence of interruptions. The latest of them was particularly irksome.

'We needed those bricks for today,' said Brassey.

'I've sent word to the brickyard to increase production.'

'It's security that we need to increase, Aubrey. How was anybody able to steal so many bricks without being seen?'

'I wish I knew, sir,' answered Filton, trembling all over. 'How were they able to light that fire, or damage the track in the tunnel, or steal that gunpowder or blow up the wagons? We're dealing with phantoms here, Mr Brassey.'

'No,' affirmed the other. 'Inspector Colbeck correctly identified our enemy. We're

187

dealing with navvies. Nobody else would have had the strength to drop all those bricks down a ventilation shaft. It would take me all night to do such a thing.'

'It would take me a week.'

'What they probably did was to unload a fair number by hand then undo the harness on the horse so that they could tip the whole cart over.'

'I suppose that the horrible truth is that we'll never know.'

'Not until the inspector returns, anyway.'

'Do you really think that he can catch these men?' said Filton, sceptically. 'He hasn't managed to do so thus far and we both saw what happened to Sergeant Leeming.'

'That incident will only make Inspector Colbeck redouble his efforts. Introducing a man into the Irish camp did have advantages. He was able to warn us about that planned attack on the French.'

'What if there's another?'

'That's very unlikely,' said Brassey. 'I think we scared the Irish by telling them that they'd lose their jobs. Work is scarce back in England. They all know that.'

'It didn't stop some of them from stealing those bricks last night and there'll be more outrages to come. I feel it in my bones.'

'Don't be so pessimistic, Aubrey.'

'There's a curse on this railway.'

'Balderdash!'

'There is, Mr Brassey. I begin to think that it's doomed.'

'Then you must change that attitude immediately,' scolded the other. 'We must show no hint of weakness. The villains are bound to slip up sooner or later. We need another spy in their camp.'

'We already have one, sir.'

'Do we?'

'Of course,' said Filton. 'Father Slattery. He knows everything that goes on in the Irish community. It's his duty to assist us.'

'His main duty is a pastoral one and nothing must interfere with that. If we asked Father Slattery to act as an informer, he'd lose all credibility. What use would he be then? Besides,' he continued, 'he obviously has no idea who the miscreants are or he'd tackle them himself. A priest would never condone what's been going on.'

'So what do we do?'

'Wait until the inspector gets back with this new man.'

'New man?'

'Yes, Aubrey. I'm assured that he will be ideal for the job.'

'Ah,' said Brendan Mulryne, swallowing his brandy in a gulp as if it was his last drink on earth, 'this is the life, Inspector. And to think I might be heaving cargo at the docks all day long.'

'You were working in the Devil's Acre last time we met.'

'I had to leave The Black Dog.'

'Why?' asked Colbeck.

'Because I had a disagreement with the landlord. He had the gall to hit me when I wasn't looking and I take violence from no man. Apart from anything else, he did it at the most inconvenient time.'

'What do you mean?'

'I was teaching his darling wife a few tricks in bed.'

Brendan Mulryne roared with laughter. He was an affable giant with a massive frame and a face that seemed to have been hewn out of solid teak by a blind man with a blunt axe. Though he was roughly the same age as Colbeck, he looked years older. There was an irrepressible twinkle in his eye and he had a ready grin that revealed a number of missing teeth. Mulryne had once been a constable in the Metropolitan Police Force but his over-enthusiasm during arrests led to his expulsion. Having caught a criminal, he had somehow seen it as a duty to pound him into unconsciousness before hauling him off to the police station. He had always been grateful to Colbeck for trying to save him from being discharged.

Since his dismissal, Mulryne had drifted into a succession of jobs, some of them firmly on the wrong side of the law but none that offended the Irishman's strange code of ethics. He would only steal from a thief or commit other crimes against known villains. It was Mulryne's way of restoring what he called the balance of society. In his heart, he was still a kind of policeman and that was why the present situation had so much appeal for him.

Having crossed the Channel the previous evening, they had spent the night in Le Havre before taking the train to Mantes. Mulryne was a much livelier companion than Victor Leeming. It was his first visit to France and he was thrilled by everything he saw. When the train rattled over the Barentin Viaduct, he gazed down with awe.

'Be-Jesus!' he exclaimed. 'Will you look at that? It's almost as if we was flying, Inspector.'

'Thomas Brassey built the viaduct.'

'Then I'll be happy to shake his hand.'

'Not too hard,' advised Colbeck. 'You've got the biggest hands I've ever seen on a human being. You can crack walnuts with a gentle squeeze. Go easy on Mr Brassey.'

'I will.' His face crumpled with sympathy. 'But I'm sorry to hear about Sergeant Leeming.'

'Victor was unlucky.'

'He taught me a lot when we were both in uniform.'

'You're a detective now, Brendan, in the

Plain Clothes Division.'

'Well,' said Mulryne, emitting a peal of laughter, 'clothes don't come any plainer than these.'

He was wearing the same moleskin trousers, canvas shirt and tattered coat that had served him in the docks, and his hobnail boots were also suitable for work on the railway. A shapeless hat completed the outfit but he had removed it when they boarded the train. Mulryne was tickled by the fact that he was dressed like a typical navvy while travelling in a first class carriage.

'I'll be carrying on the family tradition,' he said, proudly.

'Will you?'

'Yes, sir. My father was a navvy in the old days when the word had its true meaning. Father – God bless him – was a navigator who helped to cut canals. I was born in a navvies' camp somewhere along the line.'

'I never knew that, Brendan.'

'I'm a man with hidden secrets.'

'You'll certainly have to hide a few when we get to Mantes.'

'I'll soon charm my way in.'

'That's what Victor thought but they found him out.'

'It takes an Irishman to beguile the Irish, so it does.'

'It's the reason I chose you. Most of them are decent, honest, hard-working men and they couldn't have a better priest than Father Slattery.' He saw Mulryne's glum expression. 'What's wrong?'

'I didn't know I'd have a priest to worry about.'

'Father Slattery is a dedicated man.'

'Yes – dedicated to stopping the rest of us having a bit of fun. It's the reason I couldn't stay in Ireland. It's so priest-ridden. You only had to fart and they'd make you say a novena and three Hail Mary's. The place for a man of the cloth,' he declared, soulfully, 'is in a church and not on a railway.'

'He does valuable work,' said Colbeck. 'More to the point, he knows everyone. That's why you ought to meet him, Brendan. He can introduce you to the others. Father Slattery is a way in.'

'And will I be seeing you at the service on Sunday, Liam Kilfoyle?'

'Yes, Father.'

'You said that last week and the week before.'

'It slipped my mind,' said Kilfoyle, evasively.

'St Peter has been known to let certain things slip *his* mind as well,' cautioned the priest. 'How will you feel when you reach the pearly gates to find that he's forgotten all your good deeds?'

'I'll remind him of them.'

'The best way to do that is to attend Mass.'

'I worship in my own way, Father Slattery.'

'That's wonderful! When you come on Sunday, you can give us all a demonstration of how you do it. We can always learn new ways to pray, Liam.' He beamed at Kilfoyle. 'I'll see you there.'

'I hope so.'

'Are you going to let the Lord down yet again?'

Kilfoyle swallowed hard. 'I'll try not to, Father.'

'Spoken like a true Catholic!'

The old man chuckled and went off to speak to a group of men nearby. It was the end of the day's shift and Slattery was trying to increase the size of the congregation in his makeshift, outdoor church. Kilfoyle was glad to see him go. A wayward Christian, he always felt guilty when he talked to the priest. Memories of sinful nights between the thighs of another man's wife somehow thrust themselves into his mind. It was almost as if Father Slattery knew about his moments of nocturnal lechery with Bridget.

'What did that old bastard want?' said Pierce Shannon, coming over to him. 'Did he want you to train for the priesthood?'

'Nothing like that.'

'Be careful, Liam. You'd have to be celibate.'

194

'Then the job'd not suit me. I've got too much fire in my loins for the church. Father Slattery will have to look elsewhere.'

'Well, it had better not be in my direction.'

'Why not, Pierce? You might end up as a cardinal.'

'If I'm a cardinal, you're the Angel Bleeding Gabriel.'

They traded a laugh. Shannon stepped in closer.

'By the way,' he said, casually, 'it's a shame about that friend of yours, Victor Leeming. He could have been useful to us.'

'Not any more.'

'I suppose the truth is that he just didn't fit in here. Pity – he was a good worker.'

'Victor won't be doing any work for a while.'

'I liked the man. He had a good punch.'

'He was certainly a match for you, Pierce.'

'Only because he caught me unawares that one time,' said Shannon, thrusting out his chest. 'In a proper fight, I reckon that I could kick seven barrels of shit out of him.'

'Don't try to do that to Brendan,' warned Kilfoyle.

'Who?'

'Brendan Mulryne. He was helping us to shovel spoil into the wagons today. He's got muscles bigger than bloody pumpkins. He made me feel puny beside him. Brendan could fill two wagons in the time it took me to fill one.'

'What sort of man is he?'

'The best kind – joking all day long.'

'I prefer a man who keeps his fucking gob shut while he works.'

'Then stay clear of Brendan. He can't keep quiet. We got on well together. He feels the same about priests as me. He'd rather roast in Hell than be forced to listen to a sermon.'

'Where's he from?'

'Dublin.'

'And he's a real navvy?'

'With hands like that, he couldn't be anything else.' Kilfoyle saw the giant figure ambling towards him. 'You can meet him for yourself, Pierce. Here he comes.'

Shannon turned a critical eye on Brendan Mulryne, who was smiling amiably at everyone he passed and making cheerful comments as he did so. When he spotted Kilfoyle, he strolled across to him. Mulryne was introduced to Shannon. As they shook hands, the latter felt the power in the other's grip.

'I'm looking for somewhere to sleep tonight,' said Mulryne. 'The ganger told me there'd be room at Pat O'Rourke's. Do you know him?'

'Yes,' replied Kilfoyle, pointing. 'He owns that stone house at the end of the row. Pat will look after you. Built the house himself.'

'How much does he charge?'

'Almost nothing.'

'That's good because I haven't got two bleeding pennies to rub together.' He became conspiratorial. 'Hey, I don't suppose that either of you know how I can pick up a little extra money, do you?'

'In what way?' asked Shannon.

'Any way at all, friend.'

'Such as?'

'On my last job, I made a tidy sum at cockfighting.'

'Nobody will want to fight a cock as big as yours,' said Kilfoyle with a giggle. 'And, if you're talking about the kind with feathers and sharp claws, then Mr Brassey won't allow that kind of thing on any of his sites.'

'What the eye doesn't see, the heart doesn't fucking grieve.'

'I couldn't have put it better,' said Shannon, warming to him at once. 'How else have you made money in the past, Brendan?'

'All sorts of ways. Best of all was prize-fighting.'

'Really?'

'Yes, I'd take on all-comers with one hand strapped behind my back. They not only paid for the chance to take a swing at me,' said Mulryne, 'I got my share of the bets that were laid as well.'

'Very crafty.'

'I've got a devil of a thirst, Pierce. That

takes money.'

'Not here,' said Kilfoyle. 'The brandy's dirt cheap.'

'I know. I tried some on the way here. Anyway,' Mulryne went on, 'I'd best find O'Rourke so that I've got somewhere to lay my fucking head tonight. Then it's off to the nearest inn with me.'

'We'll take you there,' volunteered Shannon.

'Thank you, friend. I might hold you to that.' He caught sight of Father Slattery among the crowd and recoiled. 'Is that the bleeding priest they told me about?'

'That's him, large as life.'

'Then keep the bugger away from me.'

'Father Slattery is harmless enough,' said Kilfoyle.

'Not to me, Liam. There's a time and place for priests and this is not it. When I've worked my balls off all day,' asserted Mulryne, 'the last thing I want is a dose of religion. A good drink and a warm woman is all I need and Father Slattery looks as if he's never tasted either.'

Maria Brassey was an excellent hostess. She gave the guests a cordial welcome and served a delicious meal. When he spoke French by demand, Robert Colbeck discovered that she had an excellent grasp of the language. She was delightful company and presided over the table with her husband. After dinner, however, she knew exactly when to withdraw so that the men could talk in private.

'Have you had any success while I was away?' said Colbeck.

'A little,' replied Brassey. 'The nightwatchmen caught two men pilfering but they had nothing to do with all the damage we've suffered. I paid them what I owed and ordered them off the site.'

'That, of course, is another avenue we might explore.'

'What do you mean, Inspector?'

'Discontented former employees. Men with a grudge.'

'You'll not find many of those,' said Aubrey Filton, the other guest. 'Mr Brassey is renowned for his fairness. If the men step out of line, they know they'll be sacked. They accept that.'

'Most of them, perhaps,' said Colbeck. 'But I can see how it would rankle if someone was dismissed from a job that would guarantee two years' work for them.'

'We keep a record of every man we employ.'

'Then I'd like to take a close look at it, Mr Filton.'

The three men were comfortably ensconced in chairs in the living room of the country house that Brassey had rented. It was close enough to the site for him to get there with ease yet far enough away to be out of reach of the incessant noise that was created. Having grown up on a farm, the contractor always preferred a house that was surrounded by green fields. It made him feel as if he were back in his native Cheshire. He sipped his glass of port.

'How is Sergeant Leeming?' he said.

'Very glad to be back home,' returned Colbeck. 'Victor took a beating but no permanent damage seems to have been done. He simply needs plenty of time to recover.'

'That sort of thing would put me off police work forever,' said Filton. 'It's far too dangerous.'

'Victor is not so easily deterred.'

'And what about this new fellow?'

'Oh,' said Colbeck with a smile, 'you can rely on him. If you set off an explosion under Brendan Mulryne, you'd not scare him away. He has nerves of steel.'

'Then why didn't you bring him here in the first place?' said Brassey. 'Was he assigned to another case?'

'Yes, sir.'

'He doesn't look like a detective at all.'

'He isn't one,' said Colbeck.

'I see. He's an ordinary constable.'

'There's nothing ordinary about Brendan, I promise you. He was trained as a policeman and I had the good fortune to work with him when I was in uniform. When you have to break up a tavern brawl, there's no better man to have beside you than him.'

'I can imagine.'

Colbeck did not reveal that the man he had entrusted with such an important task was, in fact, a dock labourer of dubious reputation who led the kind of chaotic existence that two conventional middle class gentlemen could not begin to understand. The less they knew about Brendan Mulryne, the better. At all events, Colbeck resolved, his name must not get back to Edward Tallis. If the superintendent became aware of the Irishman's presence on site, Colbeck would not have to write a letter of resignation. He would probably be ejected from Scotland Yard with Tallis's condemnation ringing in his ears.

'What interests me is the next stretch of line,' said Colbeck, draining his glass. 'The one that runs from Caen to Cherbourg.'

Brassey held up a palm. 'Give us a chance, Inspector,' he said, jocularly. 'We haven't finished this one yet.'

'And may never do so,' said Filton, gloomily.

'Of course we will, Aubrey.'

'I wonder, sir.'

'Will any French companies put in a tender for the other line?' asked Colbeck. 'Are any contractors here big enough to do so?'

'Yes,' replied Brassey. 'The French were slow starters when it came to railways but they are catching up quickly, and contractors have seen the opportunities that are there. When the time comes, I'm sure that we'll have a number of competitors.'

'What about labour? Are there enough navvies in France?'

'No, Inspector Colbeck, not really. Comparatively few railways have been built here so far. As a result, there's no pool of experienced men on which to draw. We found that out when we built the Paris to Rouen railway some years ago.'

'Yes, I believe that you imported 5,000 from England.'

'It was not nearly enough,' said Brassey. 'I had to cast the net much wider in order to double that number. They were mainly French but they also included Germans, Belgians, Italians, Dutchmen and Spaniards. Do you remember it, Aubrey?'

'Very well,' said Filton. 'You could hear eleven different languages in all. It was quite bewildering at times.'

'As for the line from Caen to Cherbourg, that remains in the future. We've not really had time to think about it.'

'Somebody else might have done so,' said Colbeck.

'I'm sure that other contractors are planning surveys already.'

'Only because they want to build the line.'

'It could be a very profitable venture.'

'Assuming that we do not have another revolution,' said Filton with a tentative laugh. 'You never know with these people.'

'Oh, I think that Louis Napoleon is here to stay.'

'For a time, Mr Brassey.'

'He's a man of great ambition, Aubrey.'

'That's the impression I've had of him,' said Colbeck. 'From all that I've read about Louis Napoleon, he seems to be a man of decisive action. He knows precisely what he wants and how best to achieve it. Well, you've met him, Mr Brassey,' he continued. 'Is that an unfair estimate of him?'

'Not at all. He's determined and single-minded.'

'Just like his namesake.'

'He patterns himself on Bonaparte.'

'That could worry some people. When I said a moment ago that somebody else might have thought about the extension to Cherbourg, I was not referring to your rival contractors. They simply want to build the railway,' said Colbeck. 'What about those who want to stop it from ever being built?'

'Why should anyone want to stop it, Inspector Colbeck?'

'We'll have to ask them when they're finally caught.'

Brendan Mulryne might have been working on the railway for a month rather than simply a day. He related so easily to the people around him that he gained an immediate popularity. Part of a crowd of navvies who descended on one of the inns in a nearby village, he proved to his new friends that he could drink hard, talk their language and tell hilarious anecdotes about some of the escapades in which he had been involved. Since there were others there who hailed from Dublin, he was also able to indulge in some maudlin reminiscences of the city. The night wore on.

To earn some easy money, he issued a challenge. He said that he would pay a franc to anyone who could make him double up with a single punch to his stomach. Those who failed would pay Mulryne the same amount. Liam Kilfoyle was the first to try. Slapping a franc down on the bar counter, he took off his coat and bunched his right hand. Everyone watched to cheer him on and to see how he fared. Mulryne grinned broadly and tightened his stomach muscles. When he delivered his punch, Kilfoyle felt as if he had just hit solid rock. His knuckles were sore for the rest of the night.

Several people tried to wipe the grin from Mulryne's face but none could even make him gasp for breath. In no time at all, he had earned the equivalent of a week's wage and he showed his benevolence by treating everyone to a drink. By the time they rolled out of the inn, Mulryne was more popular than ever. He led the others in a discordant rendition of some Irish ballads. When they neared the camp, the men dispersed to their respective dwellings. Mulryne was left alone with Kilfoyle and Pierce Shannon.

'When you won all that money,' said Shannon, 'why did you throw it all away on a round of drinks?'

Mulryne shrugged. 'I was among friends.'

'I'd have held on to it myself.'

'Then you don't have my outlook on life, Pierce.'

'And what's that?'

'Easy come, easy go.'

'Does it work the same for women?' asked Kilfoyle.

'Yes,' said Mulryne, chortling happily. 'Take 'em and leave 'em, that's what I believe, Liam. Love a woman hard but always remember the queue of other lucky ladies that are waiting for you with their tongues hanging out.'

'What about French women?'

'What about them?'

'Do you like them?'

'I like anything pretty that wears a skirt.'

'They can't compare with an Irish colleen.'

'Women are women to me.'

They walked on until they came to the two parallel tracks that had already been laid. Empty wagons stood ready to be filled on the following day. Kilfoyle saw a chance to win a wager.

'How strong are you, Brendan?' he said.

'Why – do you want to take another swing at me?'

'No, I was wondering if you could lift that.' He pointed to one of the wagons. 'Only a few inches off the rails. Could you?'

'Depends on what you're offering,' said Mulryne.

'A day's wages.'

'They'll be mine to keep, if I win. There'll be no buying you a free drink this time, Liam.'

'If you can shift that wagon, you'll have earned the money.'

'I'll match the bet,' said Shannon, 'if you take it on.'

Mulryne removed his coat. 'I never refuse a challenge.'

It was the last wagon in the line. He walked around it to size it up then un-coupled it from its neighbour. Taking a firm grip of it at the other end, he gritted his teeth and pretended to put all his energy into a lift. The wagon did not budge. Kilfoyle rubbed his hands with glee.

'We've got him this time, Pierce,' he said.

'I just need a moment to get my strength

up.' Mulryne took a few deep breaths then tried again in vain. 'This bleeding thing is heavier than I thought. What's inside it – a ton of lead?'

'Do you give up, Brendan?'

'Not me – I'll have one last go.'

'You owe each of us a day's wages.'

'I'll make it two days, if you like,' said Mulryne.

'Done! What about you, Pierce?'

Shannon was more wary. 'My bet stands at one day.'

'Then get ready to hand it over,' said Mulryne, spreading arms further apart as he gripped the wagon once more. 'Here we go.'

Bracing himself with his legs, he heaved with all his might and lifted the end of the wagon at least six inches from the rail. Then he dropped it down again with a resounding clang.

Kilfoyle was amazed. 'You did it!'

'I usually only use one hand,' boasted Mulryne.

'You could have lifted it off the rails altogether.'

'Easily.'

'Here's my money,' said Shannon, paying up immediately. 'I'll have more sense than to bet against you next time.'

'Don't tell the others, Pierce.' Mulryne slapped the wagon. 'I think that this little trick might bring in even more profit. Let's have what you owe me, Liam.'

'Right,' said Kilfoyle, handing over the coins.

'And don't be stupid enough to challenge me again.'

'I won't, Brendan.'

'To tell you the truth,' admitted Mulryne, 'I never thought I could do it. But the chance of winning the bet put new strength into my arms. I'm like an old whore,' he added with a loud guffaw. 'I'll do absolutely anything for money.'

CHAPTER NINE

Robert Colbeck was interested in every aspect of the railways. While he enjoyed travelling on them, he was also very curious about those who brought them into being with the brilliance of their invention or the sweat of their brow. Bridges, aqueducts, tunnels, cuttings, and drainage systems did not burst spontaneously into life. Each and every one had to be designed and built to specification. Colossal earthworks had to be constructed. Timber had to be felled and cut to size. Marshes had to be drained. Stone had to be quarried. Untold millions of bricks had to be made on site before being used to line tunnels, create ventilation shafts, solidify bridges and aqueducts, or stabilise steep embankments. A railway was a declaration of war against a contour map of the area where it was being built. Continuous and unremitting attack was needed.

When he inspected the site with Aubrey Filton that morning, Colbeck was impressed by the amount of work that had been done since the day he had first arrived there with Victor Leeming. Nobody was slacking. Everywhere he looked, men were putting their hearts and souls into their job. Brendan Mulryne, he noticed, was now helping to dig a new cutting, shovelling methodically and building up a vast mound of earth to be taken away to the wagons. Colbeck could hear his distinctive voice above the din.

'You're making headway, Mr Filton,' he observed.

'Not enough of it, Inspector.'

'Where did you expect to be at this stage?'

'At least a quarter of a mile farther on,' said the engineer. 'The French government are slave-drivers. We have targets to meet at the end of every month.'

'Everything seems to be going well now. And we've not had any incidents for the last couple of days.'

'It's the calm before the storm.'

'I don't think so,' said Colbeck. 'I believe it may have something to do with the fact that Mr Brassey took my advice about security. In addition to nightwatchmen, he now has a handful of guard dogs.'

'Yes, they're vicious-looking brutes.'

'That's the intention.'

'I'm glad that they're kept on a leash.'

'They won't be if there's any trouble, Mr Filton. The dogs will be released. The simple fact that you've got them will make any villains think twice before committing a crime. They might be able to outrun a nightwatchmen,' said Colbeck, 'but not if he has four legs.'

They strolled on until they reached the forward end of the strenuous activity. Ground rose steadily ahead of them and would need to be levelled before the track could be laid. There would be more digging for Mulryne and the others. Colbeck thought about all the maps and charts he had seen in Brassey's office.

'How good an engineer was Gaston Chabal?' he asked.

'He was outstanding.'

'I'm sure that you are as well, Mr Filton, or you'd not be employed on such a major project. Was Chabal taken on because he was French or because he had remarkable skills?'

'For both reasons, Inspector.'

'But you can manage without him?'

'We have to,' said Filton. 'Fortunately, we have all the drawings and calculations he did for us, but it's not the same as having the man himself here. Gaston was a delightful fellow.'

'Everyone seems agreed on that.'

'Except his killer.'

'Yes,' said Colbeck, thoughtfully, 'I've been trying to put myself in his position – the killer, that is, not Chabal. Why did he choose the Frenchman as his target? If you wanted to halt the construction of this railway, whom would you murder?'

Filton was offended. 'I have no homicidal urges, I assure you.'

'The obvious person would be Mr Brassey.'

'Yes, that would be a calamity.'

'Who would come next?'

'One of his partners, I suppose.'

'And then it would be the leading engineer, Gaston Chabal.'

'Actually,' said Filton with a rare flash of pride, 'I was slightly senior to Gaston. I've been with Mr Brassey much longer and he always rewards loyalty.'

'In other words, Chabal's death was not a fatal blow to the building of this railway.'

'No, Inspector. It was a bitter blow but not a fatal one.'

'Then he must have been killed for symbolic reasons.'

'Symbolic?'

'He was French,' said Colbeck. 'That was the conclusive factor. A Frenchman thrown from the Sankey Viaduct – I believe that act has a weird symbolism to it.'

'What exactly is it?'

'I've yet to establish that, Mr Filton.'

'Do you still think his killer was an Englishman?'

'I'm as certain as I can be.'

'I wish I had your confidence.'

'Everything points that way, sir.'

'Not to my eyes. What possible connection is there between a crime near the Sankey

Viaduct and the ones that have afflicted us here? The two railways involved have nothing whatsoever to do with each other.'

'Yes, they do.'

'What?'

'Mr Alexander Marklew, for a start. He's a director of the London and North-West Railway and a major investor in this one. And there are lots of other hidden links between the two, I feel, if only we could dig them out.'

'All that troubles me is what happens on this project, Inspector. We've had setback after setback. Unless they are checked, they could in time bring us to a dead halt.'

'That's his intention.'

'Who?'

'The man I'm after,' explained Colbeck. 'The one responsible for all the crimes that have occurred. He's very elusive. All I know about him so far is that he's conceived a hatred of this particular railway and a passion for symbols. Oh, yes,' he added. 'One more thing.'

'What's that?'

'The fellow is utterly ruthless.'

Sir Marcus Hetherington left the shareholders' meeting and called a cab with a snap of his fingers. He was a tall, slim, dignified man in his seventies with white hair curling from under his top hat and a red rose

213

in the lapel of his frock coat. His short, white moustache was neatly trimmed. After telling the cab driver to take him to the Pall Mall, he clambered into the vehicle and settled back. Alone at last, he was able to let his mask of imperturbability drop. His face was contorted with fury and he released a few silent expletives.

It had been a disappointing meeting. Unlike many landowners, he had not seen the advent of railways as a gross intrusion of his privacy or a precursor of the destruction of the England he knew and loved. He was keenly aware of their practical value. Since he was paid a great deal of money by way of compensation, he was happy for a line to be built across his estates. The proximity of the railway station enabled him to reach London much more quickly from Essex than by travelling in a coach. That was a bonus.

Sir Marcus had always considered himself a forward-thinking man. Railways were set to revolutionise the whole country and he wanted to be part of that revolution. As a result, he took some of the capital he had received in compensation from one railway company and invested it in a couple of others. When the market was buoyant, dividends were high and he congratulated himself on his acumen. Once the bubble had burst so spectacularly, however, he had been one of the many victims. At the meeting he had just left, the chairman had informed the assembled throng that no dividends at all would be payable to shareholders for the foreseeable future. It was infuriating.

When he reached the Reform Club, the first thing he did was to order a stiff whisky. Reclining in his high-backed leather chair, he sipped it gratefully and bestowed a patrician smile on all who passed. In the sedate surroundings of the club, he could not let his seething rage show. He had to simmer inwardly. One of the uniformed stewards came across to him and inclined his head with deference.

'There's a gentleman asking for you, Sir Marcus,' he said.

'Did he give a name?'

'He sent his card.'

The steward handed it over and the old man glanced at it.

'Send him in, Jellings,' he said, crisply, 'and bring him a glass of whisky. Put it on my account, there's a good chap.'

Minutes later, Sir Marcus was sitting beside Luke Rogan, a thickset man in his forties with long, wavy black hair tinged with grey and a flat, but not unpleasant, face. Though well-dressed, Rogan looked decidedly out of place in a palatial club that was a home for Whig politicians and their like. There was a flashy quality about the newcomer that made him look rather incongruous beside such a distinguished figure as Sir Marcus Hetherington. When set against the educated drawl of the grandee, his voice sounded rough and plebeian.

'You've more work for me, Sir Marcus?' he inquired.

'I think so, Rogan.'

'Tell me what it is. I've never let you down yet.'

'I wouldn't employ you if you had,' said Sir Marcus, 'and you would certainly not be sitting here now. Tell me, do you read the newspapers on a regular basis?'

'Of course,' replied the other with a complacent grin. 'In my line of business, I have to, Sir Marcus. Newspapers is how I gets most of my work. Well, it's how you and me got together, ain't it? You saw my advertisement and got in touch.'

'What have you noticed in the course of your reading?'

'That the police still have no idea how a certain person was thrown out of a moving railway carriage – and they never will.'

'Their failure is gratifying,' said Sir Marcus, 'I grant you that. But we must never underestimate this fellow, Colbeck. He seems to have an uncanny knack of picking up a trail where none exists.'

'Not this time. Inspector Colbeck is like the rest of them over at Scotland Yard – he's floundering, Sir Marcus.'

'I begin to wonder.'

'What do you mean?'

'I've just come from a shareholders' meeting of a railway company,' replied the other. 'The one thing of interest that the chairman told me was that Colbeck helped to prevent a serious crime from taking place on one of their trains earlier this year. The chairman could not speak too highly of him.'

'Colbeck had some luck, that's all.'

'His success can't be dismissed as lightly as that, Rogan. When I pointed out that the Railway Detective was faltering badly with his latest case, the chairman said that he'd heard a rumour to the effect that the inspector had gone to France.'

Rogan was jolted. 'To France?'

'It was not the kind of information I wanted to hear.'

'Nor me, Sir Marcus.'

'What I want to read about is the damage done to a particular railway line on the other side of the Channel yet the newspapers have been uniformly silent on the subject.'

'You can't expect them to carry foreign items.'

'That's exactly what I do expect, man. Any periodical worthy of the name should have its own foreign correspondents. *The Times* will always report matters of interest from abroad.'

'This would hardly catch their attention,

Sir Marcus.'

'Yes, it would. An Englishman is involved – Thomas Brassey.'

'I'm sure that everything is going to plan.'

'Then why is there no whisper of it in the press? Why is there no report from France about the damage caused to a railway in which they have invested both money and national pride?'

'I can't tell you,' admitted Rogan.

'Then find out.'

'Eh?'

'Go to France, man. Discover the truth.'

'But I'm handling other cases at the moment, Sir Marcus. I can't just drop them to go sailing off across the Channel. Anyway, I've no reason to suspect that the men I engaged will let me down.'

'How much did you pay them?'

'Half the money in advance,' said Rogan, 'just like you told me, the rest to be handed over when the job was done.'

'And *has* the job been done?' pressed Sir Marcus.

'Not yet.'

'Not at all, I suspect. What was to stop these rogues from pocketing the money you gave them and taking to their heels? If that's the case, Rogan – and I hope, for your sake, that it's not – then I am out of pocket as a consequence of your bad judgement of character.'

'Sir Marcus–'

'Don't interrupt me,' snapped the other, subduing him with a frosty glare. 'There's unfinished business here, sir. If you accept a commission, you should see it through as a matter of honour. What you did for me in this country, I applaud. You obeyed your orders to the letter and were handsomely rewarded. But I begin to fear that you have let me down woefully in France itself.'

'That's not true, Sir Marcus.'

'Prove it.'

'I will, if you'll bear with me for a while.'

'My patience is exhausted.' Taking something from his pocket, he slapped it down on the little table that stood between them. 'Take that and study it carefully.'

'What is it?'

'A list of sailings to France. Choose a boat and be on it today.'

'Today?' spluttered Rogan. 'That's impossible.'

'Not if you put your mind to it, man. Now stop arguing with me and be on your way. And whatever else you do,' he added, spitting the words out like so many bullets, 'don't you dare return from that confounded country with bad news for me. Is that understood?'

Rogan gulped down his whisky then grabbed the piece of paper from the table. After pulling out his watch to check the time, he got to his feet and wiped his mouth with the back of his hand.

'Yes, Sir Marcus,' he said, obsequiously. 'It's understood.'

'I don't think we've met before, have we?' said Father Slattery, offering his hand. 'Welcome to France, my friend.'

'The name is Mulryne,' said the other, extending his vast palm for the handshake. 'Brendan Mulryne.'

'I thought it might be. I've heard the stories.'

'Don't believe a word of them, Father. You know what terrible liars the Irish are. I'm just an ordinary lad who likes to keep his head down and get on with his work.'

'Is that why you weren't at church on Sunday?'

Mulryne feigned ignorance. 'I didn't know there *was* a church.'

'Then it's blind you must be, Brendan Mulryne, for everyone in the camp knows where we hold our services. We've no building as such and the altar is an old table with a piece of white cloth over it, but we can still worship the Almighty with the respect he deserves.'

'I'm glad to hear it.'

'I would have thought that sheer curiosity would have brought you along. You must have heard us singing the hymns.'

'No,' said Mulryne. 'I was too far away. The truth is, Father, that I was attending a service in the village church.'

They both knew that it was a lie but Slattery did not challenge him. He had stopped to speak to Mulryne during a break when the navvy was wolfing down some bread and cheese and glistening with sweat. He was not pleased to be cornered by the priest.

'You're a Dublin man, I hear,' said Slattery.

'So I am.'

'And your father was a navvy before you.'

'Are you planning to write my life story?' asked Mulryne. 'You know more about me than I do myself.'

'Would you call yourself a Christian?'

'That I would.'

'And are you a loyal Catholic?'

'Since the day I was born, Father.'

'Then we'll look forward to the time when you join us for worship on a Sunday. They tell me that you've a good voice, Brendan.'

'I can carry a tune,' said Mulryne through a mouthful of bread and cheese. 'I've always been musical.'

'Then maybe you can favour us with a solo some time.'

'Oh, I don't think that the songs I know would be altogether suitable for a church service, Father Slattery. They're Irish ditties to amuse my friends. Nothing more.'

'We'll see, we'll see.'

Slattery gave him a valedictory pat on the arm before moving off. Liam Kilfoyle scrambled down the embankment to speak to Mulryne. He looked after the priest.

'What did he want, Brendan?'

'The chance to preach at me next Sunday.'

'Did you tell him you're not a church-going man?'

'But I am, Liam,' said Mulryne, taking another bite of his lunch. 'I'm a devout churchgoer. As soon as I see a church, I go – as fast as I bleeding can.' They laughed. 'It's not God I have the argument with, you see. I believe in Him and try to live my life by His rules. No, it's that army of creeping priests who get between us. They're in the way. I prefer to talk to God directly. Man to man, as you might say. What about you?'

'I'm too afraid of what God would say to me, Brendan.'

'Confess your sins and cleanse your soul.'

Kilfoyle was uneasy. 'I'll think about it,' he said. 'One day.'

'Make it one day soon.'

'You're starting to sound like a bastard priest now!'

'Sorry, Liam,' said Mulryne, jovially. 'What can I do for you?'

'It's the other way round. I may be able to do you a turn.'

'How?'

'Are you still looking to earn some extra money?'

'I'm desperate.'

'And you don't mind what you have to do to get it?'

'I draw the line at nothing,' Mulryne told him. 'As long as I get paid, I'll do whatever I'm asked. And there's another thing you ought to know about me.'

'What's that?'

'When it's needed, I can keep my big mouth shut.'

'Good,' said Kilfoyle. 'I'll pass the word on.'

The letter came as a complete surprise. Written in an elegant hand, it was addressed to Colbeck and had been sent to Thomas Brassey's office. It was passed on to the inspector as a matter of urgency. He did not at first recognise the name of Hortense Rivet. As soon as he read the letter, however, he realised that he had met the woman when he called at Gaston Chabal's house in Paris. Madame Rivet had been the engineer's mother-in-law. Since she requested a visit from Colbeck, he did not hesitate. He caught the next available train from Mantes and arrived in Paris with his curiosity whetted. As she was so anxious to see him again, Colbeck hoped that Madame Rivet might have valuable information to pass on to him.

A cab took him to the Marais and he rang the bell once again. On his previous visit to the house, Chabal's wife had opened the door with a glow of anticipatory pleasure on her face. This time, he was admitted by an old, black-clad servant with sorrow etched deeply into her face. She conducted him into the drawing room. Madame Chabal was still prostrate with grief in her bed-chamber but her mother came at once when she heard that Colbeck was there. Hortense Rivet was genuinely touched that he had responded so swiftly to her letter. As she spoke little English, they conversed in French.

'I was not sure that you were still here,' she began.

'I still have many enquiries to make in France, Madame.'

'Do you know the name of the man who killed Gaston?'

'Not yet,' he confessed, 'but we will. I'll not rest until he's caught and punished.'

She looked into his eyes for a full minute as if searching for something. Then she indicated a chair and sat opposite him. Hortense Rivet had impressed him at their first meeting. When he had told Chabal's young wife that her husband had been murdered, she had been quite inconsolable but her mother had shown remarkable self-control, knowing that she had to find the strength to help them both through the harrowing experience. Madame Rivet's beauty had been somehow enhanced by sadness. Wearing mourning dress, she was a slim and shapely woman in her early forties. The resemblance to her daughter was evident. Colbeck could see exactly what the young widow would look like in twenty years' time. It made him wonder yet again how Gaston Chabal could have betrayed such a lovely wife.

'How is your daughter, Madame?' he asked, solicitously.

'Catherine is suffering badly. The doctor has given her a potion to help her sleep. When she is awake, she simply weeps. Since we heard the news, Catherine has hardly eaten.'

'I'm sorry to hear that.'

'I wanted to thank you for the way that you broke the tidings to us, Inspector. It was difficult for you, I know, and I was not able to express my gratitude to you at the time. I do so now.'

'That's very kind of you.'

There was a long pause. She studied his face before speaking.

'You strike me as an honest man, Inspector Colbeck.'

'Thank you.'

'So I will expect an honest answer from

you. I would like you to tell me how Gaston was murdered.'

'I've already told you, Madame,' he reminded her. 'He was stabbed to death in a railway carriage.'

'Yes,' she said, 'but you did not tell us where the train was going at the time and what my son-in-law was doing on it in the first place. You spared us details that would only have caused us even more pain. I would like to know some of those details now.'

'The French police were given a full account of the murder.'

'There are reasons why I do not choose to turn to them, Inspector. The main one is that the crime did not occur in France. They only know what they have been told. You, on the other hand,' she went on, 'have been in charge of the investigation from the start. You are aware of every detail. Is that not true?'

'There are still some things we *don't* know,' he warned her.

'Tell me the things that you do.' She saw his reluctance. 'Do not be afraid that you will hurt my feelings, Inspector. I am not as frail as I may look. I have already buried my husband and seen my only son go to an early grave. They both died of smallpox. I have survived all that and found a new life for myself. What I must do now is to help Catherine through this tragedy.'

'I'm not sure that you'd be helping her by disclosing the full details of her husband's death,' said Colbeck, gently. 'They are rather gruesome, Madame.'

'What I am interested in are the circumstances.'

'Circumstances?'

'I think you know what I mean, Inspector.' She got up to close the door then resumed her seat. 'And whatever you tell me, it will not be passed on to Catherine. That would be too cruel.'

'Madame Rivet,' he said, 'we are still in the middle of this investigation and I can only speculate on what we will discover next. As for what you call the circumstances, I fear that you might find them very distressing. Some things are best left unsaid.'

'I disagree, Inspector Colbeck. I do not believe you can tell me anything that would surprise me.' She took a deep breath before going on. 'When he was working on this new railway, my son-in-law rented a room in Mantes.'

'I know. I visited the house.'

'Did it not seem odd to you that he did not live at home and travel to Mantes every day by train? It is not very far. Why did he have to be so close to the railway?'

'He worked long hours.'

'That was one of his excuses. There were several others.'

'I hear a rather cynical note in your voice, Madame.'

'It's one that I take care to hide from Catherine,' she said, grimly. 'You may as well know that I did not wish my daughter to marry Gaston Chabal. He was a handsome man with a good future ahead of him, but I did not feel that I could ever trust him. Catherine, of course, would hear none of my warnings. She was young, innocent and very much in love. For the last two years, she thought that she had been happily married.' She pulled a piece of paper from the sleeve of her dress. 'This is something you may have seen before, Inspector.'

'What is it?'

'One of the letters that were found at the house where Gaston was staying in Mantes. The police returned his effects to us earlier this week. Fortunately,' she said, unfolding the letter, 'I was able to see them first. I've destroyed the others and will make sure that my daughter does not see this one either.'

Colbeck remembered the *billets-doux* he had seen at the lodging. Out of consideration to her, he had taken it upon himself to tear up the letters from Hannah Marklew but it had never crossed his mind that he should also get rid of the anonymous correspondence from the young Parisian woman. He felt a stab of guilt as he realised the anguish he had inadvertently caused

228

and he was grateful that Chabal's wife had not been allowed to read the letters from one of her husband's mistresses. He knew how explicit they had been.

'Did you see any letters, Inspector?'

'Yes.'

'Then you must have read them.'

'I glanced at one or two.'

'Then you appreciate the sort of person who wrote them.'

'I think so.'

'Do you know who Arnaud Poulain is, Inspector?' she asked.

'No, Madame.'

'He is a banker here in Paris, a wealthy and successful man. Gaston convinced him to invest in the railway between Mantes and Caen. My son-in-law was not simply an engineer,' she went on. 'If he could persuade anyone to put money into the project, he earned a large commission. Arnaud Poulain was one of the men he talked into it. As a consequence, others followed Monsieur Poulain's example.'

'Why are you telling me this?' wondered Colbeck, guessing the answer even as he spoke. 'Monsieur Poulain has a daughter.'

'A very beautiful daughter.'

'What's her name?'

'Danielle.'

Colbeck thought of the 'D' at the end of the letters. It seemed as if Chabal had used his guile to ensnare another woman in order to secure some investment for the railway on which he was engaged.

'We may be wrong,' cautioned Madame Rivet. 'I have no proof that Danielle wrote these letters and I will certainly not confront her with them. The girl will have suffered enough as it is. I doubt very much if Gaston mentioned to her that he was married. In a liaison of that kind, a wife must always be invisible.'

'The young lady must have read about his death.'

'The discovery that he was married would have come as a terrible shock to Danielle and, I suspect, to her father. Monsieur Poulain would no doubt have welcomed Gaston into his home. The daughter was used callously as a means of reaching the father. Now, Inspector,' she continued, 'even if Danielle is not the woman who wrote this letter, the fact remains that somebody did and that does not show my son-in-law in a very flattering light.'

'I should have destroyed those letters when I had the chance.'

'You had no right to do so.'

'It would have saved you unnecessary pain.'

'The letters confirmed what I already knew,' she said, tearing the paper into tiny pieces before tossing them into a wastepaper basket. 'So, please, do not hold anything back. What were the exact circumstances of the murder?'

'M. Chabal was on his way to visit a woman in Liverpool,' he said. 'I'm not at liberty to give you her name but I can tell you that someone close to her was persuaded to invest money in the railway.'

'At least we know what they talked about in bed.' She raised both hands in apology. 'I am sorry, Inspector. That was a very crude remark and I withdraw it. I have been under a lot of strain recently, as you can understand. But,' she added, sitting up and folding her hands in her lap, 'I would still like to hear more about what actually happened that day.'

'Then you shall, Madame Rivet.'

Colbeck was succinct. He gave her a straightforward account of the murder and told her about the clues that had led him to come to France in the first place. What he concealed from her was the series of incidents that had occurred on the new railway that was being built. Hortense Rivet listened with an amalgam of sadness and fortitude.

'Thank you,' she said when he had finished.

'That is all I can tell you.'

'It was more than I expected to hear.'

'Then my visit was not wasted.'

'Catherine is heart-broken now but she

231

will recover in time. She will always nurture fond thoughts of Gaston and I will say nothing to her of the other life that he led. It is over now. He died before his wife could learn the ugly truth about him.' She let out a long sigh. 'Who knows? Perhaps it is better that way.'

Colbeck got up. 'I ought to be going.'

'It was good of you to come, Inspector.'

'Your request could not be ignored, Madame.'

'You will understand now why I wrote to you.'

'I do indeed.'

'Have you learned anything from this conversation?'

'Oh, yes. I feel as if I know your son-in-law a little better now.'

'Does that help?'

'In some ways.'

'Then there is one last thing you should know about him,' she said, rising from her chair. 'The last time I saw Gaston was in this very room. He had come home for the weekend. He did something that he had never done before.'

'And what was that?'

'My son-in-law was a very confident man, Inspector. He had the kind of natural charm and assurance that always appeal to women.' She gave a faint smile. 'You have the same qualities yourself but I do not think you exploit them as he did. But that's beside the point,' she continued, hurriedly. 'When he got back that day, Gaston was upset. He managed to hide it from Catherine but he did not deceive me.' She pointed to the window. 'It was the way that he stood over there and kept looking into the street.'

'What did you deduce from that, Madame?'

'He was frightened,' she said. 'Someone had followed him.'

Luke Rogan felt sick. He had endured a rough crossing from England and was now being jiggled about by the movement of the train. Any moment, he feared, he would be spilling the contents of his stomach over the floor of the carriage. He tried to concentrate on what lay ahead. When he had visited France before, he felt that he had left everything in order. A deal had been struck and money had changed hands. He had no reason to suppose that he had been double-crossed. The discussion with Sir Marcus Hetherington, however, had robbed him of his certainty. He was no longer quite so confident that his instructions had been carried out.

If the men had betrayed Rogan, it would cost him a lot of money and he would forfeit Sir Marcus' trust in him. He did not wish to upset his most generous client especially as

233

there was a prospect of further work from that source. Everything had gone smoothly for him in England. Rogan had to ensure the same kind of success in France. Failure was not acceptable. If the people he employed had let him down, he would have to find others to do the work in their stead and pay them out of his own pocket. The very notion was galling.

He had come prepared. Excuses would not be tolerated. Had the men in his pay not taken any action as yet, Rogan would not give them a second chance. In his bag, he carried a pistol and a dagger that had already claimed one victim. Punishment would be meted out swiftly. He had not made such a gruelling journey to be fobbed off.

Thomas Brassey was pleased to see Colbeck return to the site. Inviting him into his office, he poured both of them a glass of wine.

'One of the advantages of working in France,' he said, sampling the drink. 'England has much to recommend it but the one thing that it does not have is a supply of excellent vineyards.'

Colbeck tasted his wine. 'Very agreeable.'

'Did you enjoy your visit to Paris?'

'One would have to be blind not to do that, Mr Brassey. It's a positive feast for the eye – though some areas of the city do tend to assault the nasal passages with undue violence.'

'We have that problem in London.'

'I'm all too aware of it,' said Colbeck. 'Madame Rivet wanted to know how the investigation was progressing. She seemed to have much more faith in us than in the French police. I suppose that I should blame you for that, Mr Brassey.'

'Me?'

'Yes, sir. You set a bad example.'

'Did I, Inspector?'

'Because a British contractor builds railways for the French, they will soon expect British detectives to solve their murders for them as well. But I'm being facetious,' he said. 'The visit to Paris was very profitable. It allowed me to see that glorious architecture again and I learned a great deal about Gaston Chabal's domestic life.'

'Did you meet his widow?'

'No, only his mother-in-law. What she told me was that he had a role beyond his duties as an engineer. Apparently, he helped to find investors for this project.'

'Gaston had great powers of persuasion.'

'For which he was rewarded, I gather.'

'A labourer is worthy of his hire, Inspector.'

'He was rather more than a labourer.'

'Nobody could dispute that.'

Colbeck went on to describe, in broad out-

235

line, his conversation with Hortense Rivet, exercising great discretion as he did so. There was no need for Brassey to know that some of the shares in his railway had been bought as a result of a relationship between his French engineer and the daughter of a Parisian banker.

'How are things here, sir?' asked Colbeck.

'Mysteriously quiet.'

'The noise was as loud as ever when I arrived.'

'I was referring to the problems that have been dogging us of late,' said Brassey. 'We've had almost five days in a row now without any more nasty surprises.'

'That's good to hear.'

'How long it will last, though, is another matter.'

'Yes, it would be foolish to imagine that it was over.'

'I'd never do that, Inspector. What's made the difference is those guard dogs you suggested we might get. There are only four of them but they seem to have had the desired effect.'

'Don't forget the other form of restraint we imposed.'

'What was that?'

'Brendan Mulryne.'

'He's settled in well, from what I hear.'

'They're still not sure of him,' explained Colbeck. 'That's why they've been so well-behaved of late. They're biding their time as they try to work out if Brendan is friend or foe.'

'He's a very different animal from Sergeant Leeming.'

'But he remains suspect, Mr Brassey. Victor joins the camp as a stranger and, within a day, he starts to show too much interest in what's going on.'

'He paid dearly for that.'

'He tried to rush things, sir.'

'What about Mulryne?'

'I told him to be more circumspect. He'll not rush anything. And you must remember that he's still a new man in the camp so they're bound to have some reservations about him.'

'You mean that they've stayed their hand because of Mulryne?'

'For the time being.'

'When do you think they will strike again?'

'Soon,' said Colbeck. 'Very soon.'

Brendan Mulryne caroused as usual at the village inn that night and indulged in lively badinage with the others. In a crowd of big, powerful, boisterous, hard-drinking Irishmen, he still managed to stick out. His wild antics and devil-may-care attitude made even the rowdiest of them seem tame by comparison. They had seen him get drunk, watched him fight and heard him sing the most deliciously obscene songs. They had also stood by as he turned his battered charm on the pretty barmaids at the inn. Brendan Mulryne was a vibrant character and they were pleased to have him there.

'Are you coming back to the camp, Brendan?' said someone.

'Hold your hour and have another brandy,' he replied.

'I've no money left.'

'Nor me,' said another man. 'We're off, Brendan.'

Mulryne waved a hand. 'I'll not be far behind you, lads.'

In fact, he was deliberately lagging behind. Liam Kilfoyle had told him to do so because there might be an opportunity for him to make some money. Mulryne jumped at the invitation. When the place finally emptied, he left with Kilfoyle and began the walk back to the camp. It was not long before someone stepped out of the bushes to join them. Pierce Shannon put an arm on Mulryne's shoulder.

'I'm told you're with us, Brendan,' he said.

'I'm with anyone who pays me.'

'And what are you prepared to do for the money?'

'Anything at all,' said Mulryne, expansively, 'as long as it doesn't involve going to church or getting involved in any way with the bleeding priesthood.'

'That goes for me, too,' said Kilfoyle.

'So you don't mind breaking the law, then?' said Shannon.

Mulryne grinned. 'I'll break as many as you like.'

'We'll be in trouble if we're caught.'

'So what, Pierce? Life's far too short to worry about things like that. Just pay me the money and tell me what I have to do.'

'I'll show you.'

They strode on across the fields until the lights of the camp came into view. Lanterns twinkled and a few of the fires that had been lit to cook food were still burning away. When they got closer to the huddle of shacks and houses, Shannon stopped and waited until the last of the navvies had vanished into their temporary homes.

'This way,' he said.

He struck off to the left with Mulryne and Kilfoyle behind him. They reached the railway line and began to walk along the track. When they came to a line of wagons, Shannon called them to a halt. Mulryne gave a knowing chuckle.

'So that's it,' he said. 'It's another bet.'

'Not this time,' Shannon told him.

'I smell a trick when I see one. You're going to challenge me to lift one of those fucking wagons because you know it's filled to the brim with ballast. I'm not *that* strong,' he said, cheerily, 'and I'm not that stupid either.'

'We don't want you to lift it, Brendan.'

'Then what do you want?'

'You'll see.'

Shannon went off to scrabble around in the dark then he returned with a long, thick, wooden pole and a length of rope that he had hidden there earlier. Mulryne stared at the pole.

'What's that?' he asked.

'A lever,' replied Shannon.

'Yes, but what's it for?'

'Making money.'

Aubrey Filton had to hold back tears when he escorted the two of them to the scene. Eight wagons had been uncoupled and tipped off the line, spilling their respective cargoes as they did so. The rolling stock had been badly damaged and the mess would take precious time to clear away. Thomas Brassey gave a philosophical shrug but Robert Colbeck walked around the wagons to look at them from every angle. He bent down to pull out the long wooden pole. Beside it was a length of rope. He held both of them up.

'This is how it was done, I fancy,' he said. 'Someone levered the wagon over while someone else pulled it from the other side with a rope. Those wagons are heavy enough when they're empty. Loaded, they must weigh several tons.'

'It must have taken at least a dozen men.'

Colbeck thought of Mulryne. 'Not necessarily, Mr Filton.'

'Look at the mess they've made!'

'What puzzles me,' said Brassey, staring balefully at the broken wagons, 'is how they contrived to get past the nightwatchmen – not to mention the dogs.'

'That's the other thing I have to report, sir,' said Filton.

'What?'

'It's those guard dogs. Someone fed them poisoned meat.'

Brassey was stunned. 'You mean that they're dead?'

'Dead as a doornail, sir. All four of them.'

CHAPTER TEN

Victor Leeming was a hopeless patient. It was not in his nature to sit quietly at home while he recovered from the beating he had taken. It was wonderful to spend so much time with his wife, Estelle, and to be able to play with the children, but the enforced idleness soon began to vex him. The visitors did not help. A number of police colleagues had called at the house out of genuine concern for Leeming and it was reassuring to know that he had so many friends. What irked him was that they invariably talked about the cases on which they were working, emphasising the fact that, while they were still doing their duty, he was missing all the excitement of being employed by the Metropolitan Police Force. Leeming burned with envy. He was desperate to go back.

While his facial injuries were starting to fade, however, his ribs remained sore and he could only sleep in certain positions. Returning to work was still out of the question but that did not mean he had to be shackled all day to the house. He was anxious to know how Inspector Colbeck was getting on in France. He was interested to hear if there had been any developments in the case on this side of the Channel. He was eager to experience the surge of raw pleasure that he always got when he crossed the threshold of Scotland Yard. Victor Leeming wanted to feel like a detective again.

Superintendent Edward Tallis did not give him a warm welcome.

'Is that you, Leeming?' he said with blunt disapproval.

'Yes, sir.'

'You should be in bed, man.'

'I feel much better now,' insisted Leeming.

'Well, you don't look it. Appearance is everything in our profession,' said Tallis, adjusting his frock coat. 'It conveys a sense of confidence and is a mark of self-respect. It's one of the first things that one learns in the army.'

'But we're not in the army, Superintendent.'

'Of course, we are. We're part of an elite battalion that is fighting a war against crime. Uniforms must be kept spotless at all times. Hair must not be unkempt. Slovenliness is a deadly sin.'

'I don't believe that I am slovenly, sir.'

'No, you're far worse than that. Look at you, man – you're patently disabled. The public should be impressed and reassured by the sight of a policeman. If they see you in that state, they are more likely to take pity.'

They had met in the corridor outside the superintendent's office. Leeming had long ago discovered the futility of reminding his superior that his men were no longer in police uniform. In the considered judgement of Edward Tallis, members of the Detective Department wore a form of uniform and those who departed from it – Colbeck was the most notable offender – had to be cowed back into line. Tallis himself looked particularly spruce. It was almost as if he were on parade. In one hand, he carried his top hat. In the other, was a large, shiny, leather bag that was packed to capacity. He ran his eye over the wounded man and spoke without a trace of sympathy.

'Are you still in pain?' he said.

'Now and again, sir.'

'Then why did you drag your aching body here?'

'I wanted to know what was going on.'

'The same thing that goes on every day, Leeming. We are doing our best to police the capital and apprehend any malefactors.'

'I was thinking about Inspector Colbeck,' said Leeming.

'That makes two of us.'

'Have you heard from him, Superintendent?'

'No,' replied Tallis. 'There's a popular misconception that silence is golden. When it comes to police work, more often than not, it betokens inactivity.'

Leeming was roused. 'That's something you could never accuse the inspector of, sir,' he said, defensively. 'Nobody in this department is more active than him.'

'I agree. My complaint is that his activity is not always fruitful.'

'That's unfair.'

'I need evidence. I require signs of life. I want progress.'

'Inspector Colbeck will solve this crime in the end, sir,' said Leeming, putting a hand to his ribs as he felt a twinge of agony. 'He's very thorough. Nothing escapes him.'

'Something did,' observed Tallis. 'He obviously didn't notice that trying to pass you off as a navvy was the same as opening the door of a lion cage and inviting you to go in.'

'It was not like that at all, Superintendent.'

'Then why are you hobbling around like that with a face that would frighten the horses and give small children bad dreams?'

'What happened to me was all my own fault,' asserted Leeming.

'The duty of a senior officer is to safeguard his men.'

'I was given the chance to refuse to do what I did, sir, but I knew how important the task was. That's why I undertook it. I was warned of the dangers beforehand. I accepted the risk.'

'That's in your favour,' conceded Tallis, magnanimously, 'and so is the fact that you have not voiced any grievances since you returned from France.'

'My only grievance is that I'm not able to return to work.'

'That, too, is creditable.'

'I feel that I should be at Inspector Colbeck's side. We work so well together even if I do have to go everywhere by train. Railways upset me. Though, if you want to know the honest truth, sir,' he went on, lugubriously, 'the boat was far worse. I never want to cross the Channel again.'

'It's an experience that I am about to undergo.'

'You, sir?' Leeming was astonished.

'Yes,' said Tallis, clapping his hat on. 'I'm tired of sitting behind my desk and waiting for something to happen. And I'm fed up with being hounded from all sides by people demanding arrests. As I've had no word from Inspector Colbeck since he left, I've decided to go to France to see for myself what – if anything – he is actually doing there.' He marched past Leeming and tossed a tart remark over his shoulder. 'It had better be something worthwhile, that's all I can say!'

'Why did you give up being a barrister?' asked Aubrey Filton.

'I discovered that it was not what I wanted

to do.'

'But you seem to have all the attributes, Inspector. You've a quick brain, a fine voice and a commanding presence. I could imagine that you would excel in court.'

'To some degree, I did,' said Colbeck, modestly, 'but there was an artificiality about the whole process that worried me. I felt that I were acting in a play at times and I was not always happy with the lines that were assigned to me.'

'All the same, joining the police was a huge step to take. You were giving up what must have been a very comfortable life for a profession that, by its very nature, is full of danger.'

'Comforts of the body do not bring comforts of the mind.'

'I do not follow,' said Filton.

'Something happened that showed me the limitations of working in a court,' explained Colbeck, calling up a painful memory. 'It involved a young lady who was very close to me and who, alas, died a violent death. I was unable to save her. What that misfortune taught me was that prevention is always better than the cure. Stopping a crime from being committed is infinitely preferable to convicting the culprit once the damage is done. A barrister can win plaudits by sending a killer to the gallows but he's not able to raise a murder victim from the dead.'

'That's true.'

'As a detective,' said Colbeck, 'I've been fortunate enough to prevent murders from taking place. It's given me far more satisfaction than I ever had in court. It's also given me a peace of mind that I never enjoyed before.'

Filton was perplexed. 'Peace of mind from a job that pits you against murderous thugs?' he said. 'That's a paradox, surely.'

'You may well be right, Mr Filton.'

It was the first time that Colbeck had spent any length of time alone with the engineer and he was learning a great deal about the man. Away from the site, Filton managed to lose the harassed look in his eyes and the faint note of hysteria in his voice. He emerged as a polite, well-educated, assiduous man with an unshakable belief in the potential of railways to change the world for the better. The two men had taken a trap and driven to a tavern in the nearest village. Over a meal, they were able to talk at leisure.

'This place is quiet in the middle of the day,' said Filton. 'I'd hate to be here at night when the navvies come pouring in. It must be like Bedlam.'

'They don't seem to have done too much damage,' noted Colbeck, glancing around. 'And I daresay the landlord's profits have shot up since the railway came. He'll be sorry to see you all go when you move on further down the line.'

'If and when that ever happens.'

'It will, Mr Filton. I give you my word.'

'I'd prefer a little of that peace of mind you were talking about.'

'Mr Brassey seems to have his share of that.'

'Yes,' said Filton. 'I admire him for it. Whatever the problems, he never gets unduly alarmed. He's so phlegmatic. I wish that I could be like that. My wife says that I used to be until I started working in France.'

'I didn't know that you were married.'

'I've a wife and three children back in Southampton.'

'That might explain why you lack Mr Brassey's *sang-froid*,' said Colbeck. 'You miss your family. Mr Brassey brings his with him but yours is still in England.'

'I write to my wife as often as I can.'

'It's not the same, Mr Filton.'

'Are you married, Inspector?'

'Not yet, sir.'

'I can recommend the institution.'

'I'll bear that in mind.'

Colbeck drank some more of his wine. For a fleeting moment, he thought about Madeleine Andrews and recalled that it was she who had obtained crucial information from the woman who had called herself Hannah Critchlow. He was delighted that she had been able to help him in that way. As an engineer, Aubrey Filton could expect no assistance at all from his wife. His work separated them. Colbeck's profession actually brought him closer to Madeleine. It was something he considered to be a blessing.

'This is good food,' said Colbeck, 'and the wine is more than passable. Working in France obviously has its compensations.'

'In my opinion,' said Filton, 'they are outweighed by the many disadvantages. Whenever I'm in this country, I'm always afraid that the ground will suddenly shift from beneath our feet.'

'You only had to survive one revolution.'

'It was followed by a *coup d' état* last year, Inspector. After the revolution, Louis Napoleon came to power by democratic means. It was not enough for him. He wanted to be Master of France. So he dissolved the Chamber and seized complete control.'

'I remember it well, Mr Filton. The wonder is not that he did it but that he achieved it with so little resistance.'

'The name of Napoleon has immense resonance here,' said Filton, wryly. 'It stands for discipline, power and international renown. That speaks to every Frenchman.'

'One can see why.'

'Yes, but it has not made our work here any easier. When there are upheavals in Paris, the effects spill over on to us.'

'Your immediate problems are not French in origin,' Colbeck reminded him. 'They are essentially British. Or, if I may be pedantic, they are Anglo-Irish.'

'And how long do you think they will continue?'

'Not very long, Mr Filton. We are nearing the end.'

'How do you know?'

'Because I planted Brendan Mulryne in their midst.'

'You did the same with Sergeant Leeming.'

'That was different,' argued Colbeck. 'Victor was only there to watch and listen. He would never be taken fully into anyone's confidence. Also, he's far too law-abiding at heart.'

'Law-abiding?'

'He would never commit a crime, Mr Filton.'

'What relevance does that have?'

'Every relevance,' explained Colbeck. 'Brendan is not held back by the same scruples. To become one of them, he'll do what they do without batting an eyelid. We've already seen evidence of that.'

'Have we?'

'Think of those wagons that were overturned. Unless I'm mistaken, Brendan was involved there.'

Filton was outraged. 'Do you mean that

252

he *helped* the villains?'

'Yes, sir.'

'That's disgraceful, Inspector. Policemen are supposed to uphold the law not flout it like that.'

'Brendan is a rather unusual policeman,' said Colbeck with an appeasing smile, 'as you'll soon see. Before they would trust him, they put him to the test. Judging from the way that those wagons were toppled, I think that he passed that test.'

'So he'll be in a position to destroy even more of our property,' protested Filton. 'I thought he was supposed to be on our side. All that you've done is to import another troublemaker. How many more delays is he going to inflict on us?'

'None, I suspect. Brendan is one of them now.'

'Bracing himself for another attack, I daresay.'

'No, Mr Filton,' said Colbeck, nonchalantly. 'Waiting for the moment when he can hand the villains over to us on a plate.'

Luke Rogan festered with impatience. Having reached Mantes and spent the night there, he had to wait a whole day before he could speak to the man he had come to see. Until the navvies came off work that evening, Rogan had to cool his heels in a country he despised. Back in England, he could be

253

earning money by working for other clients. Instead, he was compelled to waste valuable time abroad. Sir Marcus Hetherington, however, could not be disobeyed.

Sending a message had been his first priority. After riding to the site on a hired horse, he tethered the animal to a tree and used a telescope to scan the scene. Hundreds of navvies were at work in the blistering sun and it took him a long time to locate the man he was after. Pierce Shannon was part of the team that was raising a high embankment. A boy was taking a bucket of water from man to man so that they could slake their thirst. Rogan kept a close eye on the boy. When he saw the lad run off to draw more water, he realised that there had to be a spring nearby. It did not take him long to skirt the railway and find the spring.

When the boy came back once more, Rogan was waiting for him to make an offer. In return for the promise of money, the boy was very willing to deliver the message. After filling his bucket, he scampered off. Rogan had no worries that his note would be read by anyone else because most of the navvies were illiterate. In any case, the terse message would have been incomprehensible to anyone but its intended recipient. He lurked near the spring until the boy eventually came for some more water.

'I gave it to him, sir,' he said.

'What was his reply?'

'He'll be there.'

'Good lad.'

After handing over the money, Rogan made his way back to his horse and rode away. When evening came, he was punctual. It seemed an age before Shannon actually turned up at the appointed place. Rogan had been waiting near the derelict farmhouse for an hour.

'Sorry to keep you, sir,' said Shannon, tipping his hat.

'Where've you been?'

'I needed a drink or two first.'

'I told you to come just as soon as you could,' said the other, reproachfully. 'Have you forgotten who's paying you?'

'No, sir.'

'Do you want to stay working in this hell-hole forever?'

'That I don't,' said Shannon. 'When you give us the rest of the money, I'll be able to turn my back on this kind of work for good. I'm minded to have a little farm back home in Ireland, you see.' He looked around at the crumbling walls. 'A house about this size would suit me down to the ground.'

'You won't get another penny until the job is done.'

'Oh, it will be, sir. I swear it.'

'Then why has there been no news of any disruption?'

'News?'

'It should have reached the English newspapers by now,' said Rogan, tetchily. 'Yet there hasn't been a single word about it.'

'You can't blame us for that, sir.'

'I can if you're trying to pull the wool over my eyes. Be warned, Shannon. Cross me and you'll be in deep trouble.'

The Irishman stiffened. 'Don't threaten me, sir.'

'Then do as you were told.'

'We have done,' said Shannon with wild-eyed indignation. 'We've done every fucking thing you suggested and much more. Just because it wasn't in your bleeding newspapers, it doesn't mean that it never happened. The person to blame is Tom Brassey.'

'Why?'

'Because he won't report anything to the French police.'

'Maybe that's because there's nothing to report.'

'Are you calling me a liar?' demanded Shannon, raising a fist.

'Give me a reason not to,' said Rogan, pulling out his gun and pointing it at him. 'Otherwise, the only farmhouse you'll ever spend time in is this one and you'll be doing it on your back.'

'Hey, now wait a minute,' said the other, backing away and holding up both hands in a gesture of conciliation. 'Be careful with that thing, sir. You've no call to point it at me. Pierce Shannon is an honourable man. I've not let you down.'

'Then tell me what you've done.'

'I will.'

Shannon used his fingers to count off the series of incidents that he had contrived, giving sufficient detail of each one to convince Rogan that he was telling the truth. When he heard about the explosion, he lowered his weapon. Shannon and his accomplices had not been idle. There was a whole catalogue of destruction to report back to Sir Marcus Hetherington.

'*Now* will you believe me?' said the Irishman.

'Yes,' replied Rogan, putting the gun away. 'I was wrong to accuse you. And I can see now why Mr Brassey wants to hide his problems from the French police and newspapers. He'd rather try to sort out the trouble for himself.'

'He even put a spy in the camp. We beat him to a pulp.'

'But you still haven't brought the railway to a standstill.'

'We will, sir. I know exactly how to do it.'

'How?'

'That would be telling,' said Shannon with a grin. 'Stay in France for a day or two and you'll find out what we did. They won't be able to keep our next fucking crime out of the newspapers. It's one thing that even Mr Brassey won't be able to hide.'

'I'll need certain proof of what you've done.'

'Then use your own eyes.'

'I'll not stay in this accursed country a moment longer,' said Rogan. 'I've got what I came for and there's too much work awaiting me in England for me to linger here. When it's all over, you know how to get in touch with me.'

'I do at that, sir – though I still don't know your name.'

'You don't need to know it.'

'Why not? You can trust Pierce Shannon.'

'Finish the task and earn your money,' said Rogan, firmly. 'Once I pay you, I never want to set eyes on you again. Go back to Ireland and take up farming. It's a far healthier life than building a railway in France.'

'I'll have no choice,' said Shannon with a laugh. 'Very soon, there'll be no bleeding railway here to build.'

Robert Colbeck had fulfilled a dream that he had harboured for many years. Dressed as an engine driver, he was standing on the footplate of the locomotive that had recently arrived with twenty wagons filled with ballast from the quarry. His only disappointment was that he was not able to drive the engine. He had only donned the clothing so that he would attract no undue attention. The footplate was the venue for a meeting that he had arranged with Brendan Mulryne. Making sure that he was not seen, the Irishman climbed up beside him.

'Drive me all the way home to Dublin, Inspector,' he said.

'I wish that I could, Brendan, but the line doesn't go that far.'

'It won't go any farther than this, if the buggers have their way.'

'Do you know what their next step will be?' asked Colbeck.

'Yes, sir.'

'Well?'

'They want to bring the whole thing to a stop.'

'And how do they intend to do that?'

Mulryne told him what he had heard. While he knew the place where the attack would be launched, he did not know the precise time. That was a detail that was deliberately kept from him. What was certain was that he would definitely be involved.

'You obviously passed the test they set you,' said Colbeck.

'Tipping over a few wagons? It was child's play.'

'Not to the people who had to clear up after you.'

'Sure, I'd have been happy to do the job

myself but that would have given the game away. If they weren't such hard-hearted villains,' said Mulryne, 'I'd have no quarrel with them. They're fellow Irishmen and that means they're the salt of the earth.'

'Do they have no suspicion of you at all?'

'None, sir, but they might start wondering if I don't join them for a drink very soon. I've made quite a bit of money from them, one way and another.' His face clouded. 'I suppose that'd be called the proceeds of crime. I won't have to hand it back, will I?'

'No, Brendan. It's yours to keep.'

'I never keep money, sir. It burns a hole in my pocket.'

'Then enjoy a drink with it,' said Colbeck. 'And, as soon as you know when they're going to strike, find a way to let me know.'

'That I will, Inspector.'

'Do you know who's paying them?'

'I don't know and I've never once tried to find out. I remembered what happened to Sergeant Leeming when he asked too many questions.' Mulryne pointed to his head. 'They think of me as a big man with a tiny brain. I'm stupid old Brendan who'll do anything for money and not worry where it comes from.'

'How many of them are there?'

'Difficult to say, sir. I've only met two.'

'There must be more than that, Brendan.'

'That's why you have to catch them in the

act. The whole gang is going to be there next time. At least, that's what Liam told me.'

'Liam?'

'I'll introduce him to you when we meet,' said Mulryne. 'You'll be pleased to make his acquaintance.'

'Will I?'

'He's one of the men who ambushed the sergeant.'

'Ah, I see.'

'Liam boasted to me about it. I had a job to hold myself back from knocking his head off there and then. Sergeant Leeming is a friend of mine. When the fighting really starts, Liam is all mine.'

'Victor will be pleased to hear about it,' said Colbeck. 'Now, off you go, Brendan. Join the others before they start to miss you. And thank you again. You've done well.'

'I ought to be thanking you, sir.'

'Why?'

'Work with Irishmen all day and drink with them all night – this is heaven for me,' said Mulryne, happily. 'Yes, and there's a barmaid at the inn who's sweet on me. What more can a man ask?'

Colbeck waved him off then allowed himself a few minutes to inspect the locomotive more closely and to run a possessive hand over its levers and valves. He had recognised the design at once. It was the work of Thomas Crampton, the Englishman whose locomotives were so popular in France. As he indulged his fancy, he wished that Caleb Andrews had been there to teach him how to drive it.

Descending at last from the footplate, he walked across the tracks and headed towards Brassey's office. Instead of his habitual long stride and upright posture, he used a slow amble and kept his shoulders hunched. Engine drivers did not look or move like elegant detectives. When success was so close, he did not wish to make a false move and attract suspicion. His talk with Mulryne had been very heartening and he was delighted that he had brought the Irishman with him. It was only a question of time before the problems at the site would be brought to an abrupt end. Colbeck wanted to pass on the good news to Brassey as soon as possible.

Reaching the office, he knocked on the door and opened it in response to the contractor's invitation. He had expected Brassey to be alone but someone else was there and it was the last person Colbeck had wanted to see. Superintendent Tallis gaped at him in wonder.

'Is that *you*, Colbeck?' he cried, staring in consternation. 'What are you doing, man? I sent you here to solve a crime, not to play with an engine.'

Madeleine Andrews had had a profitable time. It was one of the days when a servant came to clean the house and do various chores, thus releasing Madeleine to work on her latest drawing. She was not trying to sketch the Sankey Viaduct now. She was working on another sketch of the *Lord of the Isles*, the locomotive that Colbeck had taken her to see at the Great Exhibition the previous year. It had a special significance for her. When evening came, she kept glancing up at the clock, hoping that her father would not be too late.

When he went to work, Andrews always bought a morning newspaper at Euston Station. His daughter never got to read it until he came back home, and she was desperate for more news about Colbeck. If he had made any progress in the murder investigation, it would be duly reported. Madeleine was at the window when she saw her father sauntering along the street. He had made a good recovery from the injuries that had almost cost him his life, and he had his old jauntiness back. She opened the door for him and was disappointed that he was not carrying a newspaper.

'Did you have a good day, Father?' she asked.

'Yes,' he replied. 'I've been to Birmingham and back twice. I've driven among that line so often, I could do it blindfold.'

'Well, I hope you don't even try.'

'No, Maddy.' He took off his coat and hung on a hook. 'The place looks clean and tidy,' he said. 'Mrs Busby obviously came.'

'Yes. I was able to get on with my own work.'

'How is she?'

'Still worried about her husband. He has a bad back.'

'At his age?' he said, disdainfully. 'Jim Busby must be ten or fifteen years younger than me. Bad backs are for old men.' He sniffed the air. 'I can smell food.'

'I'll get it in a moment, Father. I just wondered what happened to your newspaper today.'

'What? Oh, I must have forgotten to buy one.'

'You never forget,' she said. 'Reading a paper is an article of faith and you know how much I look forward to seeing it afterwards.'

'Then I suppose I mislaid it today. Sorry, Maddy.'

'Tell me the truth.'

'That is the truth. I left it somewhere by mistake.'

'I think that you did it on purpose.'

'Don't you believe your old father?' he asked with a look of injured innocence. 'I've been very busy today, girl. You can't expect me to remember everything.'

She folded her arms. 'What did it say?'

'Nothing of importance.'

'I know you too well. You're hiding something from me.'

'Why should I do that?'

'Because you're trying to spare my feelings,' she said. 'It's very kind of you but I don't need to be protected. They've said something nasty about Robert, haven't they?'

'I can't remember,' he replied, trying to move past her.

She held his arm. 'You're lying to me.'

'There was hardly a mention of him, Maddy.'

'But what did that mention say?'

She was determined to learn the worst. Caleb Andrews knew how much she loved Colbeck and he wanted to shield her from any adverse criticism of the detective. Having been the victim of a crime himself, he was aware how long it could take to bring the perpetrators to justice. Newspaper reporters had no patience. They needed dramatic headlines to attract their readers. Robert Colbeck had so far failed to provide them. He had paid the penalty.

'There was an article about him,' he admitted.

'Go on.'

'It was cruel. That's all you need to know.'

'What did it say about Robert? Tell me. I'll not be baulked.'

'I think that Inspector Colbeck has an enemy in Scotland Yard,' said Andrews. 'Someone who envies him so much that he's gone behind his back to feed a story to the newspapers.'

'What story?' she demanded.

'A spiteful one, Maddy. According to the article, the inspector has made such a mess of this case that Superintendent Tallis has gone to France to drag him back home in disgrace.'

Tallis spat out the name as if it were a type of venomous poison.

'Brendan Mulryne!' he exclaimed.

'Yes, sir,' confessed Colbeck.

'You dared to engage the services of Brendan Mulryne?'

'He was the ideal person for the task. When I lost Victor, I had to find someone who could blend more easily into the scene.'

'Oh, yes,' said Tallis, maliciously. 'Mulryne would blend in. He's the same as the rest of them – a wild, drunken, unruly Irishman who doesn't give two hoots for authority.'

'That's unduly harsh, Superintendent,' said Thomas Brassey. 'Most of my Irish navvies are a godsend to me. They do the sort of soul-destroying job that would kill the average man yet they still manage to keep up their spirits. When I build a railway, they're always my first choice.'

Tallis was spiky. 'Well, I can assure you that Brendan Mulryne would never be *my* first choice. When we kicked him out of the police force, we should have put him in a menagerie where he belonged.'

The three men were still in Brassey's office. The confrontation with Edward Tallis was proving to be even more abrasive than usual. At the very moment Robert Colbeck's carefully laid plan was coming to fruition, his superior had turned up to throw it into jeopardy. What increased the inspector's discomfort was that his reprimand was delivered in front of Brassey. It made the contractor realise that he had been misled.

'I thought that Mulryne was a policeman,' he said.

'He was – at one time,' replied Colbeck.

'And he was a menace to us while he was there,' said Tallis. 'I'll spare you the full inventory of his peccadilloes, Mr Brassey, or we'd be here all night. Suffice it to say that the Metropolitan Police Force is run, like the army, on strict discipline. Brendan Mulryne does not know the meaning of the word.'

'He made several important arrests, sir.'

'Yes, Inspector. But he could not resist hitting his prisoners.'

'When he was in uniform,' Colbeck said, 'there was far less crime in the area he patrolled. Villains were too afraid of him.'

'I'm not surprised. He'd assault them first and ask questions afterwards. That's in blatant defiance of police procedure.'

'Why didn't you tell me all this, Inspector?' asked Brassey.

'Because I didn't feel that it was necessary for you to know, sir,' said Colbeck, awkwardly. 'For the last couple of weeks, this railway had been under siege. If these men were allowed to continue, they would bring this whole project crashing down. I believed that the one person who could save you was Brendan Mulryne and, after my conversation with him just now, I'm even more certain of it.'

'But he appears to be no more than a criminal himself.'

'He is,' agreed Tallis. 'I don't think he means to help us at all. Now that he's here, he's made common cause with the villains. He's an active part of the conspiracy against you. All that Inspector Colbeck has done is to add to your troubles.'

'That's unjust, sir!' Colbeck retaliated.

'Didn't you tell us that he'd wormed his way into their ranks?'

'Only to be able to betray them.'

'We are the ones who've been betrayed. You admitted that he's helped them to cause serious damage to railway property.'

'That was an essential part of his initiation.'

'Ruining those wagons is not what I'd call

initiation, Inspector,' said Brassey, critically. 'It's straightforward vandalism.'

'He had to convince them that he could be trusted, Mr Brassey.'

'Well, I can't trust him – not any more.'

'Nor me,' said Tallis. 'I've learned from bitter experience that the only thing you can rely on Mulryne do to is to create mischief. You had no authority whatsoever to use the rogue, Inspector.'

'Desperate diseases call for desperate remedies,' said Colbeck.

'Mulryne is nothing short of an epidemic!'

'Give credit where it's due, Superintendent Tallis. The man you traduce so readily helped us to catch those responsible for the mail train robbery last year.'

'Yes,' said Tallis, sourly. 'That was another occasion when your methods were highly questionable. You had no right to involve that reprobate in police business.'

'The end justified the means.'

'Not in my estimation.'

'The commissioner disagreed,' said Colbeck, pointedly. 'He wanted to congratulate Mulryne in person. Are you telling me that the head of the Metropolitan Police Force was at fault?'

Tallis's face twitched. 'What I'm telling you is that this charade has got to stop,' he snapped. 'Mulryne must be arrested immediately with his accomplices.'

'But we don't know who they are, sir.'

'They'll be getting drunk with him right now.'

'In your position,' advised Brassey, 'I'd think again. Only a bold man would try to apprehend an Irish navvy when he's celebrating with his friends. I agree that he should be punished, Superintendent, but you have to choose the right moment.'

'Arresting him would be madness,' argued Colbeck. 'Besides, you have no jurisdiction in this country. When we catch the villains, we'll have to hand them over to the French police.'

'Mulryne will be one of them.'

'But he's our only hope of salvation.'

'That unholy barbarian?'

'I'm bound to share the superintendent's unease,' said Brassey.

'It's not unease,' declared Tallis. 'It's sheer horror.'

'All that he needs is a little time,' said Colbeck. 'What harm is there in giving him that? I'd stake every penny I have that Brendan Mulryne will do what he's paid to do – and by the way, sir,' he added, looking at Tallis, 'all his expenses have come out of my own pocket. That should show you how much faith I have in the man.'

'I admire your loyalty but deplore your judgement.'

Brassey shook his head. 'I have an open

mind on all this.'

'Do you want this railway to be built?' Colbeck asked him.

'Of course.'

'Then trust a man who's risking his life to make sure that it is not crushed out of existence. Victor Leeming was out of his depth here and he got a beating for his pains. They couldn't punish Mulryne in the same way,' Colbeck told them. 'He's too big and strong. If they knew that he was about to betray them, they'd kill him outright.'

Brendan Mulryne was in his element. Having arrived late, he made up for lost time by ordering two drinks at a time. He was soon involved in the vigorous banter. Alive to any opportunities to make money, he performed a few feats of strength to win bets from some of the others then bought them a brandy apiece by way of consolation. The rowdy atmosphere was like a second home to him but he was not only there to revel with his friends. Every so often, he darted a glance at one of the barmaids, a buxom young woman with dark hair and a dimple in each cheek. Whenever she caught his eye, she smiled at him.

Towards the end of the evening, Liam Kilfoyle came over to him.

'Stay behind for a while, Brendan,' he said.

Mulryne chuckled. 'Oh, I intend to, Liam, I promise you.'

'Pierce would like a word.'

'As long as it's a short one.'

'He was pleased with the way you tipped over those wagons.'

'Ah, I could have done that on my own without you two pulling on that rope as if you were in a tug-o'-war contest. I like a challenge.'

'You've got one of those coming up, Brendan.'

'When?'

'Pierce will tell you – but not in here.'

Shannon was talking to some friends in a corner but he had kept an eye on Mulryne throughout the evening as if weighing him in the balance. He wished that he had known the newcomer much longer so that he could be absolutely certain about him but there was no time to spare. The surprise visit of his paymaster had acted as a stimulus. The final attack was at hand. He had other men to help him but none with Mulryne's extraordinary strength. Shannon knew a way to put that strength to good use.

When the bar started to clear, the giant Irishman made sure that he had a brief exchange with the barmaid. He spoke no French and she knew very little English but they understood each other well. Mulryne gave her a wink to seal their bargain. Her dimples were deeper and more expressive than ever. He was by no means the only man to take an interest in her but none of the others could compete. She had made her choice. At length, only the stragglers remained and the landlord began to close up the bar. Mulryne was among the last to leave and he walked away very slowly.

When Shannon and Kilfoyle fell in beside him, he put a friendly arm around each of them and gave a playful squeeze.

'Steady on, Brendan,' said Kilfoyle. 'You'll break my shoulder.'

'I was as gentle as a lamb,' claimed Mulryne.

'You don't know how to be gentle.'

'Oh, yes, I do.'

'Keep yourself more sober tomorrow,' ordered Shannon.

'I *am* sober.'

'I saw how much you drank tonight, Brendan.'

'Then you should have noticed something else,' said Mulryne. 'The more I had, the less drunk I became. It's weak men who fall into a stupor. I've learned to hold my drink.'

'You'll need a clear head.'

'My head *is* clear, Pierce.'

'I'm giving you an order,' said the other. 'If you don't want to obey it, we'll find someone else.'

'No, no,' said Mulryne, quickly. 'I'm your man. If there's money to be made – real money this time – I won't touch more than a drop tomorrow. I swear it. Is that when it's going to be?'

'Yes.'

'At what time?'

'As soon as it gets dark,' said Shannon.

'I'll be ready.'

'So will I,' said Kilfoyle. 'I've been waiting to escape from this shit hole for weeks. Now, I'll finally get my chance.'

'We all will, Liam,' said Shannon.

'This time tomorrow, I'll be rich.'

'Only if you do as you're told.'

'Thank the Lord that it is tomorrow,' said Mulryne, coming to a sharp halt. The others stopped beside. 'Had it been tonight, I'm afraid, I'd not have been able to oblige you.'

'Why not?' asked Shannon.

'You're with us now,' added Kilfoyle.

'Not tonight.'

'Why have we stopped?'

'Because I have other plans. I thought I might take a stroll in the moonlight. It looks like a perfect night for it.' He beamed at them. 'Good night, lads.'

Brendan Mulryne turned around and began to walk back towards the inn. As he did so, the barmaid came out of the front door and ran on the tip of her toes until his huge arms enveloped her. After a first kiss, the two of them then faded quietly into the shadows. Mulryne was determined to make the most of his visit to France.

CHAPTER ELEVEN

Robert Colbeck had never spent a night under the same roof as Edward Tallis before and he did not find it an uplifting experience. He slept fitfully, tormented by the thought that the whole investigation could be endangered by the precipitate action of his superior. The arrival of the superintendent could not have come at a worse time. It had taken Colbeck by surprise and undermined his position completely. It had also exposed the ambiguous involvement of Brendan Mulryne in the exercise, thereby alarming Thomas Brassey and driving Tallis into a rage that three consecutive cigars had failed to soften. It was doubtful if a night's sleep would improve the superintendent's temper.

When he came down for breakfast in the cottage where they were both staying, Colbeck did not even know if he was still employed in the Detective Department at Scotland Yard. Tallis had made all sorts of veiled threats without actually dismissing him. Colbeck's career was definitely in the balance. As they sat opposite each other at the table, there was a distinct tension in the air. It was Tallis who eventually broke it.

'I think that we should cut our losses and withdraw,' he said.

'That would be a ruinous course of action, sir,' protested Colbeck. 'Having come so far, why pull out now?'

'Because the investigation has not been run properly.'

'We are on the point of capturing the villains.'

'One of whom is Brendan Mulryne.'

'No, Superintendent. He is working for us.'

'He's not working for me,' said Tallis, angrily, 'and he never will. Setting a thief to catch a thief has never seemed to me to be wise advice. A criminal will always have more affinity with criminals than with those trying to catch them. We have a perfect example of that here. Instead of working as an informer, Mulryne has sided with his natural allies because the rewards are greater.'

'You malign him, sir.'

'I know him of old.'

'And so do I,' said Colbeck. 'That's why I picked him.'

'A singularly unfortunate choice.'

'You would not think that if you'd spoken to him yesterday.'

Tallis scowled. 'Nothing on God's earth would persuade me to dress up as an engine driver in order to converse with a man who was drummed out of the police force for using excessive violence. And that was only one of his glaring defects. You've had successes in the past, Colbeck,' he went on, chewing his food noisily, 'but this time, you have bungled everything.'

'I resent that, sir.'

'And I resent your attempt to deceive me with regard to the use of that incorrigible Irishman, Mulryne.'

'This railway line is being built by incorrigible Irishmen. Only someone like Mulryne could mix easily with them. He's done everything I asked of him.'

'You mean that you *incited* him to commit a crime?'

'No, sir.'

'Then how much licence did you grant him?'

'I told him to do whatever was necessary.'

'Even if that entailed wrecking a number of wagons?'

'It worked, sir,' insisted Colbeck. 'Don't you realise that? He's now part of their gang. Brendan Mulryne is in a unique position.'

'Yes, he can inflict even more damage on the railway.'

'He can bring the vandalism to an end.'

'He's much more likely to increase it. The kindest thing we can do for Mr Brassey is to haul Mulryne out of France altogether and take him back to whatever squalid hovel he lives in.'

'We must allow him to finish his work.'

'It is finished – as from today.'

'Even Mr Brassey thought that we should wait.'

'He's a contractor,' said Tallis, finishing his cup of coffee, 'not a policeman. He doesn't understand the way that a criminal mind works. I do. Brassey still finds it difficult to believe that he could be employing callous villains on this project.'

'That's because he has a paternal attitude towards his men, sir. Because he treats them so well, he cannot accept that they would betray him. Thomas Brassey is famed for the care he shows to anyone he employs,' said Colbeck, 'and you must bear in mind that, at any one time, he could have as many as 80,000 men on his books. If any one of them finds a particular job too onerous, Mr Brassey will not simply dismiss him. He's more likely to assign him to an easier task. That's how considerate and benevolent he is. It's the reason his men think so highly of him.'

'The law of averages comes into play here. In every thousand good men, you are bound to have a tiny minority of blackguards. Some of them are employed here,' Tallis continued, 'and they think so highly of the benevolent Brassey that they're prepared to do anything to stop this railway from being built. I'm sorry, Inspector. You may admire the way that he operates,' he said, dismissively, 'but I think that Brassey is too naïve.'

'He's a shrewd and hard-headed business-man, sir. You do not achieve his extraordinary level of success by being naïve.'

'If he has problems here, it is up to him to sort them out.'

'But there is a direct link with the murder of Gaston Chabal.'

'So you keep telling me,' said Tallis, 'but we will not find it by unleashing Mulryne on this railway. All that he will do is to muddy the waters even more.'

'Give him time,' implored Colbeck.

'We are returning to England today.'

'But that would leave Mr Brassey in the lurch.'

'He can call in the French police.'

'Then we'll never find the man who killed Chabal.'

'Yes, we will,' said Tallis. 'If we hunt for him in the country where he resides – England.'

Further argument was curtailed. Tallis got up from the table and stalked off to his room to collect his bag. Colbeck thanked the farmer's wife who had given them such a tasty breakfast and paid her for accommodating them. It was not long before he and Tallis were on their way to the site to take their leave of Thomas Brassey. During the drive, Colbeck made repeated attempts to persuade Tallis to change his mind but the superintendent was adamant. Activities in France had to be brought to an immediate halt. As a courtesy to the contractor, Tallis undertook to explain to him why.

Colbeck was faced with a dilemma. If he wanted to remain as a detective, he had to obey orders and return to London. If, however, he wanted to pick up a trail that led eventually to the killer, he had to remain in France until the information came to light. He was still wrestling with the dilemma when they arrived. Alighting from the trap, they walked towards Brassey's office. Before they could knock on the door, however, it was opened for them. The contractor had seen them through the window.

'I'm glad that you came, Inspector,' he said. 'She'll speak to nobody but you.'

'She?' said Colbeck.

'A young Frenchwoman. She seems quite agitated.'

'Then I'll talk to her at once.'

Colbeck went into the office and closed the door behind him. Tallis was annoyed at being left outside but he took the opportunity to explain to Brassey why they would be leaving the country that very day. Colbeck, meanwhile, was introducing himself to the barmaid from the village inn, who had befriended Mulryne and spent some of the previous night with him. Because they had got on so well, she had been entrusted with an important message but she would not pass it on until she was convinced that she was speaking to Inspector Robert Colbeck. Only when he had shown her identification, and explained that he was a good friend of Brendan Mulryne, did she trust him.

'*Cette nuit,*' she said.

'*Vous êtes certaine, mademoiselle?*'

'*Oui.*'

'*Merci. Merci beaucoup.*'

Colbeck was so delighted that he wanted to kiss her.

Luke Rogan knew where to find him that late in the day. Sir Marcus Hetherington was at his club, whiling away the evening by conversing with friends about the merits of certain racehorses on which they intended to place a wager. When the steward brought him Rogan's card, Sir Marcus detached himself from the group and retired to a quiet corner to receive his visitor. After crossing the Channel again when the waves were choppy, Rogan was looking distinctly unwell. He refused the offer of a whisky, vowing to touch neither food nor drink until his stomach had settled down. He lowered himself gingerly into a chair beside Sir Marcus.

'Well?' said the old man.

'It was as I told you, Sir Marcus – no need

to fear.'

'You saw the men?'

'I spoke to their leader.'

'What did he tell you?'

When Rogan repeated the list of incidents that had occurred on the railway line, Sir Marcus gave a smile of satisfaction. His money had not, after all, been squandered. He now understood why none of the destruction that had been wrought had been reported in the French newspapers.

'This is all very gratifying,' he said.

'To you, Sir Marcus, but not to me.'

'What are you talking about?'

'Taking that boat when the waves were so high,' said Rogan, holding his stomach. 'It fair upset me, Sir Marcus. I feel ill. I went all that way to find out something that I knew already. You should have trusted me.'

'I trust you – but not your friends.'

'Oh, they're not friends of mine.'

'Then what are they?'

'I'd call them the scum of the earth,' said Rogan with a sneer, 'and the only reason I employ them is that I can rely on them to do what they're told. Pay them well and they do your bidding. But you'd never want to call any of them a friend, Sir Marcus. They're ruffians.'

'Even ruffians have their uses at times.'

'Once this is over, I wash my hands of them.'

'That brings us to the crux of the matter,' said Sir Marcus. 'When will this finally be over? What they have accomplished so far is a series of delays and I willingly applaud them for that. Delays, however, are mere irritations to a man like Brassey. He's indomitable. He'll shrug off temporary setbacks and press on regardless. When are your friends – your hired ruffians, I should say – going to make it impossible for him to carry on?'

'Soon.'

'How soon?'

'Within a day or two, Sir Marcus,' said Rogan, confidently. 'That's what I was told. They're going to make one last strike before getting away from the site for good.'

'One last strike?'

'It will be much more than a simple delay.'

'Why?'

'They're going to burn down Mr Brassey's office and destroy all the surveys that people like Gaston Chabal prepared for him. Without anything to guide them, they simply won't be able to go on with the work. But there's more, Sir Marcus,' said Rogan, grinning wolfishly, 'and it will give them the biggest headache of all.'

'Go on?'

'They're going to steal the big safe from the office. It not only contains valuable documents that cannot be replaced, it holds all the money to pay the navvies.'

'So they'll get no wages,' said Sir Marcus, slapping his knees in appreciation. 'By George, this is capital!'

'No money and thousands of angry men to face.'

'Come pay day and Brassey will have a veritable riot on his hands. I take back all I said, Rogan,' the old man added with a condescending smile. 'I should never have doubted your ability to pick the right men for the job. Ruffians or not, these fellows deserve a medal. They'll have brought the whole enterprise to a juddering halt.'

There were five of them in all. One of them, Gerald Murphy, was employed as a night-watchman so he was able to tell them exactly where his colleagues were placed and how best to avoid them. Another man, Tim Dowd, drove one of the carts that took supplies to various parts of the site. Pierce Shannon, Liam Kilfoyle and Brendan Mulryne completed the gang. When they slipped out of the inn after dark, their leader noted that someone was missing.

'Where's Brendan?' he said.

'Saying farewell to his lady love,' replied Kilfoyle with a snigger. 'He's probably telling her that he'll see her later when, in fact, he'll be on the run with the rest of us.'

'Go and fetch him, Liam.'

'Never come between a man and his colleen.'

'Then I'll get the bastard.'

Shannon turned on his heel but he did not have to go back into the building. Mulryne was already walking towards him, still savouring the long, succulent kiss that he had just been given in the privacy of the cellar. He beamed at the others.

'Ah, isn't love a wonderful thing?' he announced.

'Not if it holds us up,' said Shannon, brusquely. 'Forget about her, Brendan. After tonight, you'll have enough money to buy yourself any pair of tits you take a fancy to.'

'I'm sorry, Pierce. What must I do?'

'Shut up and listen.'

Keeping his voice low, Shannon gave them their orders. Murphy was to act as their lookout and he rehearsed a whistle he would give them by way of a warning. Dowd was to bring his horse and cart to the rear of Brassey's office. Kilfoyle was charged with the task of creating a diversion by burning down Aubrey Filton's office. When all the attention was fixed on that, Shannon himself would start a fire in the contractor's office.

Mulryne was baffled. 'What do *I* do, Pierce?' he asked.

'The most difficult job of all,' said Shannon.

'And what's that?'

'Lifting the safe on to the wheelbarrow that Tim will bring.'

'Oh, that's easily done.'

'It won't be,' warned Kilfoyle. 'I've seen it. That safe will be a ton weight, Brendan.'

'I'll manage it,' boasted Mulryne. 'If it's full of money, I'll make sure that I do. Though it'd be a lot bleeding quicker if we blow open the safe there and then. We can just grab the money and run.'

'That's too dangerous,' said Shannon. 'You can't control an explosion. Besides, we've no more gunpowder left. It's far better to steal the fucking safe and take it away on the cart. By the time they discover it's gone, we'll be miles away.'

'Counting out our share of the money,' said Kilfoyle.

'I'll do that, Liam. You only get what I give you.'

'That's fair,' agreed Mulryne. 'Pierce has done all the hard work, planning everything. It's only right that he should get a little more than the rest of us.'

Shannon looked around them. 'Are we all ready, lads?'

'Yes,' they replied in unison.

'Then let's kill this fucking railway line once and for all!'

Robert Colbeck had been rescued at the last

moment. The information passed on by the French barmaid had persuaded Superintendent Tallis to stay for one more day. He accepted that it might, after all, be possible to catch the men who had caused so much disruption on the railway and, in doing so, discover who their English paymaster was. Along with Thomas Brassey and a group of his most trusted men, Tallis was in hiding not far from the contractor's office. All but Brassey were armed with cudgels or guns. Nobody expected that the Irishmen would give up without a fight.

Determined to be at the heart of the action, Colbeck had put on an old coat and hat so that he could replace the nightwatchman who normally patrolled the area. He carried a lantern in one hand and a stout wooden club in the other. He followed the identical routine as his predecessor so that it would look as if the same man were on duty. When the raid came, he knew, it would take place when he was at the farthest point from the designated target. The first hint of trouble came when he heard a horse and cart approaching. At that time of night, all the drivers should have been fast asleep while their horses were resting in their makeshift stables. Pretending to hear nothing, Colbeck turned away from Brassey's office and began a long, slow, methodical walk to the edge of the camp.

The attack was imminent. He sensed it. As soon as he reached the outer limit of his patrol, therefore, he did not amble back at the same pace. Blowing out his lantern, he ran back towards the office in the dark. Colbeck did not want to miss out on the action.

Everything seemed to have gone to plan. Murphy's whistle told them that the night-watchman was some distance away from the office. Dowd's horse and cart were in position and he had trundled the wheelbarrow up to the others. Shannon gave the signal, smacking Kilfoyle on the back so that the latter went off to stand by Filton's office, then leading Mulryne and Dowd towards their target. The door of the office had two padlocks on it but Shannon soon disposed of them with his jemmy, levering them off within seconds before prising the door open. Holding a lantern, he went across to the safe. Mulryne followed and Dowd came in with the wheelbarrow.

'Jesus!' said Dowd when he saw the size of the safe. 'I'll never be able to wheel that bloody thing away.'

'Leave it to Brendan,' said Shannon. 'That's why he's here.'

Mulryne bent down and got a firm grip on the safe. When he felt its weight, he lifted it an inch off the floor before putting it down again. He spat on both hands then rubbed them together.

'This is not really heavy,' he boasted. 'Hold up that lantern, will you, Pierce? I need all the light I can get.'

Shannon responded, lifting the lantern up until his whole face was illumined. Mulryne seized his moment. Pulling back his arm, he threw a fearsome punch that connected with Shannon's chin and sent him reeling back. He was unconscious before he hit the floor. Coming into the office, Colbeck had to step over the body. It took Dowd only a moment to realise that they had been duped. Escape was essential. Running at Colbeck, he tried to buffet him aside but the detective was ready for him. He dodged the blow and used his club to jab the man in the stomach. As he doubled up, Colbeck hit him in the face and made him stagger backwards into Mulryne's bear hug.

'Timothy Dowd,' said Mulryne, lapsing back into his days as a constable, 'I'm arresting you on a charge of attempted burglary.'

'You double-crossing bastard!' howled Dowd.

But it was the last thing he was able to say because Mulryne tightened his hold and squeezed all the breath out of him. Kilfoyle came running to see what had caused all the commotion. When he burst in, he almost tripped over Shannon's body.

'What happened to Pierce?' he demanded, bending over his friend. 'Who hit him?'

'I did,' replied Mulryne, triumphantly. 'He'll be out for ages, Liam. I caught him a beauty.'

Kilfoyle let out a roar of anger and pulled out a knife. Before he could move towards Mulryne, however, Colbeck stepped out to block his way. Kilfoyle waved his knife threateningly.

'Who the fuck are you?'

'The man who's here to disarm you,' said Colbeck, hitting him on the wrist with his club and making him drop his weapon. 'You must be Liam Kilfoyle.'

'What of it?'

'I'm a friend of Victor Leeming.'

'That dirty, treacherous, lying cunt!'

'He asked me to pass on a message,' said Colbeck, tossing the club aside so that he could use his fists. 'Attacking people from behind is unfair. This is how you should do it.'

He pummelled away at Kilfoyle face and body, forcing him back by the sheer power of his attack. The Irishman tried to fight back at first but he was soon using both hands to protect himself. When Colbeck caught him on the nose, Kilfoyle stumbled back into the arms of Superintendent Tallis as the latter came into the office.

'Have we got them all?' asked Tallis,

holding his man tight.

'Hello there, sir,' said Mulryne, effusively, as if encountering a favourite long-lost relative. 'How wonderful it is to see you again, Superintendent, even if it is on foreign soil. Forgive me if I don't shake hands but Timothy here needs holding.'

'How many of you were there, Brendan?' said Colbeck.

'Five, including me.'

'We've three of them here – that leaves one.'

'He was caught as well,' said Tallis. 'We've got the whole gang.'

'And you saved me the trouble of trying to pick up this bleeding safe,' said Mulryne, giving it a kick. 'It weighs three ton at least.'

'It shouldn't.' Colbeck picked up the fallen lantern and walked across to the safe. He opened the door to show that it was completely empty. 'Thanks to your warning, Brendan, we took the precaution of removing everything of value out of it.'

The interrogation took place in Thomas Brassey's office. It was obvious that Kilfoyle, Dowd and Murphy had no idea who had sponsored their work from England. They were mere underlings who obeyed orders from Pierce Shannon. Accordingly, the three of them were taken away and held in custody. On the following morning, they would be handed over to the French police. Shannon sat in a circle of light provided by a number of oil lamps. Colbeck and Mulryne were present but it was Edward Tallis who insisted on interrogating their prisoner. Hands behind his back, he stood over Shannon.

'Who paid you?' he asked.

'Nobody,' replied the other, rubbing his aching jaw.

'Don't lie to me. Somebody suborned you. Somebody told you to bring this railway to a halt. Who was it?'

'Nobody.'

'So you did everything of your own volition, did you?'

'What's that mean?'

'That it was all your own idea, Pierce,' explained Mulryne.

'Yes, that's right.'

'So why did you do it?' said Tallis.

Shannon gave a defiant grin. 'Fun.'

'Fun? Is it your notion of fun to cause extensive damage to the property of the man who is employing you? Is it your notion of fun to put the thousands of men on this site out of work?'

'Yes.'

'He's a bleeding liar, sir,' said Mulryne.

'Keep out of this,' ordered Tallis.

'But I know the truth. Liam told me. That's Liam Kilfoyle. He's the scrawny one that fell into your arms like an amorous woman when you came in here. Liam reckons this man met up with Pierce and offered him money to wreck this railway – a lot of money. Enough to let them all retire.'

'And who was this man?'

'Liam didn't know.' He pointed at Shannon. 'But he does.'

'Shut your gob!' snarled Shannon.

Mulryne laughed. 'Compliments pass when the quality meet.'

'If I'd known you were a fucking traitor, I'd have killed you.'

'You're in no position to kill anyone,' Tallis reminded him. 'Now stop playing games and answer my questions. Who paid you and why did he want this railway to be abandoned? He's the man who dragged you into all this? Do you want him to get off scot free?'

'Yes,' said Shannon.

'Who *paid* you, man?'

'Nobody.'

'Tell me, damn you!'

'I just did.'

'Give me a name.'

'Pierce Shannon. Would you like another? Queen Victoria.'

'I'd like you to tell me the truth.'

'I have.'

'Who is behind all this?'

'Nobody.'

Shannon was beginning to enjoy the situation. Resentful at being caught, and infuriated by Mulryne's part in his capture, he was at least getting some pleasure out of frustrating Tallis. No matter how hard the superintendent pressed him, he would volunteer nothing that could be remotely helpful. Tallis kept firing questions at him with growing vexation. Eventually, Colbeck stepped in.

'Perhaps I could take over, sir,' he suggested.

'It's like trying to get blood from a stone,' said Tallis.

'Then let me relieve you.'

'If you wish.'

Tallis withdrew reluctantly to a corner of the room and watched.

Colbeck brought a chair and placed it directly in front of Shannon. He sat down so that he was very close to him.

'When I first came to France,' he told Shannon, 'I brought my assistant with me – Sergeant Victor Leeming.'

'I knew he was a bleeding copper,' said the other with derision. 'I could smell him. I enjoyed beating him up.'

'I'm glad you mention beating someone up because that's the subject I was just about to raise with you. Would you describe your friends – Kilfoyle, Dowd and Murphy – as violent men?'

'They're Irish – they like a decent brawl.'

'The same goes for me,' said Mulryne, happily.

'I'm only interested in Mr Shannon's friends,' said Colbeck. 'At least, they're his friends at the moment. That, of course, may not last.'

Shannon was guarded. 'What are you on about?'

'The contents of your pockets.'

'Eh?'

'When we searched you earlier, you were carrying a large amount of money. A very large amount, as it happens. Where did it come from, Mr Shannon?'

'That's my business.'

'No,' said Colbeck, 'it's our business as well. And it's certainly the business of your three friends. We searched them as well, you see, and they had substantially less money on them. Even allowing for the fact that they had spent some of it on drink, they were clearly paid far less than you for any work that they did.' He turned to Mulryne. 'How much were you paid for tipping over those wagons?'

'A week's wages,' replied Mulryne.

'Mr Shannon had over two years' wages in his pocket, Brendan. Unless, that is, Mr Brassey has been particularly philanthropic. What this all indicates to me is that one person held on to most of the money he'd been paid while the other three were deprived of their fair share. That's robbery. What do you think the others would do to Mr Shannon if they knew the truth?'

'Break every bleeding bone in his body, Inspector.'

'That's the least they'd do, I should imagine.'

'I earned that money,' insisted Shannon. 'I had the brains to plan things. The others are all fucking boneheads.'

'I'll pass on that charming description of their mental powers when I talk to them,' said Colbeck, smoothly, 'and I must thank you for admitting that you were, after all, paid by someone else.' He flicked a glance at Tallis. 'Our first trickle of blood from the stone.'

Shannon sat up. 'I'm not saying another fucking word.'

'Then you're throwing away any hope of defending yourself. When we hand you over to the French police, you'll be charged under their law and in their language. When you get into court,' Colbeck went on, 'you won't understand a single word of what's going on so you'll be unable to offer anything by way of mitigation.'

'What's that?'

'It's a way of shortening the sentence you're likely to get. If you claim – as you did earlier – that everything that happened was your idea, then you'll face several years in prison. If, on the other hand, you were simply obeying someone else's orders – and if you tell us who that someone is – your sentence might be less severe. In fact, I'd make a point of telling the French police how helpful you've been.'

'And he'd tell them in French,' said Mulryne, proudly. 'He speaks the lingo. Doesn't he, Superintendent?'

'Yes,' said Tallis.

'What about you, sir? Do you speak French?'

'I'd never let it soil my lips.'

'To sum up,' said Colbeck, bestowing a bland smile on Shannon, 'it's a pity that you've elected to hold your tongue. You might need it to plead for mercy when we lock you up with your friends and tell them about the monetary arrangements you decided upon. When you get to court, how-ever,' he went on, 'you can talk all you like to no effect because they won't bother to hire interpreters for someone who was caught red-handed committing a crime. Expect a long sentence, Mr Shannon – after your friends have finished with you, that is.' He stood up. 'Let's take him over there, Bren-dan.'

'With pleasure,' said Mulryne.

'Wait!' cried Shannon, as they each laid a hand on him. 'There *was* someone who put

299

us up to this.'

'Now we're getting somewhere,' said Colbeck.

'But I don't know his name.'

'Do you expect us to believe that?'

'It's true, Inspector – I'd swear on the fucking gospel.'

'There's no need for blasphemy!' shouted Tallis. 'Keep a civil tongue in your head.'

'You must have known who this man was,' said Colbeck. 'How did he get in touch with you in the first place?'

'I was in a police cell,' admitted Shannon. 'Only for a week or so. There was an affray at a tavern in Limehouse and I got caught up in it by mistake. Anyway, this man read about it in the paper and saw that I was a navvy. He came to see me and asked me if I'd ever worked for Tom Brassey. That's how it all started.'

'Go on,' invited Colbeck.

'He tested me out then decided I might be his man.'

'What name did he give?'

'None at all,' said Shannon, 'but I did hear one of the coppers calling him "Luke" – you know, as if they were friends. I called him by that name once and he swore blue murder at me.'

'How did he pay you?'

'He waited until I'd got a job with Mr Brassey and settled in here. Then he told me what to do first so that I could prove myself. Once I'd done that,' said Shannon, 'he paid me the first half of the money so that I'd have enough to take on people I could trust.'

'And cheat easily,' said Mulryne.

'It's their own bleeding fault for being so stupid.'

Colbeck's ears pricked up. 'You say that you had the first half of the money?' Shannon nodded. 'When would you get the other half?'

'When we brought the railway to a standstill.'

'But how would you get in touch with Luke?'

'He gave me an address in London,' said Shannon. 'I was to leave a message there, saying what we'd done. Once he could confirm it, he promised to leave the second half of the money for me to collect it. And – as God's my witness – that's the fucking truth!'

'We'll need that address,' said Colbeck.

'As long as you don't tell the others about the money.'

'We don't bargain with criminals,' said Tallis.

'It's a reasonable request, sir,' Colbeck pointed out, 'and, now that he appreciates the predicament that he's in, Mr Shannon has been admirably cooperative. Some reward is in order, I believe.'

'Thanks,' said Shannon with great relief.

'We'll need that address, mind you.'

'I'll give you it to you, Inspector.'

'There you are, Superintendent,' said Mulryne, hands on his hips. 'You should have let the Inspector question him from the start. He's a genius at getting blood from a bleeding stone.'

Luke Rogan was working in his office when he heard the doorbell ring insistently. He looked out of the front window to see Sir Marcus Hetherington standing there while a cab waited for him at the kerb. Rogan was surprised. The only place they ever met was in the privacy of the Reform Club. If he had come to the office, Sir Marcus must have something of prime importance to discuss. Rogan hurried along the passageway and opened the door. Sweeping in without a word, Sir Marcus went into the office and waited for Rogan to join him.

'What's the matter, Sir Marcus?' asked Rogan.

'This,' said the other, thrusting a newspaper at him. 'This is what is the matter, Rogan. Look at the second page.'

'Why?'

'Just do as I say.'

'Very well, Sir Marcus.'

Rogan opened the newspaper and scanned the second page. He soon realised why his visitor had come. What he was looking at was a report of the arrest of four men who were accused of trying to disrupt work on the railway that was being built between Mantes and Caen. Rogan recognised one of the names – that of Pierce Shannon – and assumed that the others were his accomplices. The name that really jumped up at him, however, was not that of the prisoners but of the man who had helped to capture them.

'Inspector Colbeck!' he gasped.

'Read the last paragraph,' instructed Sir Marcus. 'The much-vaunted Railway Detective believes that he now has evidence that will lead him to the person or persons responsible for the murder of Gaston Chabal. In short,' he said, hitting the top of the desk hard with his cane, 'evidence that points to you and me.'

'But that's impossible!'

'So you assured me.'

'Shannon didn't even know my name.'

'He's obviously told them enough to steer them towards you.'

'He couldn't have, Sir Marcus.'

'Then how do you explain this report?'

'Colbeck is bluffing,' said Rogan, trying to convince himself. 'He's done this before. He pretends to be in possession of more information than he really has in the hope of making someone fly into a panic and give themselves away.'

'The newspaper certainly gave me a sense of panic,' confessed Sir Marcus. 'My wife thought I was having a heart attack when I read that – and I almost did.'

'He knows *nothing*, Sir Marcus.'

'Then how did he manage to arrest four men in France?'

'Pure luck.'

'Colbeck never relies on luck. He believes in a combination of tenacity and cold logic. He's been quoted to that effect more than once. I do not want his tenacity and logic to lead him to me.'

'That's out of the question, Sir Marcus.'

'Is it?'

'I'm the only person that knows you were my client.'

'Do you keep records?' asked the other, glancing down at the desk. 'Do you have an account book with my name in it?'

'Of course not. I know how to be discreet.'

'I hope so, Rogan.'

'Colbeck will not get within a mile of us.'

'What can he possibly have found out?'

'Nothing of value.'

'He must have squeezed something out of those Irishmen.'

'Shannon was the only one I had dealings with. The others don't even know that I exist. And all that Shannon can do is to give them a rough description of me.' Rogan showed snaggly teeth in a grin. 'That means he'd be describing thousands of men who look just like me.'

Sir Marcus relaxed slightly. He removed his top hat and sat down on a chair, resting his cane against a wall. Rogan took the unspoken hint and went to a small cupboard. Taking out a bottle of whisky, he poured two glasses and handed one to his visitor.

'Thank you,' said the old man, tasting the whisky. 'I'd hoped to toast our success but our plans have obviously gone awry.'

'We can try again at a later date, Sir Marcus.'

'This was our chance and we missed it.'

'Bide our time, that's all we have to do.'

'Until a certain detective comes knocking on our doors.'

'That will never happen,' said Rogan, airily. 'The one thing that Shannon knows is an address where he was to leave a message. Nobody at that address knows my name or where I live. It was simply a convenient way of paying Shannon the second half of his fee when his work was completed.'

'But it was not. He failed and you failed.'

Rogan was hurt. 'You can't put the blame on me.'

'You selected this idiot.'

'With the greatest of care, Sir Marcus. I asked a friend about him before I even went near him. He told me that Shannon was full of guile and quite fearless. That's the kind of man we wanted.'

'Then why has he let us down so badly?' asked Sir Marcus. 'And why is Inspector Colbeck coming back to England with such apparent confidence to hunt down Chabal's killer?'

'He's trying to frighten us.'

'He frightened me, I can tell you that.'

'You're as safe as can be, Sir Marcus,' Rogan assured him, taking a first sip of his whisky. 'So am I. London is a vast city. He could search for fifty years and still not find us. Colbeck has no idea where to start looking.'

'There's that address you gave to Shannon.'

'A dead end. It will lead him nowhere.'

'Supposing that he does pick up our scent?'

'I've told you. There's no hope of him doing that.'

'But supposing – I speak hypothetically – that he does? Colbeck has already come much farther than I believed he would so we must respect him for that. What if he gets really close?'

'Then he'll regret it,' said Rogan, coolly.

When he got back from work that evening, Caleb Andrews found a meal waiting for him. Since he had good news to impart about the murder investigation, he surrendered his paper to Madeleine and drew her attention to the relevant report. She was thrilled to read of Robert Colbeck's success in France. Her faith in him had never wavered and she had been disturbed by the harsh criticism he had received in the press. Public rebuke had now been replaced by congratulation. He was once again being hailed for his skill as a detective.

When the meal was over, Andrews was in such an ebullient mood that he challenged his daughter to a game of draughts. He soon repented of his folly. Madeleine won the first two games and had him on the defensive in the third one.

'I can't seem to beat you,' he complained.

'You were the one who taught me how to play draughts.'

'I obviously taught you too well.'

'When we first started,' she recalled, 'you won every game.'

'The only thing I seem to do now is to lose.'

He was spared a third defeat by a knock on the front door. Glad of the interruption, he was out of his chair at once. He went to the door and opened it. Robert Colbeck smiled at him.

'Good evening, Mr Andrews,' he said.

'Ah, you're back from France.'

'At long last.'

'We read about you in the paper.'

'Don't keep Robert standing out there,' said Madeleine, coming up behind her father. 'Invite him in.'

Andrews stood back so that Colbeck could enter the house, remove his hat and, under her father's watchful eye, give Madeleine a chaste kiss on the cheek. They went into the living room. The first thing that Colbeck saw was the draughts board.

'Who's winning?' he asked.

'Maddy,' replied Andrews, gloomily.

'This game was a draw, Father,' she said, eyes never leaving Colbeck. 'Oh, it's so lovely to see you again, Robert! What exactly happened in France?'

'And why did you have to solve crimes on *their* railways? Don't they have any police of their own?'

'They do, Mr Andrews,' replied Colbeck, 'but this was, in a sense, a British crime. It was almost like working over here. British contractors have built most of their railways and French locomotives are largely the work of Thomas Crampton.'

'I'm the one person you don't need to tell that to, Inspector,' said Andrews, knowledgeably. 'In fact, there are far more Cramptons in France than here in England. Lord knows why. I've driven three or four of his engines and I like them. Shall I tell you why?'

'Another time, Father,' said Madeleine.

'But the Inspector is interested in engineering, Maddy.'

'This is not the best moment to discuss it.'

'What?' Andrews looked from one to the other. 'Well, perhaps it isn't,' he said, moving away. 'Now where did I leave my tobacco pouch? It must be upstairs.' He paused at the door. 'Don't forget to show him that picture you drew of the Sankey Viaduct, Maddy.'

He went out of the room and Colbeck was able to embrace Madeleine properly. Over her shoulder, he saw that the tobacco pouch was on the table beside the draughts. He was grateful for her father's tact. He stood back but kept hold of her hands.

'What's this about the Sankey Viaduct?'

'Oh, it was just something I sketched to pass the time,' she said. 'It's probably nothing at all like the real thing.'

'I'd be interested to see it, all the same.'

'Your work is far more important than mine, Robert. Come and sit down. Tell me what happened since I last saw you.'

'That would take far too long,' he said, as they sat beside each other on the sofa. 'I'll give you a shortened version.'

He told her about his visit to Paris and his long conversation with Gaston Chabal's mother-in-law. Madeleine was startled by the revelation that the engineer appeared to have seduced another woman for the sole purpose of gaining an additional investor in the railway. She was fascinated to hear of Brendan Mulryne's success as a spy and pleased that Superintendent Tallis had been forced to admit that the Irishman had performed a valuable service.

'Mr Tallis couldn't actually bring himself to thank Brendan in person,' said Colbeck. 'That would have been asking too much. What he did concede was that the notion of putting an informer into the ranks of the navvies had, after all, been a sensible one.'

'Coming from the superintendent, that's high praise.'

'I pointed out that Brendan Mulryne would be an asset if he were allowed to rejoin the police force but Mr Tallis would not hear of it. He'd sooner recruit a tribe of cannibals.'

'Why is he so critical of your methods?'

'There's always been a degree of animus between us.'

'Is he envious of you?'

'It's more a case of disapproval, Madeleine.'

'How could he possibly disapprove of a man with your record?'

'Quite easily,' said Colbeck with a grin. 'Mr Tallis doesn't like the way I dress, the approach I take to any case and the readiness I have to use people such as Brendan

Mulryne. Also, I'm afraid to say, he looks askance at my private life.'

She gave a laugh of surprise. 'Your private life!'

'He thinks that you're leading me astray.'

'Me?'

'I was only joking, Madeleine,' he said, putting an arm around her. 'The truth is that Superintendent Tallis doesn't believe that his detectives should *have* a private life. He thinks that we should be like him – unattached and therefore able to devote every waking hour to our job with no distractions.'

'Is that what I am – a distraction?'

'Yes – thank heaven!' He kissed her on the lips. 'Now, let's see this drawing of the Sankey Viaduct.'

'You won't like it, Robert.'

'Why not?'

'It's too fanciful.'

'I love anything that you do, Madeleine,' he said, warmly. 'And it must be worth seeing if your father recommends it.'

'He only saw an earlier version.'

'Please fetch it.'

'I'm not sure that I should.'

'Why are you being so bashful? I really want to see it.'

'If you wish,' she said, getting up, 'but you must remember that it's a work of imagination. It has no resemblance to the real viaduct.' She crossed the room to pick up a portfolio that rested in an alcove. Opening it up, she selected a drawing. 'It was simply a way of keeping you in my mind while you were in France.'

'Then I must have a look at it.'

Colbeck rose to his feet and took the sketch from her hand. He was intrigued. The viaduct dominated the page but what gave him a sudden thrill of recognition was the way that it connected England and France. It was like a bridge across a wide gulf. He let out a cry of joy and hugged her to him. Madeleine was mystified.

'What have I done to deserve that?' she said.

'You've just solved a murder!'

CHAPTER TWELVE

Victor Leeming was thoroughly delighted when Colbeck called on him that morning. Simply seeing the inspector again was a tonic to him. Time had been hanging with undue heaviness on his hands and he desperately missed being involved in the murder investigation. He felt that he was letting the inspector down. They sat down together in the cramped living room of Leeming's house. He listened attentively to the recitation of events that had taken place in France, only interrupting when a certain name was mentioned.

'Brendan Mulryne?'

'Yes, Victor.'

'There was no reference to him in the newspapers.'

'Mr Tallis made sure of that,' said Colbeck. 'He refused to give any public acknowledgement to Brendan because he felt that it would demean us if we admitted any reliance on people like him. As it happens, I would have kept his name secret for another reason.'

'What's that, Inspector?'

'I may want to employ him again. If his

name and description are plastered all over the newspapers, it would make that difficult. He needs to be kept anonymous.'

'I'm not sure that I'd have used him at all,' admitted Leeming.

'That's why I didn't discuss the matter with you.'

'I like Mulryne – he's good company – but I'd never trust him with anything important. He's likely to go off the rails.'

Colbeck smiled. 'In this case,' he pointed out, 'he did the exact opposite. Instead of going off the rails, he kept Mr Brassey on them. Largely because of what Brendan did, the railway can still be built.'

'Then I congratulate him.'

'You have a reason to thank him as well, Victor.'

'Do I?'

'One of the men who gave you the beating was Pierce Shannon.'

'I'm not surprised to hear it. He was a sly character.'

'Brendan laid him out cold on your behalf.'

'I wish I'd been there to do it myself,' said Leeming, grimly.

'The other man who attacked you was Liam Kilfoyle.'

'Liam? And I thought he was a friend of mine!'

'Not any more,' said Colbeck. 'I had the

pleasure of exchanging a few blows with Mr
Kilfoyle. I let him know what I felt about
people who assaulted my sergeant.'

'Thank you, sir.'

Colbeck told him about the capture of the
villains and how they had been handed over
to the French police the next day. Thomas
Brassey and Aubrey Filton had been over-
whelmed with gratitude. The second visit to
France had been eventful. Colbeck felt
satisfied.

'So that part of the investigation is now
concluded,' he said.

'What comes next?'

'The small matter of tracking down the
killer.'

'Do you have any clues, Inspector?'

'Yes, Victor. One of them came from the
most unexpected source, but that's often the
way with police work. And I'm a great
believer in serendipity.'

Leeming was honest. 'So would I be, if I
knew what it meant.'

'Picking up a good thing where you find
it.'

'Ah, I see. A bit like beachcombing.'

'Not really,' said Colbeck. 'Beachcombing
implies that you deliberately go in search of
something. Serendipity depends entirely on
chance. You might not even be looking for a
particular clue until you stumble upon it in
the most unlikely place.'

'Serendipity. I'll remember that word. It will impress Estelle.'

'How is your wife?'

'She's been a tower of strength, sir.'

'Happy to have you at home so much, I should imagine.'

'Yes and no,' said Leeming, sucking in air through his teeth. 'Estelle is happy to have me here but not when I'm convalescing. She'd like more of a husband and a bit less of a patient.'

'You seem to be recovering well.'

Leeming's facial scars had almost disappeared now and the heavy bruising on his body had also faded. What remained were the cracked ribs that occasionally reminded him that they were there by causing a spasm of pain. He refused to give in to his injuries.

'I'm as fit as a fiddle, sir,' he said, cheerily. 'But for the doctor, I'd be back at work right now.'

'Doctors usually know best.'

'It's so boring and wasteful, sitting at home here.'

'Do you get out at all?'

'Every day, Inspector. I have a long walk and I sometimes take the children to the park. I can get about quite easily.'

'That's good news. We look forward to having you back.'

'I can't wait,' said Leeming. 'Much as I

love Estelle and the children, I do hate being unemployed. It feels wrong somehow. I'm not a man who can rest, sir. I like action.'

'You had rather too much of it in France.'

'I like to think that I helped.'

'You did, Victor,' said Colbeck. 'You did indeed.'

'Mind you, I couldn't make a living as a navvy. A week of that kind of work would have finished me off. They earn their money.'

'Unfortunately, some of them tried to earn it by other means.'

'Yes,' said the other with feeling. 'Shannon and his friends were too greedy. They wanted more than Mr Brassey could ever pay them. Pierce Shannon always had an ambitious streak. It's a pity you got so little out of him when you questioned him.'

'That's not true.'

'He couldn't even tell you the name of the man who paid him.'

'Oh, I think that he gave us a lot more information than he realised,' said Colbeck. 'To begin with, we now know how he and his paymaster first met.'

'In a police cell.'

'What does that tell you?'

'Nothing that I couldn't have guessed about Shannon, sir. He got involved in a brawl and was arrested for disturbing the peace. Men like that always get into trouble when they've had a few drinks.' He cleared his throat. 'I'm bound to point out that the same thing happened to Brendan Mulryne after he'd left the police force.'

'He might not be the only policeman that we lost.'

'I don't think that Shannon was ever in uniform, sir.'

'What about the man who employed him?'

'We know nothing whatsoever about the fellow.'

'Yes, we do,' said Colbeck. 'We know that he's able to talk to someone in a police cell which means that he's either a lawyer, a policeman or someone who used to be involved in law enforcement. I'd hazard a guess that he has friends in the police force or he'd not have been given such easy access to a prisoner. Also, of course, we do have his Christian name.'

'Luke.'

'You can find out the rest when you get there.'

'Where?'

'To the station where Pierce Shannon was detained.'

Leeming was taken aback. 'You want *me* to do that, sir?'

'You enjoy a long walk, don't you?'

'Yes.'

'And you're chafing at the bit while you're sitting here.'

'I am, Inspector – that's the plain truth.'

'Then you can return to light duties immediately.' His grin was conspiratorial. 'Provided that you don't mention the fact to Mr Tallis, that is. He might not understand. He has a preference for making all operational decisions himself.'

'I won't breathe a single word to him.'

'Not even serendipity?'

'I'm saving that one for my wife.'

'Does that mean you're willing to help us, Victor?'

Leeming struggled to his feet. 'I'm on my way, sir.'

They noticed the difference at once. It was as if a threatening black cloud that had been hanging over the site had suddenly dispersed to let bright sunshine through. In fact, it was raining that morning but nothing could dampen their spirits or that of the navvies. Hectic activity was continuing apace. They were now certain to complete the stipulated amount of work on the railway by the end of the month. The sudden and dramatic improvement made Aubrey Filton blossom into an unaccustomed smile.

'This is how it should be, Mr Brassey,' he said. 'Now that we've got rid of the rotten apples from the barrel, we can surge ahead.'

'Word spread quickly. When they heard about the arrests, the men were as relieved as we were. And you can't blame them,' said

Brassey, reasonably. 'If work had ground to a halt here, I'd have been in danger of losing the contract. Thousands of them would have been thrown out of work. Their livelihoods have been saved.'

'And your reputation has been vindicated.'

'I care more about them than about me, Aubrey.'

'You treat them like members of a huge family.'

'That's exactly what they are.'

They were at the window, gazing out at sodden navvies who laboured away as if impervious to rain. There was a new spirit about the way everyone was working. It was almost as if the many wanted to atone for the dire shortcomings of the few by demonstrating their commitment to the project. Eamonn Slattery had noticed it. The priest was standing between the two men.

'Look at them,' he said with pride. 'There's not a navvy alive who can match an Irishman when it comes to hard physical work. The Potato Famine nearly crippled our beloved country but it was a blessing to someone like you, Mr Brassey.'

'I agree, Father Slattery,' conceded the other. 'A lot of the men here emigrated from Ireland. I was glad to take them on. What's the feeling among them now?'

'Oh, they reacted with a mixture of thanks and outrage.'

320

'Inspector Colbeck deserves most of the thanks.'

'So I hear,' said Slattery with a cackle. 'And there was me, thinking that dandy was working for the Minister of Public Works. He took me in completely but, then, so did Brendan Mulryne.'

'He's the real hero here,' opined Filton. 'The others will miss him. He made himself very popular. Well, there's one good thing to come out of all this.'

'And what's that, Father?'

'I can count on a decent congregation on Sunday,' explained the priest with a grin. 'It's strange how adversity turns a man's mind to religion. They know how close they came to losing their jobs. A lot of them will get down on their knees to send up a prayer of thanks. I'll make the most of it and preach a sermon that will sing in their ears for a week. By next Sunday,' he added, philosophically, 'most of them won't come anywhere near the service.'

'Were you surprised to find out who was trying to disrupt the railway?' asked Brassey.

'I'd always suspected that Shannon might have something to do with it. He was the type. Kilfoyle disappointed me. I thought that Liam would have more sense.'

'What about the other two men?'

'Dowd and Murphy? Weak characters. Easily led.'

'They'll get no mercy in court,' predicted Brassey. 'This railway has the backing of Louis Napoleon and his government. Anyone who tries to bring it to a halt will be hit with the full weight of the law.'

'The whole sad business is finally over,' said Slattery. 'I think that we ought to console ourselves with that thought.'

'But it isn't over yet.'

'No,' said Filton. 'The murder of Gaston Chabal has still to be solved. What happened here was entangled with that, Father Slattery.'

'How?'

'The only person who knows that is Inspector Colbeck.'

'Does he know the name of the killer?'

'He will do before long.'

'You sound very confident of that, Mr Filton.'

'He's an astonishing man.'

'It was an education to see him at work,' said Brassey. 'In his own way, Inspector Colbeck reminded me of Gaston. Both share the same passion for detail. They are utterly meticulous. That's why I know that he'll apprehend the killer in due course, Father Slattery.'

'More power to his elbow!'

'The Inspector is tireless,' said Filton.

'Yes,' confirmed Brassey. 'His energy is remarkable. Even as we speak, the hunt is continuing with a vengeance.'

Robert Colbeck did not like him. The moment he set eyes on Gerald Kane, he felt an instant aversion. Kane was a short, neat, vain, conservatively dressed, fussy man in his forties with long brown hair and a thick moustache. His deep-set eyes peered at the newcomer through wire-framed spectacles. His manner was officious and unwelcoming. Even after he had introduced himself, Colbeck was viewed with a mingled suspicion and distaste.

'Why are you bothering me, Inspector?' asked Kane, huffily. 'As far as I'm aware, we have broken no laws.'

'None at all, sir.'

'Then I'll ask you to be brief. I'm a busy man.'

'So am I.'

'In that case, we'll both profit from brevity.'

'This cannot be rushed, Mr Kane,' warned Colbeck.

'It will have to be, sir. I have a meeting.'

'Postpone it – for his sake.'

'Whom are you talking about?'

'Gaston Chabal.'

Gerald Kane raised his eyebrows in surprise but the name did not encourage him to adopt a more friendly tone. He simply treated his visitor to a hostile stare across his desk. They were in his office, a place that was as cold, ordered and impeccably clean as the man himself. Everything on the leather top of the desk was in a tidy pile. All the pictures on the walls had been hung at identical heights. Kane was the secretary of the Society of Civil and Mechanical Engineers and he seemed to look upon his post as a major office of state. He sounded an almost imperious note.

'What about him, Inspector?' he said.

'I believe that you wrote to him, sir.'

'I don't see why that should concern you. Any correspondence in which I am engaged is highly confidential.'

'Not when one of the recipients of your letters is murdered.'

'I'm well aware of what happened to Chabal,' said Kane without the slightest gesture towards sympathy. 'It's caused me no little inconvenience.'

'He did not get himself killed in order to inconvenience you,' said Colbeck, sharply. 'Since you wrote to invite him to lecture here, you might show some interest in helping to solve the crime.'

'That is your job, Inspector. Leave me to do mine.'

'I will, sir – when I have finished.'

Kane looked at his watch. 'And when, pray, will that be?'

'When I tell you, sir.'

'You cannot keep me here against my will.'

'I quite agree,' said Colbeck, moving to the door. 'This is not the best place for an interview. Perhaps you'd be so good as to accompany me to Scotland Yard where we can talk at more leisure.'

'I'm not leaving this building,' protested Kane. 'I have work to do. You obviously don't realise who I am, Inspector.'

'You're a man who is wilfully concealing evidence from the police, sir, and that is a criminal offence. If you will not come with me voluntarily, I will have to arrest you.'

'But I *have* no evidence.'

'That's for me to decide.'

'This is disgraceful. I shall complain to the commissioner.'

Colbeck opened the door. 'I'll make sure that he visits you in your cell, sir,' he said, levelly. 'Shall we go?'

Gerald Kane got to his feet. After frothing impotently for a couple of minutes, he finally capitulated. Dropping back into his chair, he waved a hand in surrender.

'Close that door,' he suggested, 'and take a seat.'

'Thank you, sir,' said Colbeck, doing as he was told. 'I knew that you'd see the wisdom of cooperating with us. The situation is this. When I was in Mantes recently, I went through Chabal's effects and found a letter written by you. Since it invited him to give a

325

second lecture, I take it that you organised his earlier visit.'

'I did. It's one of my many duties.'

'Where did the earlier lecture take place?'

'Right here, Inspector. We have a large room for such meetings. My colleagues are sitting in it at this very moment,' he went on with a meaningful glint, 'awaiting my arrival for an important discussion.'

'Engineers are patient men, sir. Forget them.'

'They will wonder where I am.'

'Then it will give them something to talk about,' said Colbeck, easily. 'Now, sir, can you tell me why you invited Chabal here?'

'He was a coming man.'

'Do we not have enough able engineers in England?'

'Of course,' replied Kane, 'but this fellow was quite exceptional. Thomas Brassey recommended him. That was how he came to my notice. Gaston Chabal had enormous promise.'

'His lecture was obviously well-received.'

'We had several requests for him to come back.'

'Could you tell me the date of his visit to you?'

'It was in spring, Inspector – April 10th, to be exact.'

'You have a good memory.'

'That's essential in my job.'

'Then I'll take advantage of it again, if I may,' said Colbeck. 'Can you recall how many people attended the lecture? Just give me an approximate number.'

'I represent civil and mechanical engineers,' declared the other, loftily. 'Accuracy is all to us. We do not deal in approximates but in exact measurements. When he first spoke here, Gaston Chabal had ninety-four people in the audience – excluding myself, naturally. As the secretary of the Society, I was here as a matter of course.'

'Were the others all exclusively engineers?'

'No, Inspector. The audience contained various parties.'

'Such as?'

'People with a vested interest in railways. We had directors of certain railway companies as well as potential investors in the Mantes to Caen project. Mr Brassey, alas, was not here but Chabal was a fine ambassador for him.'

'Ninety-four people.'

'Ninety-five, if you add me.'

'I would not dream of eliminating you, Mr Kane,' said Colbeck. 'With your permission, I'd like to plunder that famous memory of yours one last time. How many of those who attended do you recall?'

'I could give you every single name.'

Colbeck was impressed. 'You can remember *all* of them?'

'No, Inspector,' said Kane, opening a drawer to take something out. 'I kept a record. If I'd secured Chabal's services again, I intended to write to everyone on this list to advise them of his return.' He held out a sheet of paper. 'Would you care to see it?'

Colbeck decided he might grow to like Gerald Kane, after all.

Victor Leeming was so pleased to be taking part in the investigation again that he forgot the nagging twinge in his ribs as he walked along. It took him some time to reach his destination. He had been sent to the police station that was responsible for Limehouse and adjoining districts. Close to the river, it was a bustling community that was favoured by sailors and fishermen. Limehouse had taken its name centuries earlier from the lime kilns that stood there when plentiful supplies of chalk could be brought in from Kent. It was the docks that now gave the area its characteristic flavour and its central feature.

When his nostrils first picked up the potent smell of fresh fish, Leeming inhaled deeply and thankfully. The bracing aroma helped to mask the compound of unpleasant odours that had been attacking his nose and making him retch. Streets were coated with grime and soiled with animal excrement and other refuse. Soap works and a leather tannery gave off the most revolting stench. Unrelenting noise seemed to come from every direction. Leeming saw signs of hideous poverty. He could almost taste the misery in some places. Limehouse was an assault on his sensibilities. He was grateful when he reached the police station and let himself in.

A burly sergeant sat behind a high desk, polishing the brass buttons on his uniform with a handkerchief. A half-eaten sandwich lay before him. He looked at his visitor with disdain until the latter introduced himself.

'Oh, I'm sorry, sir,' he said, putting the sandwich quickly into the desk and brushing crumbs from his thighs. 'I didn't realise that you were from the Detective Department.'

'Who am I speaking to?' asked Leeming.

'Sergeant Ryall, sir. Sergeant Peter Ryall.'

'How long have you been at this station?'

'Nigh on seven years, sir.'

'Then you should be able to help us.'

'We're always ready to help Scotland Yard.'

Ryall gave him a token smile. His face had been pitted by years of police service and his red cheeks and nose revealed where he had sought solace from the cares of his occupation. But his manner was amiable and his deference unfeigned. Leeming did not criticise him for eating food while on duty. Having worked in a police station himself, he knew how such places induced an almost permanent hunger.

'I want to ask about a man you kept in custody here,' he said.

'What was his name?'

'Pierce Shannon.'

Ryall racked his brains. 'Don't remember him,' he said at length. 'Irish, I take it?'

'Very Irish.'

'Hundreds of them pass through our cells.' He lifted the lid of the desk and took out a thick ledger. 'When was he here?'

'A couple of months ago, at a guess,' said Leeming. 'When he left here, he went to France to help build a railway.' Ryall began to flick through the pages of his ledger. 'The person I'm really hoping to find is a man who visited Shannon in his cell while he was here.'

'A lawyer?'

'No – a friend.'

'We don't keep a record of visitors, Sergeant Leeming.'

'I was hoping that someone here might recall him. If he was a stranger, he'd have no authority to interview the prisoner in his cell. You'd not have let him past you.'

'That, I wouldn't,' said Ryall, stoutly.

'So how was he able to get so close to Shannon?'

'One thing at the time, sir. Let me locate the prisoner first.' He ran his finger down a list of names. 'I've a Mike Shannon here. He

330

was arrested for forgery in June.'

'That's not him. This man was involved in a brawl.'

'Pat Shannon?' offered the other, spotting another name. 'We locked him up for starting a fight in the market. What age would your fellow be?'

'In this thirties.'

'Then it's not Pat Shannon. He was much older.' He continued his search. 'It would help if you could be more exact about the date.'

'June at the earliest, I'd say.'

'Let's try the end of May, to be on the safe side.' Ryall found the relevant page and went down the list. 'It was warm weather last May. That always keeps us busy. When it's hot and sweaty, people drink more. We attended plenty of affrays that month.' His finger jabbed a name. 'Ah, here were are!'

'Have you got him?'

'I've got a Pierce Shannon. Gave his age as thirty-five.'

'That could be him. Was he involved in a brawl?'

'Yes, sir – at the Jolly Sailor. It's a tavern by the river. We have a lot of trouble there. Shannon was one of five men arrested that night but we kept him longer than the others, it seems.'

'Why?'

'He refused to pay the fine so we hung on

to him until he could be transferred to prison. Shannon was released when someone else paid up on his behalf. He was released on June 4th.'

'Do you know who paid his fine?'

'No,' said Ryall. 'None of our business. We are just glad to get rid of them. His benefactor's name would be in the court records.'

Leeming was pleased. 'Thank you,' he said. 'You've been very helpful. While he was under lock and key here, Shannon had a visit from a man whose first name was Luke. Does that ring a bell?'

'Afraid not – but, then, it wouldn't. I wasn't on duty during the time that Pierce Shannon was held here. I spent most of May at home, recovering from injuries received during the arrest of some villains.'

'You have my warmest sympathy.'

'Horace Eames would have been in charge of custody here.'

'Then he's the man I need to speak to,' decided Leeming. 'If he let Luke Whatever-His-Name-Is into one of your cells, he would have been doing so as a favour to a friend. Inspector Colbeck thinks that friend might have been a policeman himself at one time.'

Ryall closed the ledger. 'Possible, sir. I couldn't say.'

'I need to speak to Mr Eames. Is he here, by any chance?'

'No, he left the police force in July. Horace said that he wanted a change of scene. But he's not far away from here.'

'Can you give me the address, please?'

'Gladly,' said Ryall. 'You probably walked past the place to get here. It's a boatyard. Horace was apprenticed to a carpenter before he joined the police force. He was always good with his hands. That's where'll you'll find him – at Forrestt's boatyard.'

The shop was in a dingy street not far from Paddington Station. It sold dresses to women of limited means and haberdashery to anyone in need of it. In a large room at the back of the premises, four women worked long hours as they made new dresses or repaired old ones. The shop was owned and run by Madame Hennebeau, a descendant of one of the many French Huguenot families that had settled in the area in the previous century. Louise Hennebeau was a tall, full-bodied widow in her fifties with a handsome face and well-groomed hair from which every trace of grey had been hounded by a ruthless black dye. Though she had been born and brought up in England, she affected a strong French accent to remind people of her heritage.

She was very surprised when Robert Colbeck entered her shop. Men seldom came to her establishment and the few who did never achieved the striking elegance of her visitor. Madame Hennebeau gave him a smile of welcome that broadened when he doffed his top hat and allowed her to see his face. Colbeck then introduced himself and she was nonplussed. She could not understand why a detective inspector should visit her shop.

'Would you prefer to talk in English or French, Madame?'

'English will be fine, sir,' she replied.

'French might be more appropriate,' he said, 'because I am investigating the murder of a gentleman called Gaston Chabal. Indeed, I have spent some time in France itself recently.'

'I still do not see why you have come to me, Inspector.'

'While I was abroad, crimes were committed on a railway line that was being built near Mantes. The men responsible have now been arrested but, had they done what they were supposed to do, they would have been richly rewarded. To get the reward,' Colbeck explained, 'the leader of the gang was told to come here.'

'Why?' she asked, gesticulating. 'This is a dress shop.'

'It's also a place where a message could be left, apparently.'

'Really?'

'For whom was that message intended?'

'I have no idea. I think there's been some mistake.'

'I doubt it. The man I questioned was very specific about this address. He even knew your name, Madam Hennebeau.'

'*How?*'

'That's what I'd like you to tell me.'

Waving her arms excitedly, she went off into a long, breathy defence of herself and her business, assuring him that she had always been very law-abiding and that she had no connection whatsoever with any crimes committed in France. Her righteous indignation was genuine enough but Colbeck still sensed that she was holding something back from him. He stopped her with a raised hand.

'Madame Hennebeau,' he said, politely, 'you obviously did not hear what I said at the start of the conversation. My visit here concerns a murder investigation. Nothing will be allowed to obstruct me in pursuit of the killer. Anyone who harbours information that may be useful to me – and who deliberately conceals it – will find that they are on the wrong side of the law. Retribution will follow.'

'But I have done nothing wrong,' she said, quivering all over.

'You are protecting someone I need to find.'

'No, Inspector.'

'He may even be hiding here at the moment.'

'That's not true,' she cried in alarm. 'There's nobody here except my women and me.'

'I may need to verify that by searching the premises. If you refuse to help me, Madame Hennebeau, I will have to return with some constables to go through every room. It may be necessary to disturb your seamstresses while we do so but that cannot be helped. As I told you,' he stressed, 'I'll let nobody obstruct me.'

'That is not what I'm doing, Inspector Colbeck.'

'I know when I'm being lied to, Madame.'

'I'm an honest woman. I'd never lie.'

'Do you want me to organise that search?'

'If I could help you, I would.'

'Then tell me the truth.'

'I do not know it myself.' She took a tiny handkerchief from the sleeve of her blouse and dabbed at her watering eyes. 'A gentleman came in here some weeks ago. He asked me if I would receive a message for him in return for some money. That's all I had to do,' she said, earnestly. 'Receive a message and hold it here for him. When it came, I was to put something in the window – a display of green ribbons – so that he could see it as he passed.'

'Was that because he lives nearby?'

336

'I cannot say. When he saw the signal, he was to pick up the message and leave a reply for whoever had been here. It all seemed so harmless to me, Inspector. I did not realise I was breaking the law.'

'You were not, Madame.'

'I feel as if I was now.'

'What was this gentleman's name?'

'He did not tell me – I swear it.'

'Could you describe him?'

'He was shorter than you, Inspector, and he had broader shoulders. He was not good-looking but he has a pleasant face. I liked him. His hair was thick and turning grey.'

'Could you give me some idea of his age?'

'Ten years older than you at least.'

'Why did he pick here?' wondered Colbeck. 'I can see that he could rely on you do what he asked, but why did he single you out in the first place? Was he ever a customer here?'

'No, Inspector,' she said.

'Then how did you meet?'

'It was some time ago,' she said, hiding her embarrassment behind a nervous laugh, 'and we did not really meet in the way that you imply. He used to wave to me through the window as he passed the shop and we became...' She licked her lips to get the words out more clearly. '...we became acquainted, as you might say. Then, out of the blue, he stepped into the shop one day.'

'When was this?'

'Weeks ago. I did not even recognise him at first.'

'Why not?'

'Because he was not wearing his uniform. When he used to go past regularly, he always looked very smart. That's why I trusted him, Inspector,' she said. 'He was a policeman.'

The Lamb and Flag was a favourite haunt of Victor Leeming's because it had three outstanding features. It was within walking distance of Scotland Yard, it served excellent beer and it was a tavern that Edward Tallis would never deign to enter. Leeming could enjoy a quiet drink there without fear of being caught in the act by his superior. When he got there, a few of his colleagues were already in the bar and they were very pleased to see him again. They chatted happily with him until Robert Colbeck came in through the door. Understanding at once that the two men wanted to be alone, the others greeted the newcomer with a respectful smile then drifted away. Colbeck brought drinks for himself and his sergeant before choosing a table in the far corner. Leeming quaffed his beer gratefully.

'I needed a taste of that,' he said, wiping the froth from his upper lip. 'I've been very busy today, Inspector.'

'I hope that I didn't overtax you, Victor.'

'Not at all. It felt marvellous to be back.'

'Albeit unofficially,' Colbeck observed.

'Quite so, sir.'

'Did you learn anything of value?'

'Eventually,' said Leeming, taking another long sip as he gathered his thoughts. 'I went to the police station and discovered that Pierce Shannon had been locked up there on May 27th.'

'Disturbing the peace?'

'And causing damage to property, most likely, but he wasn't charged with that. Because he couldn't pay his fine, he was kept in his cell, pending a transfer to prison, but the fine was then paid by an anonymous benefactor.'

'The very man who visited him in prison, I daresay.'

'I can confirm that. I spoke to Horace Eames.'

'Who is he?'

'He spends his time making lifeboats now, sir, but he used to be a policeman in Limehouse. It was Eames who let this old friend of his speak to Shannon in his cell. When he gave me his name, I wanted to make sure that we had the right man so I went to the magistrate's court to check their records.'

'Well done, Victor.'

'Sure enough, the very same person had

paid the fine.'

'That's conclusive.'

'Do you know what Luke's other name was?'

'Yes – Rogan.'

Leeming's face fell. 'You've already found out,' he complained.

'Let's call it a joint operation, Victor. We've each confirmed what the other managed to ascertain. While you were in a boatyard, I was at a dress shop in Paddington.'

'A dress shop?'

'It was the place where Shannon was told to leave a message for his paymaster. A French lady owns the shop. She and Rogan seemed to have developed something of a friendship.'

'He was a policeman in that district. So was Horace Eames at one time. They worked together.'

'I went to the station and they told me all about Rogan. It seems that he was a ladies' man,' said Colbeck. 'He developed a habit of enjoying favours from some of the women he encountered on his beat. And not the kind that ever charge for such services, I should add. In return, he kept a special eye on their property. He was a good police-man, apparently, but too fond of disobeying orders. In the end, he was dismissed from Paddington and became a private detective.'

'That's what Eames told me.'

'Did he give you an address for him?'

'He has an office somewhere in Camden.'

'What about his home address?'

'Eames couldn't tell me that, sir,' said Leeming. 'When he left the police force, Rogan moved from his house in Paddington.'

'Not all that far,' said Colbeck, taking a sheet of paper from his inside pocket. 'He needed to keep an eye on the window of that dress shop for a signal that was to be put there. It must have been chosen because of its proximity to his home.' He put the paper on the table. 'Take a look at that, Victor.'

'What is it, sir?'

'A list of people attending a lecture given by Gaston Chabal.'

Leeming picked it up. 'Where did you get this from?'

'The man who organised the event,' said Colbeck, taking a sip of his whisky. 'He's very methodical. As you can see, the names are all in alphabetical order. Check those that begin with an "R". Do you recognise someone?'

'Luke Rogan,' said the other, pointing to the name.

'Now, what is a private detective doing at a meeting that had such specialised interest? He knows nothing about civil engineering. I must be the only policeman in London who would have listened to Chabal with any alacrity.'

'So what was Rogan doing there?'

'Following him,' decided Colbeck. 'Unless I'm mistaken, he even followed the man to Paris. Chabal's mother-in-law told me that he felt someone was watching him. I believe that Rogan stayed on his tail until the moment when he had the opportunity to kill him. I'm also fairly certain that he was wearing a police uniform when he committed the murder. If Chabal was afraid that somebody was stalking him,' he added, 'the one person who would not arouse his suspicion was a police constable.'

'A bogus one.'

'Chabal was not to know that.' He had a second sip of his drink. 'Look at that list again, Victor. Can you see another name that you recognise?'

Leeming let his eye run down the neat column of names. 'Yes,' he declared, 'I know this one – Alexander Marklew.' He tapped the piece of paper. 'That's it, Inspector,' he went on with a note of triumph in his voice. 'We've found the link we needed.'

'Have we?'

'Of course. The only way that Rogan would even have known that that lecture was taking place was if someone took him there. That someone must be Mr Marklew. We've come full circle, Inspector,' he said, pausing to pour down some more beer. 'We're back with the most obvious suspect of all.'

'Who's that?'

'A jealous husband.'

'Husbands are not jealous of things they know nothing about.'

'But he *did* know. He used a private detective to find out.'

'No, Victor. I don't accept that. Alexander Marklew is a person I'd expect to be at such a lecture, but not because he realised that his wife had been unfaithful to him. Had that been the case, he'd surely have challenged Mrs Marklew about it. No,' said Colbeck, taking the list back from him, 'we must look elsewhere on this list.'

'What for?'

'The name of the man who *did* employ Luke Rogan.'

'Then all we have to do is to work through them one by one.'

'There's a more direct way than that, Victor.'

'Is there, sir?'

'Yes,' said Colbeck, pocketing the list and reaching for his whisky. 'I can pay a call on a certain private detective. Luke Rogan is the killer. His arrest must be our first priority.'

Sir Marcus Hetherington's estates were in Essex and he spent a fair amount of time at his country seat. When he was in London, however, he stayed at his town house in Pimlico. It was there, helped by his valet, that he was dressing for dinner. He was too busy adjusting his white tie in a mirror to hear the doorbell ring down below. It was only when he began to descend the staircase that he became aware of the fact that he had a visitor. A manservant awaited him in the hall.

'A gentleman has called to see you, Sir Marcus,' he said.

'At this hour? Damnably inconvenient.'

'I showed him into the drawing room.'

'What was his name?'

'Mr Rogan.'

Sir Marcus reddened. 'Luke Rogan?' he asked, irritably.

'Yes, Sir Marcus.'

Without even thanking the man, Sir Marcus brushed rudely past him and went into the drawing room, closing the door with a bang behind him to show his displeasure. Luke Rogan was admiring a painting of the battle of Waterloo that hung over the fireplace. He spun round to face the old man.

'What the devil are you doing here?' demanded Sir Marcus.

'I needed to see you.'

'Not here, man. I've told you before. You should only make contact with me at the Reform Club. If I am not there, you simply leave a note for me.'

'I preferred to call on you at home, Sir Marcus.'

'But I refrained on purpose from giving you this address.'

'I soon found it out,' said Rogan. 'When someone employs me, I like to know a little more about them than they're prepared to tell me.'

'Impudent scoundrel!'

'We're in this together, after all.'

'What are you blathering about?'

'Inspector Colbeck.'

Sir Marcus became wary. 'Go on,' he said, slowly.

'He *knows*.'

Luke Rogan had a hunted look about him. He spoke with his usual bravado but there was a distant fear in his voice. Sir Marcus took note of it. Crossing to a table, he removed the stopper from a crystal decanter and poured himself a glass of brandy. He did not offer a drink to Rogan. After replacing the stopper, he threw down half of the brandy before rounding on his visitor. His face was expressionless.

'What do you mean?' he asked with rasping authority

'Inspector Colbeck came to my office,' replied Rogan.

'When?'

'This afternoon. Luckily, I was out.'

'How did you learn of his visit?'

'The other offices are leased to a firm of solicitors, Sir Marcus. One of their clerks spoke to the inspector. He said that I would be out all afternoon and was not expected to return. As it happens,' said Rogan, 'I did call in earlier this evening.'

'What did Colbeck want?'

'To speak to me, that's all.'

'Was he on his own or did he bring men with him?'

'He came alone. I take that as a good sign.'

'A good sign!' repeated the old man with asperity. 'First of all, you assure me that he will never connect you in a hundred years with what happened in France. Then, when he comes knocking on your door only days later, you describe it as a good sign.'

'I was referring to the fact that he was on his own, Sir Marcus.'

'It only takes one man to make an arrest.'

'That may not be the reason he came.'

'Why else?'

'To make enquiries, maybe,' said Rogan, hopefully. 'My name may have floated in front of him and he came to satisfy his curiosity. I felt that I should warn you, Sir Marcus, but it may be unnecessary. I can't see how Colbeck could link possibly me with the murder.'

'I can,' said the other. 'You slipped up somewhere.'

'But I covered my tracks very carefully.'

'So you tell me.'

'I did, Sir Marcus. I know how policemen

work. I left no clues as to my name or my whereabouts.'

'Then how do you explain Colbeck's visit to your office?'

Rogan shrugged. 'I can't,' he admitted.

'So you come running here, you imbecile!' shouted Sir Marcus before downing the rest of his brandy. 'Did it never occur to you that Colbeck might have left a man to watch your office in case you returned? When you did, and learned what had happened, you might have led him all the way to my door.'

'Impossible!'

'How do you know?'

'Because I left the building by the rear exit,' said Rogan, 'and I changed cabs twice on my way here to throw off anyone who might be following. There was no one, Sir Marcus. I walked around the whole square to be sure before I even rang your bell.'

Sir Marcus put his glass on a table. Flipping his coat tails out of the way, he sank into a leather chair and ruminated for several minutes. Rogan remained on his feet, still trying to work out how Colbeck had managed to identify him as one of the culprits. Having taken such pains to hide behind anonymity, he felt distinctly uneasy, as if layers of protective clothing had suddenly and unaccountably been whisked off him. It made him shiver.

'Where will he go next?' said the old man.

'To your home?'

'No, Sir Marcus. He may have got to my office but he'll never find out where I live. Even my closest friends don't know that. I keep my address secret and change it regularly. When I go back home tonight,' said Rogan, confidently. 'I'll do so without a qualm.'

'That's more than I'll do.'

'You're perfectly safe here.'

'Not as long as Inspector Colbeck is on the case.' His gaze shifted to the painting above the fireplace and hovered there for while. 'How many men of his standing do they have at Scotland Yard?'

'None at all.'

'He must have an assistant.'

'Victor Leeming was the man beaten up in France,' said Rogan. 'He's not even involved in the case anymore. Colbeck will miss him and that's to our advantage. From what I've heard, Leeming is hard-working and resolute.'

'There must be other capable men in the Department.'

'Not one of them can hold a candle to the Railway Detective.'

'So he is irreplaceable?'

'Completely, Sir Marcus.'

The old man stood up and walked across to stand in front of the fireplace. He looked up at the swirling action in the oil painting on the wall. As rich memories were ignited, he drew himself up to his full height and stood to attention. He could hear the sound of armed conflict and it brought a nostalgic smile to his lips. When he spoke to Rogan, he kept staring up at the battle of Waterloo.

'Did you ever serve in the army?' he asked.

'No, Sir Marcus.'

'A pity – it would have been the making of you. Military life gives a man the best start in life. It shapes his thinking. It imparts courage and teaches him the virtues of patriotism.'

'Nobody is more patriotic than me,' claimed Rogan.

'Winning a battle is quite simple,' said the old man. 'You have to kill your enemy before he can kill you.' He turned round. 'That way, you remove any threat to your life, liberty and prospects of happiness. Do you understand what I'm saying, Rogan?'

'Extremely well, Sir Marcus.'

'We have an enemy. He's trying to hunt the pair of us down.'

'What do wish me to do?'

'Get rid of Inspector Colbeck,' said the other. 'He's the one man with the intelligence to find us and I'll not let that happen. It's time for him to meet his Waterloo, I fancy. You have your orders, Rogan.'

'Yes, Sir Marcus.'

'Kill him.'

CHAPTER THIRTEEN

Superintendent Edward Tallis was in a buoyant mood for once. He had just received a letter from Thomas Brassey, expressing formal thanks for all the help that had been rendered by the Metropolitan Police Force. The commissioner had then complimented him on his wisdom in dispatching Robert Colbeck abroad and, even though Tallis had been strongly opposed to the notion, he was happy to claim some credit for it now that the French expedition had paid such dividends. But the main reason for the superintendent's good humour was that he was at last in possession of a murder suspect.

'Luke Rogan,' he said, rolling the name off his tongue.

'I have men out looking for him at this very moment, sir.'

'But you do not know his home address.'

'Not yet,' replied Colbeck.

'He sounds like a slippery customer.'

'He is, Superintendent.'

'A former policeman, operating on the wrong side of the law. That's very distressing,' said Tallis, clenching his teeth. 'It sets a

351

bad example. He needs to be caught quickly, Inspector.'

'Rogan is not the only person we need,' Colbeck reminded him. 'He was merely the agent for someone else. The man who employed him is equally culpable.'

'Unfortunately, we do not have his name.'

'You are holding it in your hands, sir.'

They were in the superintendent's office and there was no sign of a cigar. Cool air blew in through a half-open window. When he had delivered his verbal report, Colbeck had also shown his superior the list of those who had attended Gaston Chabal's lecture. Tallis looked at it more closely and noticed something.

'Why have you put crosses against some of the names?'

'Those are the men I've been able to eliminate, sir.'

'How?' asked Tallis.

'Some of them – Alexander Marklew, for instance – invested a sizeable amount of money in the Mantes to Caen Railway. They are hardly likely to connive at the destruction of the project when they have a financial stake in it.'

'I accept that.'

'As for the other names I have set aside,' said Colbeck, 'that was done so on the advice of Mr Kane.'

'He's the secretary of this Society, isn't he?'

'Yes, sir. Once I had persuaded him to cooperate with me, he was extremely helpful. Mr Kane pointed out the civil engineers who were in the audience that day. Men who make their living from the railway,' Colbeck reasoned, 'would not be inclined to inflict damage on one. They would be violating an unwritten code.'

'So how many names are left?'

'Just over thirty.'

'It will take time to work through them all.'

'If we arrest Rogan, we'll not have to do so. He'll supply us with the name we want. It obviously belongs to a man of some wealth. He spent a large amount on this whole venture.'

'Luke Rogan must have been highly paid to commit murder.'

'I suspect that he needed the money,' said Colbeck, 'which is why he was prepared to take on the assignment. Judging by the size of his office, his business activities were not very profitable. It was very small and he could not afford to employ anyone to take care of his secretarial work.'

'Then why was he chosen?' said Tallis, frowning. 'Wouldn't his paymaster have gone to someone who was more successful?'

'No, sir. That would have been too risky for him. Most private detectives would have refused to have anything to do with such blatantly criminal activities. They are far too honourable. They would have reported to us any such approach. What this man required,' Colbeck said, 'was someone who was less scrupulous, a mercenary who could not afford to turn down such a generous offer. He found what he wanted in Luke Rogan.'

'How soon do you expect to apprehend him?'

'I could not say. He's proving rather elusive.'

'Was there nothing in his office to indicate his whereabouts?'

'Nothing whatsoever,' replied the other. 'I searched the place thoroughly this morning. Rogan was canny. He left no correspondence in his office and no details of any clients.'

'He must have had an account book of sorts.'

'Kept at his home, I presume.'

'Wherever that might be.'

'Mr Kane had an address for everyone on that list so that he could inform them about future events that took place. Luke Rogan had supplied what purported to be his home address but, when I got there, the house did not even exist.'

'What about the police in Paddington?'

'They confirmed that Rogan had always been rather secretive.'

'But they must have known where his abode was,' said Tallis, returning the sheet of paper to Colbeck. 'A police constable would have to register a correct address.'

'That's what he did, sir.'

'Did you visit the place?'

'There was no point,' said Colbeck. 'When he was dismissed from the police force, he moved from the house. Nobody seems to know where he went. Luke Rogan is not married so he has only himself to consider. He can move at will.'

'He must live *somewhere*, Inspector.'

'Of course. I believe it will not be too far from Paddington.'

'Then roust him out.'

'We are doing all that we can, sir.'

'How many men are out looking for him?'

'Hundreds of thousands.'

Tallis glared at him. 'Are you trying to be droll?'

'Not at all,' said Colbeck. 'I'm working from the figures in last year's census. London has a population of well over three million.'

'So?'

'We can discount the large number of people that are illiterate and any children can also be taken out of the equation. It still leaves a substantial readership for the daily newspapers.'

'Newspapers?'

'You obviously haven't read your copy of *The Times* this morning,' said Colbeck, indicating the newspaper that was neatly folded on the desk. 'I took the liberty of placing a notice in it and in the others on sale today.'

'I was about to suggest that you did exactly that,' said Tallis, reaching for his newspaper. 'Where is the notice?'

'Page four, sir. Why restrict the search to a handful of detectives when we can use eyes all over London to assist us? Somebody reading that,' he said, confidently, 'is bound to know where we can find the elusive Luke Rogan.'

When the cab reached the railway station, Sir Marcus Hetherington alighted and paid the driver. He then bought a first class ticket and walked towards the relevant platform. On his way, he passed a booth from which he obtained a copy of *The Times*. Stuffing it under one arm, he marched briskly on with his cane beating out a tattoo on the concourse. A porter was standing on the platform, ready to open the door of an empty first class carriage for him. Sir Marcus gave him a nod then settled down in his seat. The door was closed behind him.

While he enjoyed travelling by rail, he hated the hustle and bustle of a railway station and he always tried to time his arrival so that he did not have to wait there for long in the company of people whom he considered undesirables. Sir Marcus was not so aristocratic as to believe that trains should be reserved exclusively for the peerage but he did consider the introduction of the third class carriage a reprehensible mistake. It encouraged the lower orders to travel and that, in his opinion, gave them a privileged mobility that was wholly undeserved. When he saw a rough-looking individual, rushing past his carriage with a scruffy, middle-aged woman in tow, Sir Marcus grimaced. To share a journey with such people was demeaning.

Moments later, the signal was given and the train sprang into life, coughing loudly before giving a shudder and pulling away from the platform. Another latecomer sprinted past the carriage to jump on to the moving train farther down. Sir Marcus clicked his tongue in disapproval. Now that they were in motion, he was content. He had the carriage all to himself and the train would not stop until it reached his destination. Opening his newspaper, he began to read it. Since he took a keen interest in political affairs, he perused every article on the first two inside pages with care. When he turned to the next page, however, it was a police notice that grabbed his attention.

'What's this?' he gulped.

The notice requested the help of the public to find Luke Rogan, the prime suspect in a murder investigation, who operated as a private detective from an office in Camden. A detailed description of the man was given and, to his chagrin, Sir Marcus could see that it was fairly accurate. Anyone with information about Rogan's whereabouts was urged to come forward.

'Damnation!' cried Sir Marcus.

He flung the newspaper aside and considered the implications of what he had just read. It was disturbing. If everyone in the capital was looking for Luke Rogan, he could not escape arrest indefinitely. The trail would then lead to Sir Marcus. He began to perspire freely. For a fleeting second, the shadow of the Railway Detective seemed to fall across him.

'If you come down to Euston Station with me,' offered Caleb Andrews, 'I'll show you how it was done.'

'I think I already know,' said Colbeck.

'There are some empty carriages in a siding, Inspector. I could demonstrate for you.'

'Robert is far too busy, Father,' said Madeleine.

'I'm only trying to help, Madeleine. What you have to do, you see, is to prop the door open while the train is in motion. Someone did just that a few months ago on a train I was driving from Birmingham,' he explained. 'Some villains got on with a strongbox they'd stolen. After a couple of miles, they jammed open the door and flung the strongbox out so that they would not be caught with it.'

'I remember the case,' said Colbeck. 'When they came back later to retrieve their booty, the police were waiting for them. A farmer had found the strongbox in his field and raised the alarm.'

'The point I'm trying to make is that the box was heavy – almost as heavy as that Frenchman. Yet it was slung out with ease.'

'How do you know?' asked Madeleine. 'You weren't there.'

'I was driving the train.'

'But you didn't actually see them throw anything out.'

'Stop interrupting me, Maddy.'

'You make a fair point, Mr Andrews,' said Colbeck, trying to bring the conversation to an end, 'and I'm grateful. But we've moved on a long way from the Sankey Viaduct.'

'You should have come to me at the time, Inspector.'

'I'm sure.'

Colbeck had paid a return visit to Luke Rogan's office to see if there had been any sign of the man. The uniformed policeman who had been keeping the place under surveillance assured him that Rogan had not entered the building by the front or rear doors. Since he was in Camden, only a few streets away from her house, Colbeck decided to call in on Madeleine but it was her father's day off so he had to contend with Caleb Andrews. It was several minutes before he was finally left alone with Madeleine.

'Can I make you some tea, Robert?' she asked.

'No, thank you. I only popped in for a moment.'

'I'm sorry that my father badgered you.'

'I never mind anything that he does,' said Colbeck, tolerantly. 'But for him, we'd never have met. I always bear that in mind.'

'So do I.'

'You were the strongbox thrown from that particular train.'

'I'm not a strongbox,' protested Madeleine with a laugh.

'I was speaking metaphorically.'

'You mean, that I'm very heavy and difficult to open.'

'No,' said Colbeck, giving her a conciliatory kiss. 'I mean that you possess great value – to me, that is.'

'Then why didn't you say so?'

'I was dealing in images.'

'Well, I'd prefer you to speak more directly,' she chided him. 'It would help me to understand you properly. I still don't know what you meant about my drawing of the viaduct helping you to solve a murder. All you would tell me was that it was symbolic.'

'Highly symbolic.'

'It was a sketch – nothing more.'

'Show it to me again,' he invited, 'and I'll explain.'

'In simple language?'

'Monosyllables, if your prefer.'

Madeleine fetched her portfolio and extracted the drawing of the Sankey Viaduct. She laid it on the table and they both scrutinised it.

'What you did was to bridge the Channel between England and France,' he pointed out. 'All the way from Dover to Calais.'

'I drew that picture out of love.'

'But it's a symbol of something that certain people hate.'

'And what's that?'

'I'll tell you, Madeleine. The railway that's being built from Mantes to Caen will not end there. In due course, an extension will be added to take it to Cherbourg.'

'I don't see anything wrong in that.'

'There's an arsenal there.'

'Oh.'

'The railway that Thomas Brassey is constructing will in time provide a direct route between Paris and a main source of arms and ammunition. That's bound to alarm some people here,' he continued. 'It's less than forty years since we defeated France and that defeat still rankles with them.

Louis Napoleon, who rules the country, is an Emperor in all but name. Emperors need imperial conquests.'

Madeleine was worried. 'Do you think that France would try to *invade* us?' she said, turning to look up at him. 'I thought we were completely safe.'

'I'm sure that we are,' said Colbeck, 'and I'm equally certain that Mr Brassey is of the same opinion. If he believed for one moment that he was endangering his native country by building that railway, he would never have taken on the contract.'

'Then why did someone try to wreck the project?'

'Because he is afraid, Madeleine.'

'Of what?'

'Potential aggression from the French.'

'But you just said that we had nothing to fear.'

'Other people see things differently,' he said, 'and it was only when you showed me this drawing that I realised how they could view what was happening in northern France. A railway between Paris and Cherbourg is a source of intense concern to some Englishmen.'

'All that I can see is my crude version of the Sankey Viaduct.'

'Look beyond it,' he advised.

'At what?'

'The railway that will connect the French

capital to a port with military significance.'
He gave an apologetic smile. 'I'm afraid that
I'm going to have to use a word that you
don't like.'

'Will it explain what all this is about?'

'I think so, Madeleine.'

'What's the word?'

'Metaphorical.'

She rolled her eyes. 'We're back to that
again.'

'Your drawing is to blame,' he said, indicating it. 'You've created what someone clearly
dreads – a viaduct between England and
France. In his mind – and we have to try to
see it from his point of view, warped as it
might be – the railway between Paris and
Cherbourg will be a metaphorical viaduct
between the two countries. It's a potent
symbol of French imperial ambition.'

'Is that why a man was killed?' she said,
trying to assimilate what she had been told.
'Because of symbols and metaphors?'

'Chabal was an engineer with an important role in the project.'

'According to father, lots of engineers
work on a new railway.'

'Quite true. Mr Brassey has a whole team
of them.'

'Why was this particular man murdered?'

'He had the wrong nationality – he was
French.'

'Did he have to be thrown from the

Sankey Viaduct?'

'I think so.'

'You're going to tell me that that was symbolic as well, aren't you?' she said. 'It's something to do with whatever you called it a few moments ago.'

'A metaphorical viaduct. I'm only guessing,' he went on, 'and I could be wrong. There are just too many coincidences here. Someone is so horrified at the prospect of that railway being built that he will go to any lengths to stop it.'

'What sort of a man is he, Robert?'

'One who has an implacable hatred of the French.'

'Why?'

'He probably fought against them.'

Nobody else was allowed in the room. It was on the first floor of the mansion and it overlooked the rear garden. It was kept locked so that none of the servants could get into it. The first thing that Sir Marcus Hetherington did when he let himself in was to lock the door behind him. He gazed around the room and felt the familiar upsurge of pride and patriotism. What he had created was a shrine to England's military glory. Banners, uniforms and weapons stood everywhere. Memorabilia of a more gruesome kind were contained in a glass case. Its prime exhibit, a human skull, was something that he cherished. It had belonged to a nameless French soldier who had fallen at the battle of Waterloo. Sir Marcus had killed him.

He wandered around the room, examining various items and luxuriating in the memories that they kindled. Then he crossed to the window. It was a fine day and sunlight was dappling the back lawn, but he was not looking at the garden. His gaze went up to the flag that was fluttering in the breeze at the top of its pole. He gave it a salute. Turning back, he surveyed his collection once more, drawing strength from it, finding consolation, recapturing younger days. On the wall above the mantelpiece was a portrait of himself in uniform. It never failed to lift his heart.

Crossing to a rosewood cabinet, he opened the top drawer and took out a wooden case that he set down on the table. When he lifted the lid of the case, Sir Marcus looked down fondly at a pair of percussion duelling pistols with plated turn-off barrels and walnut stocks inlaid with silver. The weapons gleamed. Packed neatly around them was a small supply of ammunition. He removed the pistols from the case and held one in each hand. The sensation of power was thrilling. It coursed through him for minutes. When it finally began to ease, Sir Marcus started to load the pistols.

Now that he was involved in the investigation once more, Victor Leeming was eager to take on more work. He spent the morning on the hoof, tracking down some of the people who had attended the lecture given by Gaston Chabal. It had been a largely fruitless exercise but it made him feel useful again. Instead of meeting the inspector at the Lamb and Flag, he agreed to visit Colbeck's house in John Islip Street so that they could have more privacy. Robert Colbeck's father and grandfather had been cabinetmakers with a string of wealthy clients. When he inherited the house, he also inherited examples of their work. In the drawing room where he and Leeming sat, a large cupboard, two matching cabinets and a beautiful mahogany secretaire bore the Colbeck name.

'How are you feeling today, Victor?' asked the inspector.

'Tired but happy to be so, sir.'

'You must not overdo it.'

'Knocking on a few doors is no effort,' said Leeming. 'I just wish that I had more to report. None of the four people I called on could possibly have hired Luke Rogan. You can cross them off the list.'

'That saves me the trouble of bothering with them.'

'How many names are left?'

'Less than twenty. We are slowly whittling

them down.'

'Why are you so sure that the man we want actually attended that lecture? If he detested the idea of that railway being built in France, wouldn't he avoid a man who was talking about it?'

'On the contrary,' said Colbeck. 'He'd want to find out as much about it as he could. Also, of course, he'd be keen to take a closer look at Gaston Chabal. The man represented everything that he loathed and feared. No, he and Rogan were there together, I'm certain of it. They may not have sat beside each other – they probably took care to stay apart in order to conceal their relationship – but they were both at that lecture.'

'Then we are bound to find him in the end.'

'Oh, yes.'

Colbeck stirred his tea before tasting it. Leeming had already finished one cup and was halfway through the second. He chewed on the slice of cake that he had been offered.

'What did Mr Tallis have to say about it all?'

'He was pleased, Victor. Or, to put it another way, he smoked no cigars, had no tantrums and was almost disarmingly civil. All that he craves is a little success,' said Colbeck. 'It stops him from being pilloried in the newspapers.'

'Talking of the newspapers, sir, I saw that

notice you put in this morning's edition. It's sure to get a response.'

'Not all of it entirely reliable, alas.'

'No,' said Leeming, wearily. 'The promise of a reward does things to some people. They invent all sorts of stories to try to get their hands on the money. But they won't all be fraudulent. There may be some wheat among the chaff, sir.'

'I'm counting on it.'

'You gave a good description of Rogan. It tallied with the one I had from Horace Eames.'

'I also relied on what Madame Hennebeau told me. She was clearly very fond of the man but, then, so were a number of women.'

'Luke Rogan will be on the run by now. You'll have flushed him out of his hiding place good and proper.'

'That was the idea behind using the press,' said Colbeck. 'I wanted to scare Rogan and drive a wedge between him and his employer. When he realises that we've identified his hired killer, the man who set everything in motion will want to distance himself from Rogan. My guess is that he'll go to ground immediately.'

'Here in London?'

'Well, it won't be in France, we may be certain of that.'

While his visitor drained his teacup,

Colbeck told him about the conversation he had had earlier with Madeleine Andrews regarding her sketch of the Sankey Canal. Leeming was almost as confused by his talk of symbols and metaphors as she had been, but he trusted the inspector to know what he was talking about. What interested him was Colbeck's theory that the man who had engaged Rogan had probably served in the army at one time.

'I wish you'd told me that before, Inspector,' he said.

'Why?'

'I could have asked the people I interviewed this morning if they knew anyone who'd been at that lecture with a military background. It's a small world – engineers and such like. They all seem to know each other.'

'That's in our favour.'

'Do you have any more names for me?'

'Haven't you done enough work for one day?'

'No,' said Leeming, ignoring the stab of pain in his ribs. 'I'm only just starting to warm up, sir. Use me as much as you wish.'

'Mr Tallis would admonish me, if he knew.'

'You employed Brendan Mulryne behind his back and got away with it. Unlike him, I do work at the Detective Department.'

'But you're supposed to be on sick leave, Victor.'

'I'm sick of sick leave. Give me some more names.'

'As you wish,' said Colbeck, taking a slip of paper from his pocket and handing it over. 'There are four more people for you to chase down. Be sure to find out if any of them bore arms against the French at one time. That would make them fifty or more at least.'

'I'll remember that.'

'And take a cab. You don't have to go all over London on foot. Keep a record of your cab fares and I'll reimburse you.'

'You can save your money with this chap, sir,' said Leeming as he saw the first address on the list. 'He lives in Pimlico. That's well within walking distance of here.'

'It is indeed. What's the man's name?'

'Hetherington – Sir Marcus Hetherington.'

The publicity in the newspapers had given him a real fright. Before his landlady or his neighbours could report his whereabouts to the police, Luke Rogan gathered up everything of value and stuffed it into a bag. Then he changed out of the slightly garish attire he usually wore and put on a pair of dungarees, a moth-eaten old coat and a floppy hat. It was a disguise he often used in the course of his work as a private detective and it was so nondescript as to render him almost invisible. After checking his appearance in the mirror, he fled from his house in Bayswater without leaving behind the unpaid rent.

He left his belongings at the house in Paddington of a woman he had befriended during his days as a policeman. He gave her a plausible explanation about why he was dressed as a workman but she needed no convincing. She was a lonely widow who was so pleased to see him that she offered him accommodation for as long as he wished. As she never read a newspaper, there was no possibility that she would link her former lover with a series of horrific crimes. In the short term at least, Rogan had somewhere to hide.

Sir Marcus Hetherington had ordered him to kill Colbeck in order that the murder investigation would lose the man who directed it and make it founder. In view of what the inspector had done, Rogan was now fired by revenge as well. He was anxious to strike back at the person who had exposed him in the newspapers as a wanted felon and spread his name across the whole of London. He knew that he could never return to his old life again. Colbeck had robbed him of his occupation. In recompense, he would deprive the detective of his life.

Rogan had been patient. He knew what his intended victim looked like and where to find him. Lurking outside Scotland Yard until the inspector had emerged, he waited until Colbeck had summoned a cab then flagged down one of his own and ordered it to follow the first vehicle. What he learned was that Colbeck lived in John Islip Street and that, very soon after his arrival, he had a visitor. While the two men were inside the house, Rogan loitered in a doorway on the other side of the street and bided his time. He felt under his coat for the knife that was thrust into his belt. Having already killed Gaston Chabal, it could now be used to dispatch another man.

Inside the house, the detectives came to the end of their conversation.

'I'll be on my way, Inspector,' said Victor Leeming, rising slowly to his feet. 'Thank you for the tea and cake.'

'When this is all over, we'll celebrate with something a little stronger,' promised Colbeck. 'Before that, I'll want to know how you fared this afternoon.'

'Where will I meet you?'

'At the Lamb and Flag.'

'What time?'

'Shall we say six o'clock?'

'I'll be there, sir.'

'Good.' Colbeck got to his feet and led the way into the hall. 'I'll go back to Scotland Yard to see if anyone has come forward as a result of that notice in the newspapers.'

'And I'll ring some more doorbells.'

'Are you glad to be back in harness again, Victor?'

'Yes, sir – even if I can only manage a trot.'

They put on their respective hats and left the house together. Leeming looked up and down the street. 'Not long to go now.'

'I hope not.'

'We'll soon catch Luke Rogan.'

'Yes,' said Colbeck. 'We're getting close. I can feel it.'

They exchanged farewells then parted company. Leeming walked at a gentle pace towards Vauxhall Bridge Road while Colbeck went off in the opposite direction, intending to stop the first empty Hansom cab. As none was in view, he continued to stroll briskly along the pavement. He reviewed all the evidence they had so far gathered and it left him with a feeling of guarded optimism. His only worry was that Rogan might leave London to avoid arrest and, possibly, flee the country altogether. If necessary, Colbeck was more than ready to pursue him abroad.

It was minutes before he realised that he was being followed. He did not remember seeing anyone when they came out of the house but he sensed a distinct presence now. When an empty cab came towards him, therefore, he let it pass. Colbeck wanted to know who was on his tail. Moving to the kerb, he glanced back down the street then crossed diagonally to the other side. Out of the corner of his eye, he had seen him. The man had pretended to tie up his bootlace so that he could keep his head down but Colbeck knew at once that it was a ruse. He was being shadowed.

As he walked on, he maintained the same pace, giving no indication that he was aware of someone behind him. They were now on the same side of the street. The gap between them slowly closed until Colbeck could hear the tramp of hobnail boots behind him. That was the danger signal. If he was simply being followed, he knew that the man would stay well back to avoid being seen. The fact that he was moving steadily closer meant that he was going to attack.

Colbeck did not know if the man was a thief or someone with a personal grudge against him. Police work had made him many enemies and he had often received threats from convicted criminals as they were hauled out of the dock to begin a prison sentence. It did not matter who the stalker was. The way to deal with him, he believed, was to invite the attack. When he reached a corner, he turned sharply and went down a narrow lane. He heard footsteps quicken behind him. After a few more yards, Colbeck swung round to confront the man. The sun forewarned him. It glinted on the knife that had suddenly appeared in the stalker's hand. The man lunged forward and thrust hard with his weapon but he could not sink it into the back of an unsuspecting victim this time. Colbeck was ready for him.

Jumping quickly back out of the way, he whisked off his top hat and flung it hard into the man's face to confuse him for an split-second. He grabbed the hand that was holding the knife and turned the point away. They grappled fiercely and it was clear that the man was used to a brawl. Strong and wily, he did everything he could to over-power Colbeck, punching, gouging, spitting into his face, biting his hand and trying to stamp on his toes with his boot. Colbeck responded by tightening his grip. When he managed to manoeuvre the man off balance, he swung him hard against the brick wall. Shaken by the impact, his attacker dropped the knife. Colbeck used a foot to kick it away.

As they grappled once more, Colbeck realised that he was not ideally dressed for a fight. His tight-fitting frock coat did not allow him much flexibility. His adversary, by contrast, had much more freedom of move-ment. He used it to push Colbeck against the wall then hit him with a relay of punches. Before the detective could fight back, he was kicked in the shin then tripped up. As he fell to the ground, Colbeck heard the ominous sound of torn cloth but he had no time to worry about his coat. The man dived on him and went for his throat, getting both thumbs on his windpipe and pressing hard.

It was the first moment when Colbeck had a proper look at his face. Breathing heavily, the man bared his teeth in a grin of triumph and applied more pressure. Colbeck knew that it must be Luke Rogan. The man was intent on murder. Desperation gave him an extra surge of strength and he rolled suddenly to the left, toppling Rogan and weakening his grip. Colbeck punched him hard in the face until he put up both hands to defend himself. The searing pain in Colbeck's throat had gone but he still had to contend with a powerful adversary. What brought the fight to an end was the arrival of several onlookers. Hearing the commotion, a small crowd began to gather around them. They were witnesses. Rogan had to get away.

Smashing a fist into Colbeck's face, he struggled to his feet and pushed his way past the spectators before running off down the lane. Colbeck was still dazed. By the time he was helped to his feet by two men, he saw that Luke Rogan had vanished. One of the bystanders looked at his torn coat and blood-covered face.

'You all right, guv'nor?' he asked.

'Yes, thank you,' said Colbeck, dusting off his coat.

'Like me to call a policeman, sir?'

Colbeck gave a hollow laugh.

The superintendent had never seen him looking dishevelled before. In all the years they had known each other, Robert Colbeck had striven for a stylishness that Edward Tallis felt was out of place in the Detective Department. Smartness was always encouraged but not to the point of ostentation. Colbeck did not look quite so elegant now. His frock coat was torn, his trousers were scuffed and his face was cut and bruised. Looking into the mirror, he was using a handkerchief to wipe away the blood from his cheek when Tallis burst into his office.

'They told me you were back,' he said, staring in amazement at the unkempt figure before him. 'Whatever happened to you, man?'

'I tried to arrest Luke Rogan, sir.'

'You found him?'

'No, sir,' replied Colbeck. 'He found me.'

'How do you know that it was him?'

'Because he attempted to kill me.' He pointed to the knife that lay on his desk. 'In the same way that he murdered Gaston Chabal.'

Colbeck told him what had happened and how he had been face to face with the wanted man described that morning in the newspapers. When he heard that Rogan had escaped, Tallis wanted him apprehended immediately.

'I'll send out men to scour the area,' he said.

'Too late, Superintendent. I've already done that.'

'I'll not have anyone assaulting my men.'

'He'll be long gone by now,' said Colbeck. 'He ran off as if the hounds of hell were on his tail.'

'And so they will be,' vowed Tallis. 'Dear God! What is the world coming to when a detective inspector can be the victim of a murderous attack only a few blocks from his own doorstep?'

'It's not exactly a daily event, sir.'

'Once is enough.'

'I agree.'

'We knew that Rogan was a villain but it never crossed my mind that he'd be capable of this audacity. Why did he strike at you?'

'Because he identifies me as his nemesis,' said Colbeck. 'Rogan thought he'd committed the perfect murder until we began to breathe down his neck. If he read a newspaper this morning, he'd have seen my appeal for information that would lead to his capture. That could make a man feel vengeful.'

'He's not the only one, Inspector. When I look at you in that state, I feel vengeful as well. Rogan will pay for this.'

'It's a pity I can't send him a bill from my tailor.' Colbeck examined the long tear under his arm. 'This will need to be repaired and the coat will have to be cleaned. I can't wear it like this.'

'This must not be allowed to happen again.'

'It won't, sir.'

'From now on, you'll have a bodyguard.'

'But it's not necessary.'

'Someone is determined to kill you.'

'Luckily, he failed.'

'He's sure to try again.'

'I think that's the last thing he'll do.'

'Why?'

'Because he knows that I'll be on my guard now,' said Colbeck. 'He'd never have a chance to get that close again.'

'We'll look under every stone in London for him.'

'That could be a wasted exercise, Inspector.'

'Why?'

'Because I don't think he'll stay in the city.'

'He must, if he wants to ambush you again,' said Tallis.

'No, sir. It's too dangerous. Luke Rogan won't show his face here again. He's probably on his way out of London right now.'

'Where do you think he will go?'

'There's one obvious place.'

'Is there?'

'Yes, Superintendent,' said Colbeck. 'He'll want a refuge. He'll scurry back to the man who dragged him into this in the first place. They have a common bond, after all. When we catch them, both will face the prospect of a death sentence.'

Sir Marcus Hetherington was livid when he was told that he had a visitor by the name of Luke Rogan. Storming out of the library, he went to the front door of his mansion and saw the sorry figure waiting in the porch. Rogan was still wearing the old coat and dungarees. Since he was holding his cap in his hands, the bruises on his forehead and the black eye were clearly visible. Sir Marcus spluttered.

'Whatever brought you here?' he asked.

'We need to settle our account, Sir Marcus.'

'This house is sacrosanct. You're not allowed anywhere near it.'

'I think I am,' said Rogan, pugnaciously.

'And how did you get those bruises?'

'Invite me in and I'll tell you.'

'You're not coming in here.'

Fearing that his wife might see the man, Sir Marcus took him past the stable block at the rear of the house. They went into an outbuilding some distance away so that they could talk without being seen. Rogan told him about the failed attempt on Colbeck's life. The old man was incensed.

'Can't you do *anything* you're told?' he yelled.

'I got rid of that Frenchman for you,' retorted the other.

'Yes, but you didn't bring that railway to a halt, did you? Nor did you stop the police from finding out your identity, thus putting both our lives in danger. And now – *this!*'

'Colbeck saw me coming.'

'You swore to me that you'd kill him.'

'I tried, Sir Marcus. How do you think I got these bruises?'

'The worst thing of all is that you come running here, like a snivelling child who's been beaten at school.'

Rogan became truculent. 'I didn't come for sympathy,' he said. 'I came for what's owed to me. Now that I have to get out of London, I need every penny.'

'I'm not paying you for something you didn't do.'

'You have to, Sir Marcus. You gave me your word.'

'I've paid you enough already,' said the old man, 'and the money was not well spent. You blundered. And to cap it all, you have the temerity to disturb me in my own home. That's unpardonable.'

'We're in this together.'

'Our association is ended forthwith.'

'You don't get off the hook that easily, Sir

Marcus,' said Rogan, squaring up to him. 'If you don't pay me what's due, I'll write a note to Inspector Colbeck and tell him whose idea it was to kill Gaston Chabal and toss him off that viaduct.'

'You wouldn't dare!' howled Sir Marcus.

'What do I have to lose?'

'You're the man they're after, not me. There's a description of you in the newspapers this morning. If you were so careful, how did the police track you down to your office?'

'Give me the money!'

'No!'

'If I go down, Sir Marcus, you'll come with me.'

There was a silent battle of wills. Sir Marcus glowered at him but Rogan met his gaze with unflinching steadiness. The old man was enraged by the lack of respect he was being shown. Hitherto, Rogan had always been deferential. He was now scornful of their social differences. He would not be cowed. Sir Marcus reached a decision. When he had first employed him, Rogan had been an asset to him. He had now become a liability.

'Who knows that you came here?' he asked.

'Nobody.'

'Are you sure?'

'Quite sure, Sir Marcus.'

'Someone must have brought you from the railway station.'

'I walked.'

Sir Marcus was duly impressed. It was almost two miles to the house. If Rogan had walked all the way, it showed how eager he was to get there. Since the house was in an isolated position, the chances that anyone had seen him coming there were very slim. The only other person who had set eyes on the visitor was one of the servants. Feigning repentance, Sir Marcus nodded his head.

'I am indebted to you,' he conceded. 'There's no denying that.'

'I need my money,' said Rogan.

'You'll get it – on the understanding that you'll go far away from here and never return. Is that agreed?'

'You'll never see me again, Sir Marcus.'

'Do I have your word on that?'

'I won't even stay in the country.'

'In that case,' said the old man, 'I'll get what I owe you and I'll add something more. Wait here until I get back.'

Victor Leeming arrived at the Lamb and Flag to find a tankard of beer waiting for him. Colbeck was sitting at a table. When he saw the inspector's face, Leeming was shocked.

'You look worse than me, sir!' he said.

'I feel it, Victor.'

'What on earth happened?'

'I had a chance meeting with Luke Rogan.'

Leeming sat down in the other chair and listened to the story.

He was annoyed that he had left Colbeck alone after their meeting in John Islip Street. He felt guilty.

'I should have made sure you caught a cab,' he said.

'I can look after myself.'

'But you might have been killed, sir.'

'A little shaken up, that's all,' said Colbeck. 'What really upset me was that I tore my coat and muddied my trousers. Luckily, I keep a change of clothing in my office. I'd never have ventured in here otherwise.' He drank some whisky. 'What did you learn?'

'You can cross three of the names off that list, sir.'

'Excellent – that takes us down to single figures. Some of the other men working on the case have been busy as well. They managed to eliminate another eight suspects between them.'

'You may be able to get rid of even more.'

'Why?'

'Because I think I struck gold at the first address.'

'The one in Pimlico?'

'Yes, Inspector,' said Leeming before taking a long drink of beer. 'It's a town house owned by Sir Marcus Hetherington. He's gone back to his estates in Essex so I wasn't able to speak to the gentleman himself, but I talked to a servant.'

'And?'

'Sir Marcus had a long and distinguished career in the army.'

'How old would he be?'

'Well into his seventies, apparently.'

'Then he could be our man.'

'I'm fairly certain of it,' said Leeming. 'When I mentioned the name of Luke Rogan, the servant claimed that he had never heard of him. But I had a strong suspicion that he was lying. He's obviously very loyal to his master.'

'Did you press him in the matter?'

'No, sir. I went away. When I'd visited the other three addresses, I took a cab back to Pimlico and spoke to the same man. This time I showed him that description of Luke Rogan in the newspaper and reminded him that it was a crime to hold back evidence from the police. That rattled him, I could see.'

'Did he buckle?'

'Eventually,' said Leeming. 'He remembered something that had slipped his mind. It seems that a man who called himself Rogan had called at the house only yesterday. That settles it for me, sir.'

'And me,' said Colbeck. 'How quickly can

you drink that beer?'

'Why, sir?'

'We're going to catch a train to Essex.'

It was some while before Sir Marcus Hetherington returned and Rogan began to worry. When he stepped outside, however, he saw the old man coming towards him with a small bag in his hand. The sight made him relax. Sir Marcus ushered him back inside and closed the door behind them. Then he held out the bag.

'This is all you get, mind,' he warned. 'Your final payment.'

'Thank you,' said Rogan, snatching the bag.

'Count it out to make sure that it's all there.'

'I will, Sir Marcus.'

There was a little table in the corner. Luke Rogan sat beside it and tipped out the bundle of notes and coins. He began to count the money but did not get far. Taking out a pistol from inside his coat, Sir Marcus shot him in the head from close range. Blood spurted everywhere and stained the banknotes on the table. Rogan slumped forward. Sir Marcus was relieved, convinced that he had just rid himself of the one person who could connect the series of crimes to him. Rogan had deserved what he got. The old man had no sympathy.

Putting the gun aside, he took down an empty sack that was hanging from a nail and used it to cover Rogan's head. Then he opened the door, checked that nobody was about and took hold of the body under the armpits. Rogan was a solid man but Sir Marcus was still strong enough to drag him to the disused well nearby. The corpse plummeted down the shaft and disappeared under the water. The money was soon thrown after Rogan. When he had strewn handfuls of straw down the well, Sir Marcus reclaimed his pistol and went off to change for dinner.

An hour later, he and Lady Hetherington were at either end of the long oak table in the dining room, eating their meal and engaging in desultory conversation. Sir Marcus was chastened by the turn of events. In being forced to kill Rogan, he felt that a chapter in his life had just been concluded. He had to accept that his plan to destroy the railway in France had failed. But at least he was safe. He could now resume his accepted routine, going through the social rounds in Essex with his wife and making regular trips to his club in London. Nobody would ever know that he had once been associated with a private detective named Luke Rogan.

When the servant entered the room, and apologised for the interruption, he shattered his master's sense of security.

'There's an Inspector Colbeck to see you, Sir Marcus.'

'Who?' The old man almost choked.

'Inspector Colbeck. He's a detective from Scotland Yard and he has a Sergeant Leeming with him. They request a few moments of your time. What shall I tell them, Sir Marcus?'

'Show them into the library,' said the other, getting to his feet and dabbing at his mouth with a napkin. 'Nothing to be alarmed about, my dear,' he added to his wife. 'It's probably something to do with those poachers who've been bothering us. Do excuse me.'

The servant had already left. Before he followed him, Sir Marcus paused to kiss his wife gently on the cheek and squeeze her shoulder with an absent-minded affection. Then he straightened his shoulders and went out. The detectives were waiting for him in the library, a long room that was lined with bookshelves on three walls, the other being covered with paintings of famous battles from the Napoleonic Wars. Many of the volumes there were devoted to military history.

Robert Colbeck introduced himself and his companion. He gave Sir Marcus no opportunity to remark on his facial injuries. His initial question was all the more unsettling for being delivered in a tone of studied politeness.

'Are you acquainted with a man named Luke Rogan?'

'No,' replied Sir Marcus. 'Never heard of him.'

'You've never employed such an individual?'

'Of course not.'

'I notice a copy of *The Times* on the table over there,' said Colbeck with a nod in that direction. 'If you've read it, you'll have encountered Rogan's name there and know why we've taken such an interest in him. I've a particular reason for wanting to apprehend him, Sir Marcus. Earlier today, he did his best to kill me.'

'Did you instruct him to do that, Sir Marcus?' asked Leeming.

'Don't be so preposterous, man!' shouted the other.

'It's a logical assumption.'

'It's a brazen insult, Sergeant.'

'Not if it's true.'

'Sergeant Leeming speaks with authority,' said Colbeck, taking over again. 'He called at your house in Pimlico this afternoon. According to the servant he met, Luke Rogan visited the house yesterday and spent some time in your company. I think that you are a liar, Sir Marcus.' He gave an inquiring smile. 'Do you regard that as an insult as well?'

The old man would not yield an inch. 'You

have no right to browbeat me in my own home,' he said. 'I must ask you to leave.'

'And we must respectfully decline that invitation. We've spent far too long on this investigation to pay any heed to your bluster. The facts are these,' Colbeck went on, brusquely. 'You attended a lecture given by Gaston Chabal, who was working as an engineer on the railway between Mantes and Caen. Because that railway would one day connect Paris with a port that also houses an arsenal, you spied a danger of invasion. To avert that danger, you tried to bring the railway to a halt. That being the case, Chabal's murder took on symbolic significance.' His smile was much colder this time. 'Do I need to go on, Sir Marcus?'

'We are well aware of your military record,' said Leeming. 'You fought against the French for years. You can only ever see them as an enemy, can't you?'

'They *are* an enemy!' roared Sir Marcus.

'We're at peace with them now.'

'That's only an illusion, Sergeant. I knew the rogues when they held sway over a great part of Europe and plotted to add us to their empire. Thanks to us, Napoleon was stopped. It would be criminal to allow another Napoleon to succeed in his place.'

'That's why you had Chabal killed, isn't it,' said Colbeck. 'He had the misfortune to be a Frenchman.'

Sir Marcus was scathing. 'He embodied all the qualities of the breed,' he said, letting his revulsion show. 'Chabal was clever, arrogant and irredeemably smug. I'll tell you something about him that you didn't know, Inspector.'

'Oh, I doubt that.'

'Not content with building a railway to facilitate the invasion of England, he showed the instincts of a French soldier. Do you know what they do after a victory?' he demanded, arms flailing. 'They rape and pillage. They defile the womenfolk and steal anything they can lay their hands on. That was what Chabal did. His first victim was an Englishwoman. He not only subjected her to his carnal passions, he had the effrontery to inveigle money from her husband for the project in France. Rape and pillage – no more, no less.'

'Considerably less, I'd say,' argued Colbeck. 'I spoke to the lady in question and she told me a very different story. She became Gaston Chabal's lover of her own free will. She mourned his death.'

'I saved her from complete humiliation.'

'I dispute that, Sir Marcus.'

'I did, Inspector. I had him followed, you see,' said the old man, reliving the sequence of events. 'I had him followed on both sides of the Channel until I knew all about him. None of it was to his credit. When he tried to take advantage of the lady during her husband's absence, I had him killed on the way there.'

'And thrown from the Sankey Viaduct.'

'That was intentional. It was a reminder of our superiority – a French civil engineer hurled from a masterpiece of English design.'

'Chabal was dead at the time,' said Leeming, shrugging his shoulders, 'so it would have been meaningless to him.'

Sir Marcus scowled. 'It was not meaningless to me.'

'We need take this interview no further,' decided Colbeck. 'I have a warrant for your arrest, Sir Marcus. Before I enforce it, I must ask you if Luke Rogan is here.' The old man seemed to float off into a reverie. His gaze shifted to the battles depicted on the wall. He was miles away. Colbeck prompted him. 'I put a question to you.'

'Come with me, Inspector. You, too, Sergeant Leeming.'

Walking with great dignity, Sir Marcus Hetherington led them upstairs and along the landing. He unlocked the door of his shrine and conducted them in. Colbeck was astonished to see the range of memorabilia on show. The sight of the skull transfixed Leeming. Sir Marcus turned to the portrait of him in uniform.

'That was painted when I got back from Waterloo,' he said, proudly. 'I lost a lot of friends in that battle and I lost two young sons as well. That broke my heart and destroyed my wife. I'll never forgive the French for what they stole from us that day. They were *animals*.'

'It was a long time ago,' said Colbeck.

'Not when I come in here. It feels like yesterday then.'

'I asked you about Luke Rogan.'

'Then I'll give you an answer,' said the old man, opening a drawer in the cabinet and taking out the wooden case. He lifted the lid and took out one of the pistols before offering it to Colbeck. 'That's the weapon I used to kill Mr Rogan,' he explained. 'You'll find his body at the bottom of the well.'

Leeming was astounded. 'You *shot* him?'

'He'd outlived his usefulness, Sergeant.'

'It's beautiful,' said Colbeck, admiring the pistol and noting its finer points. 'It was made by a real craftsman, Sir Marcus.'

'So was this one, Inspector Colbeck.'

Before they realised what he was going to do, he took out the second gun, put it into his mouth and pulled the trigger. In the confined space, the report was deafening. His head seemed to explode. Blood spattered all over the portrait of Sir Marcus Hetherington.

Madeleine Andrews was dismayed. It was two days since the murder investigation had been concluded and she had seen no sign of

Robert Colbeck. The newspapers had lauded him with fulsome praise and she had cut out one article about him. Yet he did not appear in person. She wondered if she should call at his house and, if he were not there, leave a message with his servant. In the end, she decided against such a move. She continued to wait and to feel sorely neglected.

It was late afternoon when a cab finally drew up outside the house. She opened the door in time to watch Colbeck paying the driver. When he turned round, she was horrified to see the bruises that still marked his face. There had been no mention of his injuries in the newspaper. Madeleine was so troubled by his appearance that she took scant notice of the object he was carrying. After giving her a kiss, Colbeck followed her into the house.

'Before you ask,' he explained, 'I had a fight with Luke Rogan. Give me a few more days and I'll look more like the man you know. And before you scold me for not coming sooner,' he went on, 'you should know that I went to Liverpool on your behalf.'

'Liverpool?'

'The local constabulary helped us in the first stages of our enquiries. It was only fair to give them an account of what transpired thereafter. I can't say that Inspector Heyford was overjoyed to see me. He still hasn't recovered from the shock of accepting

Constable Praine as his future son-in-law.'

Madeleine was bemused. 'Who are these people?'

'I'll tell you later, Madeleine,' he promised. 'The person I really went to see was Ambrose Hooper.'

'The artist?'

'The very same.' He tapped the painting that he was holding. 'I bought this from him as a present for you.'

'A present?' She was thrilled. 'How marvellous!'

'Aren't you going to see what it is?' Madeleine took the painting from him and began to unwrap it. 'Because I was engaged in solving the crime, Mr Hooper gave me first refusal.'

Pulling off the last of the thick brown paper, she revealed the stunning watercolour of the Sankey Viaduct. It made her blink in awe.

'This is amazing, Robert,' she said, relishing every detail. 'It makes my version look like a childish scribble.'

'But *that* was the one that really helped me,' he said. 'You drew what was in Sir Marcus Hetherington's mind. Two countries joined together by a viaduct – victorious France and defeated England.'

'Is this Gaston Chabal?' she asked, studying the tiny figure.

'Yes, Madeleine.'

'He really does seem to be falling through the air.'

'Mr Hooper has captured the scene perfectly.'

'No wonder you were so grateful to him at the start.'

'He was the perfect witness – in the right place at the right time to record the moment for posterity. That painting is proof of the fact.'

'It's a wonderful piece of work. Father will be so interested to see it. He's driven trains over the viaduct.'

'I didn't buy it for your father, I bought it for you. It was by way of thanks for your assistance. Do you really like the painting?'

'I love it,' she said, putting it aside so that she could fling her arms around his neck. 'Thank you, Robert. You're so kind.' She kissed him. 'It's the nicest thing you've ever given me.'

'Is it?' he asked with a mischievous twinkle in his eye. 'Oh, I think I can do a lot better than that, Madeleine.'

The publishers hope that this book has given you enjoyable reading. Large Print Books are especially designed to be as easy to see and hold as possible. If you wish a complete list of our books please ask at your local library or write directly to:

Magna Large Print Books
Magna House, Long Preston,
Skipton, North Yorkshire.
BD23 4ND

This Large Print Book, for people
who cannot read normal print,
is published under the auspices of

THE ULVERSCROFT FOUNDATION